Land of Butterflies

David Lyons

RAVEN
CREST
BOOKS
PUBLISHING

Copyright © 2022 David Lyons

The right of David Lyons to be identified as the author of this work has been asserted by him in accordance with the Copyright, Designs and Patents Act 1988

All rights reserved.

This is a work of fiction. Names, characters, businesses, places, events and incidents are either the products of the author's imagination or used in a fictitious manner. Any resemblance to actual persons, living or dead, or actual events is purely coincidental.

No part of this publication may be reproduced, stored in a retrieval system or transmitted in any form or by any means including photocopying, electronic, recording or otherwise, without the prior written permission of the rights holder, application for which must be made through the publisher.

ISBN: 9798375530895

Dedicated to my brother Martin

ACKNOWLEDGEMENTS

I would like to extend Becky and Omar a massive thank you, for firstly believing in the story and for their tireless dedication, professionalism and support throughout the publishing process.

CHAPTER 1

In a time long ago, in a land where wildflowers and honeysuckle grew, a place now only accessible through the fantasies of our imagination, butterflies ruled the earth and everything lived in peaceful harmony there. This past time may be too distant for you to approve or for me to pretend to know with any level of precision; but let's just say our minds can dream and contemplate a single day three hundred million years ago when the sun shone, just as it does today, and the breeze carried the scent of wildflowers across endless meadows.

Chet and Cecily would dance their way across the blistering white sand to the coolness of the waves and scream with laughter once their small hot toes touched its soothing white foam. If only those heavenly days could be trapped in a bottle and kept hidden in some secret place to visit and once more breath in the summer smell of almond suntan oil and hear the hectic sound of screeching seagulls. Life was such a fun place then for seven-year-old twins Chet and Cecily. It was a private world of wonder - where no outside force could wield any control over their gaiety and happiness. Their little family was the centre of their universe and for them every important happening in the wide world only took place inside that precious protective circle. Their pretty little cottage on the edge of Robin Hood's Bay with its bright red roses that climbed at will over the front door and whitewashed walls whose colour was ritually touched up each spring was the living personification of an image from the top of an old biscuit tin. From the rear garden, the cottage had a full unhindered panoramic view to the white sands of the bay. The sound of the waves was the children's night-time lullaby and their first morning chime and soothed their passage to the land of dreams once their heads touched their feather pillows.

Their idyll ended so suddenly and cruelly once their father died and they were submersed into a world of darkness and despair. Those heady days of vanilla ice cream that melted too quickly in dainty wafers and the taste of dandelion and burdock that was the true flavour of summer, at once vanished into a distant hazy memory.

Their father, Rutherford, was a very tall, pencil thin man with sparse white, blond hair and large blue eyes that were permanently hidden behind thick black rimmed spectacles. He owned a small but very select shoe shop in the village of Robin Hood's Bay and painted the timberwork on the outside of the shop Harrods green as his aspirations lay in the perfection of that establishment. The finest brands of leather shoes were to be found here and looked as though they should always be kept displayed in glass cabinets and never be subjected to the undignified rigours of movement as they encased a humble foot. They perched on brown timber shelves with aged chipped paintwork and woodworm and shone without the presence of a single finger stain, radiating an aroma of the finest leather. The shelves had known far too many years of service but continued to house their ranks and the shoes sat with a haughty elegance staring down their length to the toe cap valuating the worthiness of prospective owners.

Their father was proud of his little shop and even though he didn't earn much more than a humble living, was content with his lot. The children never wore trainers or tennis shoes as their father called them. It was the finest leather for them or their bare feet. Most times they preferred their bare feet but they hated stone bruises and wearing a leather shoe with a stone bruise, well, that was a different level of pain all together. After school a few evenings a week the children would race along the winding cobbled streets of the village to the shop and sit in the small and very cramped back storeroom doing their home-work. Here amongst the smell of cardboard boxes and shoe polish they could listen to their father laugh and talk with his customers. The atmosphere inside the little shop made the customers feel at home midst the quaintness of a bygone era that once again sprang to life once they were cocooned in its nucleus. Turning the small circular brass doorknob opened up a world of yesteryear recognised mostly by his customers of a more discerning vintage. Entering this time capsule rekindled part of their youth for fleeting moments and secretly many imagined the feel of their father's or mother's hand leading them inside for their first pair of good shoes.

The customers always returned to the shop as Rutherford made buying shoes one of life's most important rituals. Everything had to have that personalised touch of perfection even right down to the red paper bags with the name of the shop printed in large gold lettering that he had specially made in London. They were at a huge extra cost that the business couldn't really afford but he felt it gave the place a certain panache.

Rutherford had a special knack of flicking the red bags open that the children often tried to imitate but never succeeded in mastering. This action executed properly made the whole procedure of purchase seem even more important.

"They will keep you going for a while," he would always say, and the children would mouth the words quietly together in the back room as their father said them. The children, unable to restrain themselves, would laugh aloud afterwards much to their father's displeasure.

If the flow of business was slow and if it were a sunny day, the shop would close early. The timber "closed" sign that Chet made from a piece of bleached and weathered driftwood, where the "c" was far too close to the "d" making it looked like "dosed" was hung on the door and they would all set off to the beach. The crystal-clear blue waves that rolled almost silently onto the white sand of Robin Hood's bay was just a short walk away. Their father always stopped at "the best little ice cream shop in the country" to buy three 99s. He loved 99s even more than the children did and would tell them repeatedly about all the ice cream shops to avoid when buying a 99. He had sampled the wares of all the ice cream shops in Robin Hood's Bay over time and rated them out of ten. Most of them didn't make it past four but this shop by the beach with its tatty old plastic ice cream cone that stood outside for display was a ten. The sun had bleached the old plastic cone almost white over far too many hot summers and the owner of the shop was a customer of Rutherford's as well which made his rating doubly good.

"Shoes ok?" their father would always ask, with a genuine concerned look and stare down to inspect the ice cream vendors feet as the man pulled on the handle of his antiquated ice cream machine to fill the cone to and beyond the brim. The children would stare at the milky white ice cream rising in layers around the cone and wish that the vendor would break his own generous record and make the top one inch higher. He never disappointed and they would lick their lips imagining the scrumptious taste that was soon to be theirs to savour.

"Shoes couldn't be any better. Syrup?" the man would say and look over his thick black rimmed spectacles that always had smudges of ice creamed finger stains on the lenses.

"Yes! Yes!," the children would say and jump up and down in anticipation.

"Thought so," the man would reply with a smile and pour very liberal amounts onto the 99s until it began to spill down onto his shoes. The man's three legged black and white cat always stood by in expectancy waiting for this overflow and meowed and purred with satisfaction as he kept the floor and the ice cream vendor's shoes sparkly clean.

The sky was black on the brink of thunder and the children decided not to visit their father at the shop but ran home quickly through the heavy persistent rain drops.

That evening their father stood by the shop door and stared out at the deluge of rain drops crashing onto the dark wet cobbles and decided to wait it out until the weather's anger abated a little. He lovingly restocked his shelves and listened to the water race headlong down the tin gutters. A gutter joint was broken some time ago on a downpipe that faced the street and on evenings such as this he always made an intention to fix it but then always forgot once the sun's smile returned once more. The escaping water from the broken gutter left a dark mould stain on the wall in the shape of Italy and shoes had to keep their distance from its hazardous coast line.

The highlight of Rutherford's day was evening dinner with his family - listening to the children's stories, Maximillian's interventions with a story of much greater importance than any being relayed and Jilly's occasional smile to him through it all. Rain or no he turned the little brass door handle closed and locked the shop to the world. He could feel the icy rain drops run past the collar of his shirt and down the back of his neck as he gave the handle a final twist to make sure it was properly secure. Once satisfied he ran across the wet cobblestones, jumping newly formed puddles that sprang up everywhere before him. He didn't hear the motor bike and side car that raced crazily through the rain. The sound of its screeching brakes was the last sound Rutherford heard. He died instantly on the cold wet cobbles that were lit by the weak beams of an amber streetlight.

"It wouldn't have mattered if you had both gone to see your father that day. What is to be will be and there is nothing you could have done to change that. It was his time. We all have our ordained time to die and sadly that was his." Maximillian tried to console the children as they continually blamed themselves for their father's untimely death.

"We must stick together now and be brave, that is what he would wish for. Remember he is with you always – watching over you, even though you can't see him." Maximillian continued.

The children took a little comfort from their grandfather's words but deep down in their hearts they wondered if their father would still be alive if they had gone to visit him on that fateful afternoon.

Not very long after Rutherford's death the postman's old rusty bicycle with its tatty wicker basket became a familiar sight at the front door of the pretty little cottage, as bills began to arrive through the letter box demanding payments for one thing or another. The family soon realised that Rutherford's perfect little shoe shop had been in debt and was swiftly taken over by heartless creditors. Soon after this their little chocolate box cottage in Robin Hood's Bay with its rose garden their father had lovingly planted and watered through hot summers to maturity and the swing, that hung from the chestnut tree that had gone through countless ropes and a few timber seats, all were sold to meet debts. They could have found rented accommodation in the village, but Jilly wanted to take the family away from Robin Hood's Bay as the memories were too painful for her to bear.

At the furthest end of their garden a rarely observed weeping willow tree stood and beyond this an area of wild un-kept grass where the crickets chattered in summer. The children flattened paths through the grass to secret hideaways where they could become the heroes of their favourite fairy tale. Lost in their imaginings they would play there for hours while the bumble bees and butterflies meandered over their heads. Now it was all to change, and this special area was to be lost to them and their reveries. Life had gone from being carefree and happy to a bleak forsaken wilderness overnight.

Chet and Cecily's grandfather Maximilian was an unsuccessful explorer and Egyptologist who claimed to have crisscrossed all the continents and oceans of the world in search of something he sadly, never found. He became the unlikely head of the household once his son Rutherford died.

They would all miss the village's narrow winding streets,

quaint coffee shops and the ice cream shop with the old, faded plastic display cone and the three-legged cat but mostly they would miss friendly smiles of neighbours they had known for so long.

With only two weeks remaining before the deadline to vacate their home Maximillian was in a quandary and paced up and down inside his garden shed – his unlit pipe clenched tightly between his teeth. His ever eager imagination dallied on the thought that maybe somewhere amongst his life's collected treasures there might be one valuable object that could save the day. Cardboard boxes filled to the brim with what he once assumed were valuables had been sealed decades earlier with tape and now housed small families of mice. The tatty old boxes were eagerly pulled open, and their contents scattered over the shed's bare wooden floor. Some of the mice ran up along his arms and inside his shirt but he took no notice in his eagerness to uncover that one needed treasure. Piles of random neatly stacked items that moments earlier were deemed priceless to him were now pulled down and inspected in terms of value rather than sentiment.

"Nothing!!," he shouted. His face red and glowing from sweat and frustration. Strands of hair that were previously very neatly covering his bald patch now hung down on one side of his head like thin white abseiling ropes. Without thinking, he quickly relocated them back to their original position with the swift movement of the palm of his hand - an action that occurred so often it became mechanical. The articles were all only of nostalgic content and when looked upon with sensible eyes were of very little monetary value.

"My watches. Yes, they are surely worth something. Maybe one of them could be a true gem, and that painting. Yes, that painting has to be worth a fortune. I remember the man I bought it off in Rudrapur telling me about the bargain I was getting as he sunk his teeth into the handful of Krugerrands I traded with him at the time. All is not lost - I really peak when I am in a tight pinch" he thought and lit his pipe with his old gas lighter and gave a smug smile of satisfaction.

Later he thought about the sale over and over in his mind as he and Chet sat waiting in the local barbershop on a tatty old red leatherette bench that was badly repaired far too many times with differing colours of sticky tape. On that particular occasion neither of them needed a haircut but the barber was a knowledgeable person who always seemed to find solutions to everyone's problems no matter how difficult and Maximillian needed advice badly. Chet would have liked to let his hair grow long like Jason Ekker's from The Ekker Five, his favourite band but he was never allowed that luxury.

"When I grow up I am letting my hair grow right down to my feet and longer," Chet would scream as he was regularly dragged off to the barber. On this occasion Chet was boiling with anger and sat with his arms folded and gave a scowl that would fry an egg as he waited his turn to have what little hair he had left on his head removed by force.

A tatty overly read week old newspaper stared up at him from the floor. It had the damp footprints of the last ten clients clearly etched on its surface. Maximillian stared down at the newspaper and because of the distance they were apart it was in perfect focus for his eyes without his reading spectacles. The property page was open and photos of houses for sale were displayed in rectangular columns. Through the stains his eyes homed in on one advert photo and he stooped down and snatched the paper up in his hand. "Perfect that's it" Maximillian shouted and jumped up out of his seat holding the newspaper over his head. Chet looked at him with disinterest and tightened the fold on his arms and scowled a two-egg fry.

"Come on we're off," Maximillian said and grabbed Chet by the hand and yanked him out of his chair.

"We will come back another time Tim," Maximillian shouted to the barber who just nodded and smiled in acknowledgement as he was in the midst of giving a haircut but more importantly imparting one of his valued opinions to a very attentive customer and wouldn't allow his train of thought to be broken by entering into a second conversation.

"If the sale at Turnbull's works out as I have planned, I have just found us the perfect little house my lad," Maximillian said as he rushed home waving the newspaper back and forth like a cutlass in an autumn breeze that housed the final aromas of freshly cut grass for that season.

Chet marked off the days to the auction on a calendar that had the image of a pouncing lion as its motif that Maximillian got free inside his "Explorer's Updates" magazine. It was the final date to get a tick from Jilly's precious red kitchen biro and so heralded the day they all waited for and Maximilian dreaded with every core of his being.

For the sake of peace, and to save her fraying nerves Jilly reluctantly agreed to allow the children to join them. A train journey however short was a great adventure for the children but one to London was beyond their imaginings. Jilly's wicker picnic basket was filled with ham and cheese sandwiches and small fat fairy cakes with raisins but no icing. The children weren't overly fond of ham and cheese sandwiches and only Maximillian liked raisins. They would have much preferred ice cream from the train's canteen that was long overdue redecoration and smelt like week old watery gravy. But as hunger crept up on them they ate the sandwiches without a smile and further down the tracks the fat fairy cakes disappeared also. Maximillian gave a low grumble when he reached for his first fairy cake and found the space in the empty basket.

As time ticked by slowly on the grey enamelled train's clock and the sound of the iron wheels on the tracks became less noticeable a new terror slowly crept up on Maximillian.

"What if the watches are useless and the painting is a fake," he kept saying to himself over and over as he blankly looked out through the window of the moving train to scenes that were not registering in his brain. His black strong coffee went cold on the Formica tabletop without him taking one sip.

"Whatever is the matter with you? That is the fourth cup you have let go cold," Jilly said in a scolding tone. "And I only brought two flasks of hot water," she continued with a scowl that made the wrinkles on her forehead more noticeable.

Her pretty face with kind blue eyes that would only acknowledge the good in every situation had gone gaunt and pale since Rutherford's death. She no longer found fun in most every circumstance that came her way as she used to in the past. Jilly was a farmer's daughter who passionately hated farming and indeed disliked being anywhere in the near vicinity of farm animals. Agricultural smells made her suddenly reach for her perfumed handkerchief which she always kept on her person and she shunned all instances that had any possibility of her getting animal excrement on her hands or clothes. Acceptance of animal aromas is a must for all farm folk as it is par for the course but not for Jilly. She always insured that she was never in close proximity to any animal but most especially horses.

Her father, a rugged no nonsense country man with limited compassionate feelings, who always wore collarless shirts and a neck scarf, put her astride a horse when she was very young and even though she cried in terror to be taken down, her father, who was practicing tough love on this occasion, made her stay on board. The feel of the horse's back, the tensed muscles, and the power of the creature that stood beneath her still gave her night terrors. The almost overpowering strong smell of its sweat as it danced about on all legs, filled to bursting point with nervous energy and the menacing sound of its metal shoes as they crunched the pebbles beneath them into dust, made Jilly imagine its release of frustrated anger was directed towards her. It exhaled large angry clouds of white breath into the cold morning air and saliva dripped in large white blobs from the edges of the iron bit it frantically chewed on. Moving its weight suddenly from foreleg to foreleg she felt it could sense and smell her fear and doubled its efforts to heighten her anxiety. Her face would flash with terror as her mind brought her back to those terrifying moments. Her hands would become clammy as she imagined the feel of strength, muscle and nervous tension that was about to explode beneath her.

When she was taken down from the horse in tears by her father, she gave the animal a sudden solemn stare that the horse understood meant goodbye forever. That was the last time Jilly sat on a horse or indeed was within twenty metres of one.

When the coveted final day of her farm life arrived, she stood at the bus stop in her plain grey calico dress holding her brown cardboard suitcase, hugged her parents goodbye and set off for new adventures far from the farmyard and its odious aromas.

"I will never marry a farmer," she would always tell her friends and she was true to her oath.

The basement shoe storeroom of Lewis's in Manchester was a dimly lit sweltering hot place with no windows or air conditioning. It was not by any stretch of the imagination an ideal place for a first romantic encounter. Jilly first met Rutherford there when they worked their first day at the store together dowdily unpacking shoe boxes. She had very many suitors at the time. Even members of the Manchester United football team were known to loiter around the shop signing autographs in efforts to attract her favour but to no avail. She and Rutherford made a dashing pair around town and only had eyes for each other.

Before Rutherford's death Jilly would always leave her long white, blond hair loose to fall in perfect natural curls down her back. It danced lightly on her shoulders and was the envy of every woman who saw it but since Rutherford's death she kept it tied up tightly in a bun and covered with a selection of bland headscarves.

Once the ice creams that Maximillian bought them from the train's canteen were eaten with only traces now visible around their mouths, the children grew restless and questioning. Jilly was asleep or at least pretending to be, so Maximillian became the centre of their questioning attention.

"Tell us about the maharajah," they said in unison and continued the chant until Maximillian reluctantly agreed.

"All right, all right. Keep it down or the conductor will put us off the train here in the middle of nowhere and we will never find our way back home again," Maximillian said earnestly. The children suddenly grew quiet, pondering the prospects of being abandoned in the middle of nowhere and solemnly stared out at the endless lonely fields that raced past the grimy window of the train with no house in sight.

"He was a man I used to know…long, long time ago," he continued as his facial expression changed dramatically to display the depth of his imaginings.

"Tells us about his daughter," Cecily said.

"Ermmm well she was 9 years old or so and very beautiful. Just like you." Maximillian smiled.

"What colour hair did she have?" Cecily continued.

"Black. Black as the blackest coal," Maximillian said and pointed to the long black overcoat a nearby passenger was wearing. The man was deeply engrossed in a pink newspaper, his mind on the stock market floor. Cecily thought about the answer for a moment and ran her fingers through her own hair. Cecily and Chet had white, blond hair just like their parents and blue eyes that shone like the brightest sapphires. They were two months and seven days away from their eighth birthday. Chet kept an accurate account of the time as he wished it could pass more quickly so he could reach his coveted age of thirteen since he imagined teenagers had the most fun hence this was the age he hoped to get to as soon as possible. They were tall for their age. "Gangly" Maximillian called them and Cecily hated the expression. They were so alike as twins they almost thought as one and finished each other's sentences as they spoke to mutual satisfaction. They always wore similar coloured clothes and as Cecily wasn't fond of pink, this choice never presented itself to test Chet's willingness to comply with the colour coordination. They kept to themselves at playtimes in school, completely indifferent to the fact the other children thought them strange and odd. They enjoyed their own company and as of yet hadn't found anyone their own age to match up to their exacting standards of acceptance to their inner fold.

"And her name?" Chet asked

"Rawinda," Maximillian replied and stared blankly through the train's grotty window at the passing scenery. "And her father the maharaja gave me a wax pear for saving her life. Typical. Just a badly cast wax pear. And that is all. Some valuable treasure would have come in very handy now in our time of distress" he continued muttering angrily to himself.

"Is that the same tatty looking old pear you keep on top of your bookcase in your shed?" Cecily asked and tried her best not to laugh at his grievance.

"Yes, one and the same. An old pear is what I got for my troubles," and he gave a slight scoffing laugh and looked up to the ceiling of the train in dismay.

"Anyway, as I was saying Rawinda was her name," Maximillian continued and made himself more comfortable in his seat as he prepared to deliver the story. He wore his lucky old brown cord trousers that moths had many a feast on and too many hot washes had shrunken, so as he crossed his legs the skinny white presence of his ankles came into full view. He had also completely forgotten the reason why these trousers had been given that honoured title of lucky, but he wore them just the same.

The children looked at each other in wonder as they had never heard a name like Rawinda before.

"How did you save her?" Chet shook Maximillian's sleeve to focus his attention back to the story as

Maximillian's mind couldn't help wandering back to the possible worrying outcome of the forthcoming auction.

"It was a long time ago children, I have almost forgotten. But I will tell you what I remember. I was in India at the time doing a bit of exploring. I was told by a Spanish flamenco dancer who said she was descended from King Charlemagne and that her ancestor had sealed up a gold mine packed to the brim with riches that were just waiting to be discovered. I gave her a small…," Maximillian coughed and pulled his beard into a point "reimbursement for her information then searched the area she told me about, looking for clues to find this treasure with no success and one day just by chance I bought a map from a very tall one-legged Scott's man in Bombay that supposedly led to the gold mine. He had a very angry monkey on his left shoulder who wore a thick gold coloured chain around its neck and a bright yellow parrot that screeched very rude obscenities on his right shoulder. And rightly rude they were too let me tell you. I stopped to watch the spectacle, as it's not every day you come upon a scene like that. I got talking to the Scott's man, as you do, and he told me his poker was going through a dry patch and he needed some readies double quick time, if you know what I mean."

The children nodded in the affirmative, their mouths wide open in anticipation.

"Well anyway. Bought the map from him, gave him almost all the money I had for it. He said it was a real bargain in the broadest Scottish accent I have ever heard. Got myself a few Sherpa's and a few strong mules and set off into the unknown on one of the hottest summers days I ever remember. My head felt like it was on fire beneath my pith helmet. We travelled for a month. I caught…well you don't want to know about that but let me tell you it was an unpleasant experience."

Maximillian gave a nervous cough at the memory "anyway finally we reached Elephant's Head Mountain. It was a mountain on the map that was supposed to look like an elephant's head. In a way it did but you would need a very good imagination.

Anyway, we made camp for the night in a clearing at the base of the mountain and decided to start our explorations the following day. I remember it being so hot that I couldn't sleep. There was not even a breeze to blow out a match. The flies took a rota for the night shift and were relentless. I don't do it often as you both know but that night I downed half a litre of whiskey and finally I drifted off to sleep. Next morning lo and behold I was on my own with a headache to beat the band and a mouth as dry as the Mojave Desert. Sherpas gone, mules gone, and water gone but I still had the map. Thought 'this is going to be a bit tricky all right' but I forged ahead all the same. I would have taken a drink from the Scotsman's old boot that morning - I have never known such thirst."

"It was the whiskey grandad," Chet said and smiled, trying not to laugh.

Maximillian coughed and gave him a stern look "Well anyway, the map led me to a cave in the side of the mountain…"

"But what about the maharajah's daughter?" Cecily said getting impatient.

"I am getting to that if you can wait. Just typical you can't wait for anything." Maximillian pretended to look annoyed.

"Anyway, as I was saying, I was in a cave on the side of Elephant's Head Mountain. It was a dark damp place filled to the brim with spiders and what seemed like the smell of dead cat."

"Eugh gross grandad," Cecily said.

"All of a sudden, a very young girl raced into the cave and fell to her knees very distressed and out of breath."

"The maharajah's daughter?" Chet interrupted.

"One and the same." Maximillian gave them his most mystical look and stroked his white beard pulling it into a point at the tip.

"Who was after her?" Cecily said and twisted the ends

of her hair, something she always did when she felt nervous. The rattling sound of the train's iron wheels on the tracks grew silent as it slowed to a halt at a busy platform. Maximillian peered out through the window looking for a clue as to where they were. The children kept their eyes firmly fixed on him waiting for the continuation to his story and hadn't noticed the train come to a halt.

"Wait, this is our stop. Quickly we will end up in Dover." Maximillian got up suddenly and ushered them all off the train.

CHAPTER 2

The hustling noisy streets of London were a world apart from the quiet little village of Robin Hood's Bay. No friendly greetings were exchanged by the people they encountered in what the children thought were almost hostile surroundings. Expressionless faces dashed hither and tither their minds concentrating on their own cares, oblivious to the presence of others. The sounds of frustrated car horns and heated engines, hoarse street hawkers and occasional lunatics, heightened the sense of anxiety for all. Cecily tried to stroke a passing stray dog she assumed had the same temperament as the ones she was familiar with back in Robin Hood's Bay, but it showed its teeth to her and growled a hair's breadth away from attack.

"Follow me," Maximillian commanded to Jilly and the children, his pipe firmly clenched between his teeth to a degree of tension so that the words that left his mouth were muffled. Had they not been familiar with his tone of voice his orders would have been lost midst the clanging sounds of London. Jilly and the children followed the stream of white aromatic pipe tobacco that lingered in Maximillian's wake. Occasionally he would go out of sight as he hurriedly shuffled along, weaving his way knowledgeably through the crowd. The children were very impressed with his insightful command of the goings on of a busy city street. When he occasionally got out of sight they followed the familiar aroma on his pipe tobacco and felt secure knowing he wasn't too far ahead.

"Come on, get a move on will you," he would shout from a distance and wave his hand in the air without looking around. Jilly would roll her eyes to the sky and the children would laugh and before long there it was, Turnbull's sales rooms. Standing imposingly and staring down its nose at the chaotic dishevelled group that dared draw near its hallowed doors.

"Well, this is it," Maximillian said with an equal mix of

achievement and trepidation.

A large gold and silver sign on the right-hand side of the imposing front door said:

MIXED SALE OF INTERESTING ITEMS

Maximillian stared at the sign and took a few quick nervous puffs from his pipe and surrounded himself with white clouds of smoke. His head was just about visible amidst it and he gave a loud uncustomary cough.

"We had best go in. The sale starts in thirty minutes," Jilly said and was the first to brave her way forward climbing up the four shiny stone steps that lead to the front door as she held tightly onto Cecily's hand. Maximillian blessed himself as he ushered the children ahead of him and was last up the short flight of steps that lead to the large burgundy coloured front door. A rich red carpet lay beyond the door and covered the length of an imposing hallway that appeared and smelled of affluence. Jilly took command and followed the interior signs that pointed the way and they all entered the spacious auction room timidly making themselves as inconspicuous as possible.

"There are very few people here," Jilly said as she looked nervously around at the small crowd and the many empty seats. She observed the important looking snooty faces dotted randomly around the room and imagined the uniform of the day had to be red braces, pinstriped shirts and brown suede shoes. Ladies in their Hermes scarves tied in differing styles ran their fingers knowledgeably through the sales catalogue without making any facial expressions.

"They will bid via the internet," Maximillian said nervously and looked equally worried at the very small turnout.

Four vacant chairs at the back of the room near the door looked inviting and they all sat down meekly as though their presence was imposing on the pleasure and concentration of those already there.

"Not to worry if they don't sell," Jilly said and reassuringly patted her father on the shoulder. He jumped suddenly as she touched him. Every muscle in his body was like a tight wound spring ready to erupt and flood the room. He put his unlit pipe into his mouth and was about to light it up with his old tin lighter when Cecily pointed to the no smoking sign that was placed fortuitously on the wall behind him.

"Oh yes of course," he said and returned the pipe back into his pocket again giving it a forlorn glance as he did so.

"What lots are ours grandad?" Chet said and swung his legs back and forth as he sat comfortably in his chair.

Maximillian took the catalogue from the inside pocket of his blue safari jacket.

"Lots 150, 151, 152, 153 154 and 300," he replied. "The painting is lot 300." His voice gave an unfamiliar quiver as the words drained out through his almost tight lips.

Chet gave Maximillian a nudge with his elbow "It will be fine," Chet said "Remember Del Boy and Rodney's watch," Chet continued with a quiet giggle.

Maximillian laughed loudly and for a brief moment forgot his current woe. Some of the more haughty types gave Maximillian a disapproving look and he stuck his tongue out at them in reply.

They tossed their heads and turned away indignantly. Chet laughed out loud.

They were all very excited at the arrival of lot 1 and bored beyond belief at lot 100 but they sat there and waited.

"Soon now," Jilly said at lot 148.

Maximillian took an uncustomary large swallow and went slightly pale. Beads of cold sweat appeared on his forehead and he wiped them lifelessly away with the back of his hand. He imagined he could feel the whole room stare at him in expectation of his pending embarrassment. As each pair of eyes innocently met his he gave it a cold questioning stare in response. The auctioneer wore a frameless monocle, and the children were amazed as they watched it, never once moving an inch from its perch covering his right eye. Of course, they had seen people wear them before on TV but seeing one first hand was an interesting experience.

"Look at that. It never moves. Why doesn't if fall off?" Chet enquired from Maximillian.

"He is used to wearing it that's why. Now I used to wear one once you know and became very accustomed to it as well," he replied.

The children looked towards the ceiling and gave a deep sigh. Maximillian noticed.

"Ahh you never believe me, but it is all true you know," he said slightly miffed at their disbelief.

"Sure grandad. We believe you," Cecily said with a sympathetic smile.

"How much do we need to raise?" Jilly whispered to Maximillian as she shifted about in her chair.

"150,000 would be good. That should amply cover the price of that nice little house I found in the paper, he replied but his words sounded defeated as each one formed on his lips.

"That much! I can't see that happening. I think this is a waste of time," Jilly said and looked about her at the crowd that looked too lofty to be interested in a handful of old watches and a painting that she last remembered seeing blocking a draught in the window of Maximillian's garden shed.

"Have faith. I am usually right," he said sheepishly and reached for his pipe but stopped before his hand touched the pocket.

Jilly looked at him sharply and was about to say something but just gave a small sigh instead.

"You are always right," she said and patted him on the arm.

"Lot 150. A very fine gold pocket watch as seen here on the screen dating from late1800. It is in working order. So who will give me a bid of 1000?" the auctioneer smiled and looked about him waiting for an opening offer. There was none.

"Well 500 then let's start small," he continued with a roughish smile.

Jilly grasped Maximillian's arm and he made no response. He sat like a block of cold marble.

"Ahh yes, 500. The auctioneer's eagle eyed stared out through his monocle and netted the first bid. His long thin nose pointed in the direction of the raised paddle and he took a bid. 600, 650,700,750,800" the auctioneer kept taking bids until they reached 800 and then the bidding dried up suddenly.

"It's on the market now. Don't make a mistake and lose this one. You will regret it. One night you will sit by the fire and lament on not buying this watch," the auctioneer persisted but try as he did, he couldn't drag one last bid from the disinterested crowd.

"Sold to the lady with the peacock feather in her red hat for 800. Well done madam, the auctioneer continued proud of his achievement. Maximillian, Jilly and the children were less impressed and looked at each other in dismay.

"We have a long way to go to reach 150,000," Jilly said and looked straight ahead to the screen where the next lot was now being shown. Maximillian made no reply but took his pipe out and placed the shank between his teeth and gripped on tightly. Chet and Cecily looked at each other in despair. The next four watches made a total of 5000 between them and that was mainly due to the cajoling and persistence of the game auctioneer.

"There is only the painting left now and that can't be worth much either," Jilly said. "It will be ok though, we will manage somehow," she continued and forced herself to produce a smile that dallied for a brief moment on her pale lips before vanishing completely.

Maximillian's worst fears had come to pass, and disaster was unfolding around him but he tried to look calm and kept his unlit pipe firmly between his teeth. He could hear his heart pounding in his ears and a feeling of nausea began to turn his complexion ashen grey. At lot 290, ten lots before the painting was due to be sold an Indian gentleman in a crisp white suit who wore a jet-black turban on his head entered the room and sat to the left-hand side of the entrance door. Jilly and Maximillian didn't notice him as they were far too deep in their individual thoughts of pending penury.

Maximillian was imagining the workhouse and all its horrors - that's if they still existed. Cecily didn't notice him either she kept staring at the auctioneer's monocle hoping it would fall from his face just that one time. But Chet noticed him and stared. The Indian gentleman noticed Chet staring and smiled towards politely him. Chet looked away shyly.

"You tried, what more could you do. I knew this crowd was too small and look, most of them are staring at their phones anyway." Jilly tried to console Maximillian, but her words did nothing to lift his spirits and he slumped low in his chair with his head bent downwards, the bowl of his pipe resting against his chest.

"Lot 300 a very nice painting 20cm x 20cm of an Indian scene in oil. We are not sure who the artist is but it is well painted and would look superb on any wall." The auctioneer gave a sweeping gesture with his hand as with great personal effort he pretended to admire the image of the painting displayed on the screen for the crowd to peruse.

"Ermm, let's see who will open this fine painting at let's say 5000," and the auctioneer gave his most alluring smile and looked pleadingly towards the indifferent audience.

"Is that all they think it is worth?" Jilly whispered to Maximillian in shock and grabbed his sweaty hand tightly.

"I think we are in some certain trouble now my girl," Maximillian replied and continued looking towards the floor.

Chet took another glance at the Indian gentleman who was at this moment concentrating very intently on the auctioneer.

"I can't go much lower than 5,000. Ok 4,000 then. If I don't get a bid I will have to withdraw the lot," the auctioneer's voice threatened the crowd and his alluring smile disappeared.

Chet kept looking at the Indian gentleman and then all of a sudden, he stared intently at Chet.

"150,000." The Indian gentleman spoke up with an air of importance and lifting his paddle made a bid.

A loud gasp came from the crowd and Maximillian bit clean through the shank of his pipe, the bowl filled with unlit tobacco falling to the red carpet.

"150,000," the auctioneer said in bewilderment and then sheepishly continued, "are there any further bids?" and his alluring smile returned to his lips once again. Knowing that it was highly unlikely that the price would go one bid higher he scanned the room for a second bid for appearances sake. With no further offers he knocked the gavel down with an extra loud bang on his wooden rostrum. The force of the blow knocked the head clean off the gavel and it rolled along the red carpet and landed at the feet of a very haughty lady who gave it a contemptuous stare before duplicating the sentiment towards the still excited auctioneer.

"Sold to the gentleman at the back," the auctioneer said and quickly wrote down the Indian gentleman's paddle number.

Jilly, Maximillian and the children jumped around with delight and cheered. A few members of the crowd smiled at the excitement. But only a few.

"Who bought it?" Maximillian said looking about the room.

Chet looked towards the seat where the Indian gentleman had been, but he was gone. Chet could see a card left on the vacant seat so he walked over and picked it up. It was a small white card with the image of two gold butterfly's wings printed in the centre.

"He was there. I saw him. The man who bought the painting was sitting in that seat. He smiled at me," Chet said as he returned to the group and pointed to the empty seat.

"He was wearing one of those hats. You know like the

ones you showed us in your photos from India," Chet said excitedly.

"A turban?" Maximillian's voice became very serious.

"Yes. And he was nice, he smiled at me. I found this on his seat," Chet continued and handed the card to Maximillian. His eyes flashed with caution once he saw the image and he looked him about sharply.

"We must get home now. It has been a long day," he said in a voice that poorly concealed his concern. The children didn't notice his sudden change of attitude, but Jilly did.

"What is wrong?" she enquired quietly to Maximillian so the children didn't hear.

"I will try and find out who purchased the painting then we must get to the train station as quickly as possible. Don't alarm the children everything will be fine," he replied but Jilly could sense the anxiety in his voice.

Even though Maximillian tried to persuade the auctioneer to divulge the identity of the purchaser, the auctioneer didn't break company policy and give out a name so the new owner of the painting remained a mystery. But Maximillian had his suspicions.

The rectory that Maximillian noticed advertised in the newspaper on the floor of the barbershop was being sold cheaply as the local coal mine was all but worked out leaving the village as dried up as the fallen petals from an old, withered rose. A ruthless estate agent who wore a ruffled old pinstriped suit that owed its style to the Chicago gangsters of the fifties and sported a waxed moustached that extended out inches on either side of his alcohol flushed cheeks and cherry red nose, was Maximilian's advisor. He claimed the foundations of the house were built on a coal seam which, at a time in the not-too-distant past, occasionally produced diamonds. And one as big as a marble was found buried three feet from the gable wall of the rectory. He claimed that if the area was explored properly it could produce riches beyond Maximillian's wildest imaginings. The estate agent gave a nervous cough as he relayed these fantastic pieces of information and took a hip flask from the inside pocket of his crumpled jacket and took a long drink from it. He noticed Maximillian observe his action with surprise and quickly spoke to make account for it.

"It's for the cough. Was doing a bit of salmon fishing last week and stayed out too long in the water.

Don't really like the stuff at all you know. For medicinal purposes only - that's me." He blinked nervously as he spoke. Maximillian gave him a questioning stare as his gaze dallied on the estate agent's red whiskey nose. The estate agent rubbed his nose manically and then put the hip flask away to the darkness of his inside pocket.

"Anyway," he said and gave another nervous cough. "You look like a man of the world. Indeed a travelled man I would hasten to say. A man who knows a sure thing when he sets his eyes on it." The estate agent twirled the corners of his moustache as his left eye twitched beyond his control.

Flattery was of course the surest bait needed to hook and reel in the very gullible Maximilian, who pompously rose on his toes once or twice as the flooding praise went straight to his head like a twenty-year-old malt.

"Ah well I do admit I have seen quite a bit you know," Maximilian replied and glowed a knowing smile in the direction of the estate agent who tapped his red nose with his index finger in a gesture to suggest his recognition of that deep understanding that only exists amongst likeminded men.

"I can always tell a man after my own heart. A kindred spirit - you might even say." The estate agent eagerly held out his hand. "You will bag a real bargain here sir but I imagine you are very well used to being on the right end of winning deals. If you get my meaning." The estate agent's eyes twitched anxiously and he manically scratched at an area of psoriasis on the back of his hand.

Maximilian glowed like a cat who lay with content in front of a warm log fire and pompously rose on his toes again. Now pumped to the brim and beyond with praise he felt certain the diamonds were just inches beyond his reach and that further excavations would uncover the mother-load for sure. He felt that a diamond found at three feet deep was at best unusual but on the other hand he reasoned with himself that he heard of diamonds being picked directly off the top of the ground in places like Sri Lanka.

"So nature being as unpredictable as it is, why couldn't this happen here right on my doorstep?" he thought.

"It's a deal my good man," Maximilian said and shook the estate agent's sweaty hand. Maximilian quickly wiped his hand on his trouser leg afterwards.

Removing the chimes that hung by the back door was the most poignant action of their last moments in the cottage in Robin Hood's Bay. Detaching the butterfly shaped chimes finally took away the last embers of the place's soul. But the family felt their enchanting little sound would come to life once again in their new home and restore their sense of belonging in unfamiliar surroundings.

The ice cream vendor brought his three-legged cat with him in his vintage army truck to assist in their move. The truck generally only travelled short distances to vintage rallies and all the family, even the ice cream vendor prayed it would safely arrive at its destination as it navigated the steep Welsh hills. After some major puffing of steam from its antiquated radiator, which all but blocked out their view from the front windscreen, it finally crawled to a halt outside their new home.

Everyone gave a deep sigh of relief as the handbrake was pulled on making a long slow ratcheting sound. Even the cat lowered its tail down to a relaxed position, for the first time throughout the whole journey, and purred.

Architectural quaintness wasn't a prerequisite in the Welsh mining village as it had appeared to be in Robin

Hood's Bay. Houses were built for function in a bland unimaginative style in cold grey pennant sandstone. Their appearance could, if allowed, suck the very joie de vie from a soul. The rectory gave off a slightly more appealing architectural flare but only slightly. It was a tall narrow house with small windows that kept the interior in a state of perpetual purgatory and advantageously minimised the view out to the bleak slag heaps in the surrounding landscape beyond. The Welsh village sat on the pinnacle of a hill that felt the cold in the wind. A wind that could blow a gale in any season. Chet and Cecily's new bedroom no longer resounded to the comforting sound of the waves as it did in their old bedroom. Now the whistling cold wind called out its foreboding presence to them. Its sound was amplified through the space in the window frame left ajar by a broken latch. A few weather-hardy shrubs sat unloved and unattended in a border on the short path to the front door and made for an unsavoury welcoming committee. Maximillian erected his garden shed on the only level space in the rear garden and arranged all his life's collectables exactly as they were placed when the shed was back in Robin Hood's Bay.

After allowing a few days to unpack and settle in Maximillian immediately set to work on his desired plan: a plan he had mulled over in his brain before the ink on the deed to the rectory had dried. He tunnelled under the front and back gardens of the old rectory until the house all but fell down, leaving subsidence cracks on two of the exterior walls. He even tunnelled under the gardens of the surrounding houses with and without his neighbour's permission. He once felt confident that the diamonds were just inches beyond his reach but now he wasn't so certain anymore. He leaned down heavily on his spade in the cold November evening breeze that blew through the naked branches of the surrounding beech trees and he pulled his jacket close around his chest. From where he stood, he could count thirty-eight separate excavations that were all at least a couple of metres deep. The red sandy earth piled up high on all sides of each hole. Bewildered eyes peered out at him from behind the sanctuary of laced curtains on the neighbouring houses. Maximillian gave them a friendly wave knowing they were watching and that disgruntled conversations abounded behind those closed doors. The memory of his parents who were long dead now gnawed at his conscience as he looked around at the devastation he had caused with his diggings. His parents were accountants who lived their lives by the manual of perfection and who worried until their demise about their hapless son who lived in a dream world where reality and normality played little part. He tried to eliminate the certainty of their disapproval from his mind by whistling a random melody. Maximilian with his long snow white hair and Father Christmas beard retired with a sulky face to his shed at the end of the garden to rethink his strategy on the best approach to finding the hidden diamonds.

He always wore his favourite blue safari jacket with its infinity of pockets that he purchased many years previous in a back street market in Bombay. On the rare occasions that he removed the jacket before bedtime - it always seemed like he was stripping away part of his personality. Each pocket had a separate, never changing purpose that even the children knew. His bulging top right hand pocket was home to his tobacco and a battered old navy gas lighter. Wear had produced a hole on the bottom left side of this pocket out of which the gas lighter always peeped its shiny face but never had the chance to escape - as yet. The children would stare at this hole and wonder how much longer the pocket could safely restrain its captive. When Maximillian gave out one of his monster bear hugs the children could catch the sweet aroma of the tobacco wafting heavenly from this pocket.

His pipe was kept in the sanctuary of an inside pocket, as it was very precious to him. He told the children that

Marilyn Monroe, a famous actress, once gave it to him for saving her poodle from certain death under the iron wheels of an oncoming runaway train. He also said she gave him a kiss on the cheek with her bright red lipstick which he didn't wash off for weeks, but the children didn't want to hear this detail. Every time they saw the pipe they imagined the small dog's bloody body crushed and broken lying on some desolate train track and they would shudder at the thought. His top left-hand pocket housed two small knives with multiple attachments, very useful for opening tobacco tins, ale bottles and such like.

Maximillian's face was born to suit a smile and his wide green eyes always lit up at the prospect of having an attentive listener for one of his fantastic stories. Stories that everyone, even the children, assumed to be major stretches of his ever vivid imagination. However, on occasions some of his farfetched yarns were proven to be fact, thus leaving his audience at odds as to what was true and what was fiction.

The right-hand side of his white beard around his mouth was stained dark brown from tobacco smoke and gave his face an asymmetrical appearance. Cecily tried to clean it on one occasion with kitchen bleach but he didn't allow that to happen a second time as he had to keep his face and beard submerged in the mouldy old water barrel at the gable of the house for hours to relieve his pain after her efforts. He had a portly belly which he vainly denied existed and tried unsuccessfully to hide. The children would poke it with their fingers and he would suck in and try to pull it back to shape.

"Did a lot of long distance running in my time you know. I could have been a contender except for my missing toe. No big belly on me," he would always say earnestly and bang his stomach with the edge of his right hand to prove its firmness.

"Sure grandad," they would reply and laugh.

The sweet aroma of his pipe tobacco would drift through the air to the children's nostrils as he sat in a tattered old armchair in the corner of his shed reading books on Egypt. Sometimes he would invite them in and tell them stories about his adventurous past. These invites usually occurred after he had collected his old age pension and would have some chocolate hidden for the children in the mouth of a stuffed lion that he said he shot in the wilds of India. The inside of the garden shed was an Aladdin's cave to the children. They were very familiar with the exact placements of his collected objects and assisted when they were being rearranged back to their natural positions in the newly relocated shed. Some of the mice had once again hidden themselves back in the repaired cardboard boxes and had journeyed with them to this new location. Maximillian had a detailed list drawn up for any mistakes in placement his mind may have overlooked. Everything had to be just so or no peace would be had in future in his repose on his tatty old armchair. The children's assistance in this affair was more for the pleasure of their company than their knowledge of his obsessive arrangements.

African shields and spears with brightly coloured tribal decorations hung on a gable wall and surrounded a potbellied stove that sat nervously in the centre appearing to fear their displeasure. A large red monarch butterfly skilfully made from papier-mâché and coloured to absolute perfection hung over the window and appeared for all the world to be alive even though by scale it was a hundred times larger than the figure it mimicked. Sun bleached photographs of Pyramids and men in traditional Egyptian dress covered the opposite gable wall and in between this lay countless objects waiting to be explored if only the children were given permission - which they never were.

"Just leave that there will you. Leave it. Leave it. I didn't carry all that stuff halfway around the globe to have you pair of urchins smash it all to smithereens," Maximillian would shout loudly.

The children would rarely take any notice of these sudden outbursts of displeasure, so it was outside for them after that, more often in the middle of an adventurous story from which the storyteller was having the greater pleasure.

"Why can't you just leave things alone and listen to the story?" he would ask as he pulled the rusty old door latch closed leaving them on the outside. The children would laugh and race away quickly, their mouths filled to bursting point with chocolate.

One of his stories stuck fast in their imagination however, the story of the ancient world that supposedly existed some three hundred million years ago, in a time where the earth abounded in beauty and peace, was a constant favourite of theirs and rated right up there with ice cream cones. Maximillian needed little prompting to rehash this yarn as its content was by far his favourite subject. Each retelling gained new ground and some added point of interest. He told them of the discoveries made in pieces of coal that when cracked open gave up the most unusual ornamental objects that had been trapped hidden inside the coal for hundreds of millions of years. Small chalices, cups and other objects made from a combination of all the known metals that we are familiar with today. These objects had lay hidden for 300 million years or more inside the coal until they were discovered completely by accident. Maximillian explained to the open mouthed expressions on the children's faces as they sat cross legged on the floor in front of him, that it takes 300 million years for coal to form in the earth as millions of years ago the earth was covered with massive swampy forests where plants, giant ferns and mosses grew. The children's eyes lit up with wonder as the only sound that disturbed Maximillian's delivery was the cracking of the logs as they burned in the open fire. Even the honeysuckle branch that tapped loudly against the window in the wind went unnoticed.

Maximillian explained to their eager ears that fallen trees and other vegetation were trapped on the bottom of the swamps building up layer after layer and creating a dense material called peat. The constant layering of the peat created high temperatures and the pressure this created transformed the peat into rock solid coal. Implying with certain assurance that these items must have been lost by someone way back in a long-forgotten age and with the passage of time were covered over by vegetation and trapped locked inside the coal formation.

"Wow grandad," Chet said with a look of wonderment even though he had heard the self-same words in a similar order with the same degree of mystery many times over in the past.

"And no school? You said there was no school in those olden times," Cecily replied earnestly.

Maximillian mumbled as Jilly gave him a stern look of disapproval.

" Ermm, did I say that? I may have been wrong about that little part of the story. There would have to be school of course. All children must attend school." Maximillian spoke and gave Jilly one of his nervous smiles that always admitted guilt for one thing or another.

"Of course, there was school, children. How else could civilization have advanced to what it is today?"

Jilly's voice brought a reasoning to the moment that the children disliked and they sighed deeply.

Maximillian gave a loud cough and spoke again with authority "Well anyway where was I? Ermm, oh es. Inscriptions on the items, when deciphered tell of a time of peace and beauty. It was a world of fascination by my reckoning. A place we can only aspire to in our imaginations. Butterflies played a large part of this world but how I am not quite sure."

"Whatever do you mean?" Jilly suddenly became interested and dried her hands on her tea towel.

"The inscriptions show the butterflies as superior to humans. Maybe back in that time they even ruled over our race. No one knows for certain. Just remember we will find treasures in pieces of coal yet children, let me tell you," he informed the children in his most sincere voice. Jilly looked to the ceiling in dismay "Diamonds and ancient ornaments in pieces of coal? And butterflies ruling humanity. You have such an incredible imagination. Really incredible," and she laughed as she continued with her washing up once again.

This is the reason Maximillian would always try to relay his wondrous intentions and most fascinating insights to the children far out of Jilly's ear shot.

Chapter 3

Dawn shone through the children's bedroom window many times and lit the timber floor and tatty old red rug as days went by uneventfully. The family gradually became familiar with their new home and surroundings. They stopped making comparisons to their cottage at Robin Hood's Bay after a while. Jilly gave up on her reminiscences of its almost perfectly proportioned kitchen and the children stopped talking about but would never forget their white sandy beach. Soon the Indian gentleman and the card with the butterfly wings were a memory to the children. Occasionally Jilly would ask about the card, usually after she had cooked Maximilian's favourite dinner, lamb stew. This was when he was ritually in his highest spirits but on never getting a satisfactory answer from him about it, she grew weary of asking and let the riddle, however intriguing fade away.

"This will have to stop. Can't you see how close your excavations are to the foundations of our house? One of these days, mark my words this place will be down on top of us all literally like a ton of bricks. I fell into one of your blasted holes today while I was hanging out my washing. I could have broken my leg," Jilly exclaimed, her mood low one bitterly cold evening as a draught blew a gale through a large crack at the side of her kitchen window. She pointed a frozen finger to a cut and purple bruise just below her left knee. The children cloaked a giggle and Maximillian gave them a stern look to be serious for his sake.

"That is shocking let me take a look." Maximillian's voice was most concerned.

"No, it is fine, leave it but these holes or whatever they are will have to be filled in and you will have to start acting responsibly as I can't take any more of this insanity," and Jilly began to cry. Her tears put a new dimension on the scene, and everyone became very serious as Jilly rarely ever showed her emotion through tears.

"Ok I will stop and fill in all my excavations,"

Maximillian put a comforting arm around her shoulder.

"And why do you go down into the old mine day after day wandering around down there on your own. You must know that it is dangerous and probably illegal. That shaft or whatever it is that you found still open should be reported to the proper authorities. You should not go in there anymore. What happens if you get lost down there? I fear for your sanity. Is this all about your grief for Rutherford? Is this craziness your way of trying to forget what happened to him? If it is I will understand but you must explain now, I must know the truth. Why won't you tell us exactly what you are looking for. And then to make things worse when you leave that blasted mine you continue with this insane digging around the house." Jilly dried her eyes as she spoke and blew her nose loudly into one of Cecily's favourite handkerchiefs. Cecily's mouth tightened to the thinnest line possible as she watched, but she kept her emotions to herself as this wasn't the time for protest.

The children felt that this surely must be the moment when all Maximillian's secrets would finally be uncovered and they would now surely know the answers to all the question they had been asking him for ages. Maximillian wrung his hands tightly together exploring some of the cracks made in his fingers by the pick and shovel he used in his excavations.

"Of course, you have a right to know what I have been doing but I was afraid you would all think I was insane at best," he said and continued to scrutinize a long black coal scar in the palm of his hand.

"If there is some explanation for all of this then I can put it to rest and try to understand you because your actions have been troubling me now for a long time," Jilly said and wiped her eyes with a towel that Cecily timidly handed her.

"You are all very familiar with the story I have told you many times about the lost civilization 300 million years ago?"

The children nodded their heads as though they would

drop off if given just a little more exertion. Jilly folded her arms so tight her finger went pale.

"My interests were aroused long ago when I heard that in a stone quarry near Aix-en-Provence in France in the 18th century, workers were digging 15 metres deep in the 11th and 12th layers of compacted limestone when they uncovered man-made objects, coins, tools, fragments of tools, wooden handles all of which contradicts the time frame of human's current existence on earth. Some years later when I was having a dalliance with a certain lady…" he stopped short and coughed regretting this unnecessary disclosure. The children gave Jilly a sudden questioning stare and she pretended not to notice. "Ermm well, I was staying in Buckhannon, West Virginia at the time and in a nearby mine a bronze bell was found fully intact in a piece of coal. Later it was carbon dated to the Carboniferous Period 323 to 298 million years ago, even before the dinosaurs. There are many more cases of similar findings around the world, all examined by experts and all found to be absolutely authentic, proving that there was a lost civilization that existed 300 million years ago. This has always fascinated me and that is why I dig and explore." Maximillian looked at them all individually waiting for their response.

"Fascinating story. But do you honestly think you will find something here. Something so small in this vast coal mine?" Jilly said looking unimpressed.

"And what about the lady?" Cecily moved closer to Maximillian and twirled the ends of her hair.

Maximillian gave a cough, "What was that? Lady? What lady? That was a slip of the tongue."

Cecily continued to twirl the ends of her hair with more fervour and continued to stare at him. Maximillian tried not make eye contact with her but it was difficult.

"Wow grandad I want to help. I will find it" Chet said.

"It appears there is no need for help now as I completely agree with your mother and am going to stop my digging.

But thank you anyway my boy," and he patted Chet on top of his head flattening some hairs that bore the traces of an encounter with his pillow.

"I felt fate led me here. Firstly, finding the advert for the house by chance and then getting the money to buy it from that mysterious gentleman. I felt that it was all leading up to something - it could all be part of a great celestial plan but now I realise that I have been foolish. I will confine my interest in this subject to my books and I will report that open shaft to the authorities tomorrow. And that will be an end to it all." The others were all very silent as Maximillian was not customarily this serious about his intentions.

"The maharajah I told you all about is called Parth and is the world's leading collector of artefacts such as this and owns many objects found in pieces of coal that date to 300 million years ago. Would you like to hear how I met him?" Maximillian smiled and tried to lighten the mood of the room.

"Yes grandad. Yes." The children jumped up and down in delight.

"After I qualified from university many years ago, I decided to ply my trade as an archaeologist in Egypt and set off for the Valley of the Kings hoping to get involved in one of the digs there. My backpack that contained all my worldly objects, and I arrived in Luxor in mid-July to a heat that can only be compared to the heat coming from the oven when you open the door on Christmas Day to check to see if the turkey is cooked." The children smiled as they knew the intensity of that heat as they regularly opened the oven door on Christmas Day to check on the progress of the turkey much to Jilly's displeasure.

"Very hot grandad," Cecily said and stared at the black metal cooker.

"Yes, very," he replied and smiled. "I got a cheap place to stay very close to the Nile and found out pretty quickly the reason for its reduced room rate…mosquitos. I was bitten all over. Thought I'd die at one point but I struggled on. A local fellow gave me a lotion and I was soon tickety boo again but I smelt pretty rank. I still bear the scars mentally." His voice sought sympathy and he grew silent for a moment to ponder on his distressing memory. Jilly looked up to the ceiling and the children laughed which shook Maximillian out from his moment.

"Ermm anyway," he continued looking a bit miffed at being mocked "I heard about a new dig on The East Valley which is where most of the royal tombs were discovered and is the place you want to be if you are interested in Egyptology. , mosquito lotion in hand and smelling like a pole cat off I set to new adventures. I was lucky to find a new team who were well financed and beginning a dig for the tomb of Ramses VIII. A tomb that has never been discovered even to this day might I add. As you can probably imagine there was a lot of digging involved, so the glamour I imagined on day one, became a very tough ordeal after the first week. I made friends with a tall Indian man called Parth. I had an idea he was from a cast not accustomed to digging out in the hot sun, but he kept about his business working hard every day and never once discussing his past. He had a much better tolerance for mosquitos and the sun than I."

"So, he was the maharajah grandad?" Cecily asked and began to twirl the ends of her hair.

"Yes he, young Cecily," he replied and put on his pretend serious face and continued with a cough that gave due warning for no further interruptions to his story.

"Let him finish Cecily," Jilly said glancing her eyes towards the clock that was hanging over the back door. Maximillian saw her looking at it but it was his story and time was irrelevant now that he had centre stage and a captive audience.

"Anyway, ermm; yes, where was I – ermm; yes anyway. He was a very handsome man but not vain. Breeding just flowed out of him like twenty-year-old champagne from an oak barrel, even though he made no effected effort to display its existence. His features were in perfect proportion as though he had been carved by a sculptor. And his gracious manner was something that cannot be taught or mimicked but came from lineage such as his."

Chet yawned loudly. Maximillian squinted his eyes and directed a stare in his direction. Chet smiled sheepishly in return.

"Anyway, we were digging a trial hole in a sandy area and came upon some limestone which is a good thing when you are looking for ancient tombs. Parth and I, with the help of a few sherpas, cleared an area to see if we could find an entrance. Parth noticed something shining in the rocks below us and went down into the deep trench to explore further. I called out to him that the sand was giving way but he wouldn't listen and kept going deeper until the sand finally did give way and he was covered completely and out of sight. We dug like crazy and were certain he was a gonner but, like that cat with nine lives, he was fine when I pulled him out still grasping onto this thing he saw in the rocks.

He wouldn't open his hand even for the doctors, so no one knew what he had found. Days later a royal party arrived from India, and we all found out that Parth was a very important maharajah and an heir to all sorts of titles and kingdoms. So they took him out of the hospital and to the airport.

That was the last time I saw Parth in Luxor. When I visited him in hospital moments before he was taken away by the royal party he gave me a very brief glimpse of what he had found."

"What was it grandad? What was it?" The two children jumped up and down like their legs were on spring coils.

"It is getting late they best be off to bed," Jilly said and with a stretch stood up from the table.

"Yes you are right Jilly it's bedtime for children. I will tell you the rest of the story some other time."

"No, no," the children stared dagger looks at their mother who ignored their irritation.

Maximillian smiled and took out his pipe that he had repaired with sticky tape and lit it with his tin gas lighter and hid himself behind a cloud of smoke.

Early morning fog settled across the land and the sun just began to lazily peep through as Maximillian closed the back door of the rectory very quietly making sure the stubborn latch didn't do its party trick and give its familiar loud click. He could feel the first weak rays of the sun warm his face as he tiptoed across the noisy gravel towards the garden gate. He looked back at the rectory and the closed curtains on the children's bedroom and smiled. His rambling letter to the authorities advising about the open coal shaft was received and their brief reply stated that this was the day the local council was charged to lock it up for good and make it safe. There was only a matter of hours left to have one last final explore deep in the mine before that avenue of pleasure was sealed off to him forever. He bid good morning to the local postman who gave him a second questioning look as it was unusual to see Maximillian out and about at such an early hour.

"I must get up earlier in future," he thought as he observed the flowers in the gardens he passed raising their heads to honour the morning sunshine. The coal mine was a contrast in temperature and got colder and damper the deeper down he descended. His strong German army torch and the short climbers pick he bought from Millets were primed for their last action but Maximillian's expectations were very low as this morning's expedition was just an exercise in closure for him. Randomly he hacked at areas in the coal face with his shiny new pick breaking off small lumps of dusty black coal as he moved deeper into the abandoned mine. Occasionally he took one in his hand and gave it a casual inspection before moving on to examine a different area.. His old Omega Seamaster watch had its alarm set for 12 - the time he set to vacate the mine least he be seal in and trapped.

The alarm gave a low whimpering tone to herald the hour and Maximillian shone his torch about the main shaft at an eerie view of claustrophobic damp abandonment that would unnerve almost anybody else and began to make his way back to the daylight and fresh air once again. For the heck of it, knowing that this would be his picks last action, he gave an area of the exit shaft a blow and broke a standard size piece of coal from the black wet face and took it up in his hand. In shock he checked it over a few times, dropping his pick in the heat of his shock discovery. A thin silver handle protruded out from the piece of coal and glistened in the light from his torch. Maximillian rubbed his eyes leaving traces of coal dust on both sides of his cheeks and inspected the object again.

"Couldn't be. No; no; can't be," his voice echoed out through the cavernous, lonely mine.

"Bloody well is," he said again and jumped up and down on the spot in exhilaration. "Finally, I have found something important," he shouted aloud to the shadows, his torch made shadows on the wet sludge that sat centimetres thick on the floor. Forgetting his pick, now abandoned for future generations to discover, he fled the shaft as though his pants were on fire.

"Good day to you all," he said cheerily to the council men as he moved out through the entrance which they were just about to seal. They all looked at each other in bewilderment watching him as he skipped along the narrow grassy path home in a gait not suited to his age.

"Where the blazes did he come from?" one of the council men said and took off his flat cap and scratched his bald head.

It was a Saturday morning, so the children and Jilly were up late and sitting at breakfast with Radio 2 blaring from the small radio that sat on the windowsill. Maximillian pushed open the back door like a whirling tornado and his excitement flooded the room without him saying one single word. Jilly dropped her spoon of porridge midway to her lips and it fell to the stone flag floor in a crash.

The children howled in laughter at her sudden shock.

"What on earth is the matter with you. Can you not open the door calmly like everyone else. And look at you; you have been down the mine again even though you promised you would never go there again," Jilly said with an irate temper that made her ears wiggle and the children became suddenly silent.

"The shaft is sealed now for good. No one can enter the mine anymore. I just had one last look that's all and guess what I found?" Maximillian could not hide his excitement and jumped around the kitchen floor, more agile than any of them could ever have imagined, leaving coal stain tracks behind him with each bounce like elephant footprints in snow.

"What is it. What is it?" the children spoke as one; asking the question over and over, their voices rising in crescendo as their faces began to flush red with eager excitement.

"What?" Jilly said sternly and folded her arms and stared at the mess he was making on her recently washed floor.

"Look," Maximillian said and held out the piece of coal with the thin silver handle protruding from its core. "Finally, I have found it. Told you all I would. Some of you didn't believe me though," he said and looked directly at Jilly who remained defiant and kept her arms tightly folded.

Without further words Maximillian cleared some of the breakfast things from the table and took a small jewellers hammer from a kitchen drawer and began to chip at the piece of coal with extreme caution. He took his knife from the pocket of his safari jacket and began to scrape gently at the silver handle like he was cleaning a sparkle from the tip of Cecily's nose. The object was now growing in stature and beginning to show its self-more clearly with each delicate precise scrape of Maximillian's blade.

"It's stuck in the coal grandad, isn't it?" Chet put his nose as close as he dared to the action.

Jilly unfolded her arms and took an interest in the procedure stepping over her spoon of porridge as she got closer to Maximillian for a clearer view of proceedings.

"What is it?" she dared to show interest and allow herself to ask the question.

Just then the coal cracked open and the object was set free from its long held captivity and Maximillian gave it a rub with one of Jilly's best tea towels. On this occasion she didn't mind; too much.

"It's a bell grandad, isn't it?" Cecily stared at the object with intent.

"That it is young Cecily. That it certainly is," Maximillian said and handed it with pride to Jilly who took it and gave it a close scrutiny, her eyes squinting and her mouth superglued tight as she stared.

"And it was…in that piece of coal?" She spoke with hesitation her eyes growing large with wonder.

"This bell has been lodged in that piece of coal for 300 million years at least." Maximillian stood to his full height and arched his back and smiled with a sense of major accomplishment towards the children who gave him their approving smiles of praise in return. He soaked up their appreciation and bounced up and down on his toes with a certain pomp.

"You thought it was a lot of nonsense I know. Thought I was cracked as a frog but now what do you say?" Still needing Jilly's approval Maximillian held his breath.

"A bell. 300 million years old," Jilly said with wonder and gave it a shake to see if the bell still made any sound. It did and gave off the quaintest soothing little ring that made them all smile.

The room suddenly got dark as the sunlight from the kitchen window was all but blotted out by thousands of coloured butterflies that scrambled frantically on top of each other to try and gain access to the kitchen by any means. Some of them squeezed under the very narrow space at the bottom of the kitchen door. Others came in through the air vent that was over the cooker but most of them flew down the chimney and within minutes the room was teeming with peaceful fluttering butterflies.

"They are following the sound of the bell," Cecily laughed as she tried to grab one in her hand.

Maximillian eased the door open past their mass and gently tried to push some of them out with his hands but he only managed to remove a small amount who flew directly back into the kitchen once again. Jilly tunnelled her way through the fluttering wings, ringing the small silver bell as she moved towards the door and out into the back garden. The butterflies all followed the slight quaint sound of the bell as thought they were the rodents following the pied piper of Hamelin. They circled her in a tight horde that reached five metres above her head as she moved towards the middle of the garden. Taking care not to allow any further sound to emanate from the tiny bell she placed it with reverence onto the grass and moved away from it back towards the rectory. The butterflies ignored her movements and stayed in a huge mass encircling the bell in a fluttering shimmering myriad of colour. Jilly closed the door and they all stood by the kitchen window watching.

"What is happening grandad?" Chet spoke as he put his nose to the glass for the best view out to the butterflies.

"We don't know darling. I think they came to the sound of the bell." Jilly looked at Maximillian's pale expressionless face as she spoke.

"Don't know at all Chet my lad. I will have to consult my books on such like and see if I can make anything of it." He stroked his grey beard into a point as he spoke.

"Look they are leaving." Cecily pointed her small index finger and touched the condensation on the glass of the kitchen windowpane and rubbed a space on it wide enough for her to have a clear view out.

The butterflies vanished into nothingness as quickly as they arrived leaving the silent silver bell alone on the grass to experience its freedom from captivity for the first time in a long age.

FOUR YEARS EARLIER. IN INDIA.

The one-legged Scott's man kept control of his most serious expression and waited until Maximillian was out of sight and then, as if an inner explosion had occurred, a laugh raced from his toes and out through his mouth. He fell to the ground and lay wriggling in howling merriment as he counted the money Maximillian had just given him.

"This is just too easy, so many fools and too little time." His strongest Scottish accent breaking through his laughter. The monkey grabbed the parrot who was caught off guard and began to strangle it with both hands. The parrot gasped for air and screeched until the Scott's man pulled them apart and placed them back on either shoulder again. "Why can't the pair of ye live in peace.

Yiz are wrecking me head. I'll put yiz in the zoo that's what I'll do if yiz keep this up," he said and they both became very quiet.

"Elephant Mountain; now there is a name for you. This is the one; I can feel it. Treasure I have searched all my life to find," Maximillian thought quietly to himself as he walked through the crowded hot streets of Bombay with his head tossed high and his back arched in triumph.

"King Charlemagne's gold mine and I am the only one who knows where it is." His sudden laugh made the folk near him stare but he didn't notice. He gave the tattered old map one further inspection and put it safely into the inside pocket of his safari jacket. Taking centre stage in a crowded local bar that smelt of body odour, stale beer and cheap cigarettes he placed his pipe in the corner of his mouth and began to speak above the chattering and clinking sounds of the unwashed.

"I need five good men to join me on an expedition. Five of the best mind, no slackers," and he looked at an overweight drunk who began to show an interest in the proposal but on hearing the word slackers sat down heavily again. "We set off tomorrow morning at first light and we could be gone for a month or maybe more." His words carpeted an air of confidence before him, fuelled by his new acquisition of the treasure map. "Good pay to the right men," he continued and everyone jumped to their feet at once until he was surrounded by everyone in the bar except for the fat man who turned his head the other way. To get a better view of his prospective hirelings he jumped up onto the bar counter and looked at the group who all stared up at him with the wild eyes of hungry wolves. "You all look a bit useless," he whispered to himself "but you, you, you, you and…" he delayed, "and you will have to do the job fine enough I suppose. Meet me at the Bombay Palace Hotel at first light."

"And the money sahib," one of the chosen five spoke up through brown chipped teeth.

"You will be handsomely paid in the morning if you turn up," Maximillian replied and jumped down from the bar counter giving a little groan as he landed awkwardly and left with a slight limp.

The crowd mumbled between themselves with looks of hardened deceit on their faces.

That night by the weak yellow light of the remnant of a red candle Maximillian studied the map memorising each line and word on the parchment until his eyes closed for sleep without permission.

He felt he could find his way now without ever having to look at the map again; even creating the scenery he would encounter in his imagination.

"And a fine Bombay morning sahib. A fine one your British excellency. Five bells have tolled," a far too cheery voice for that hour of the morning called from the other side of the bedroom door.

"Breakfast is ready very presently," the voice continued and grew faint as it moved further away from the bedroom door overshadowed by heavy leather souls on wood and back down the hallway again.

"Great, good man I am ready for it." Maximillian pulled

back the green, moth-eaten bed cover and lowered his thin white feet onto the bare wooden floorboards.

The motley group of five waited for him on the veranda of the hotel, all looking the worst from their night of alcohol and cigarettes. They coughed and yawned and looked much lazier than he had remembered. They hid their eyes from the morning sun as he scrutinized them, his enthusiasm dwindling just a little as their rag bag appearance was much worse than he recalled.

"I have mules and a horse over there in the hotel yard. Follow me." Maximillian kicked at the dry dust the breeze had gathered in small piles on the street as he led the tired looking bunch towards the yard. Maximillian saddled up his grey horse, an animal that had been his true companion on many a forlorn disastrous campaign.

"We ride mules?" The spokesman for the group let his questioning, hungover voice be heard again.

"Well yes. There's five extra for you. I hope you can ride?"

"Ahh yes sahib we ride. Maybe on horse better but mule will have to do." The spokesman continued.

"And the money sahib. Today you said the money, your Britishness," the spokesman persisted, his voice creaking from and the absence of alcohol.

Maximillian took a shabby worn alligator skin wallet from his pocket and gave some money to each of them. They didn't look overly impressed as they counted and grumbled in low undecipherable tones.

"This is just the beginning more money after work. You understand?" Maximillian put the wallet back into his pocket. They packed the mules with a month's provisions and mumbling to each other again in low aggrieved tones they mounted the mules awkwardly like men who couldn't ride.

"Are you certain you've ridden before?" Maximillian was not impressed with the poor shapes they were making.

"Like the wind. Like the wind your fine Britishness," the

spokesman replied and hung on to his mount's mane for dear life with both hands.

"Ermm," Maximillian replied unconvinced and putting his pipe firmly in his mouth rode off at point.

Unbearably hot days followed that burned a body from the inside out and long scorching nights where the imagining of one cool breath kept Maximillian sane. Mosquitos had all but devoured him. How he wished for a bottle of that rank ointment he was given in Luxor. The five Indians were untroubled by the mosquitos and did not have one bite on their tanned hides. Maximillian knew they must have some lotion or other that they were not sharing with him. He noticed them snigger at his discomfort and knew the rank aroma of the lotion that hung like a putrid cloud over the camp but as they didn't offer he didn't ask.

After a long and draining week that stole more from his reserves than a three-month hike, a tall mountain peeped its head out above the foliage of the steaming dense forest.

"Elephant mountain sahib; your Britishness." The spokesman's voice delighted in offering the welcome news and pointed a skinny wattle that he used to coax his reluctant mule forward.

"Praise the Lord for that." Maximillian spoke with pain through his swollen bloodied mosquito bitten lips.

The sounds of Indian flying foxes and nightjar birds filled the dusk of the evening as they reached the base of Elephant Mountain and they could just about see the outline of the sheer walls of a magnificent white palace glowing in the bright moonlight on the very pinnacle of the hill.

"Very fine maharajah lives there your Britishness," the spokesman said as he noticed Maximillian stare and he smiled his broadest beam through his chipped dark brown tobacco-stained teeth.

Camp was set near sandstone rocks from which a thin sliver of ice-cold water trickled like life blood.

They all stood in line waiting with dry tongues to fill their tin mugs with its elixir. No champagne from Harry's Bar ever tasted so good to Maximillian and he had sampled many a vintage there.

The night brought the severest heat Maximillian had ever remembered. The surrounding hills blocked out what little breeze floated across the scorched landscape and the sandstone held the days heat like a sponge and filtered it out all night like gigantic radiators. He knew he would need his best self the following day and sleep was essential so to knock himself out, Maximillian made the uncustomary decision to drink whiskey to that glass beyond excess. He slept alright but woke with a head like thunder in a galvanised bucket.

"Blast. They have taken everything." He raced headlong through the quiet morning jungle where the animals and vegetation were preparing for yet another blistering day, to see if he could catch glimpse of the five Indians. They were long gone. They took the mules and all the provisions, not leaving one skin of water behind to preserve life. Maximillian quickly checked his pocket for his wallet. It was still there, and he gave a sigh of relief. His grey horse was loose and grazing peacefully in the distance all tacked up with the reins dragging on the damp dewy grass. He knew they tried to take it as well but his trusty steed would not be ridden by anyone other than Maximillian and he hoped it had bitten or kicked one of them hard when they tried. And it had.

"Looks like it's you and me again old fellow," and he patted it on the neck. The horse, contented to be in Maximillian's company continued to graze and gave him a casual look with the corner of its eye.

He lay down heavily on the grass beside the horse and spread his arms and legs out wide on the ground. The peaceful sound of it grazing calmed his anguish. The sun was just coming up over the horizon as Maximillian drifted off to sleep. The horse pushed its top lip gently against his cheek and he awoke suddenly.

"Making sure the sun doesn't burn me alive old boy," Maximillian said and rubbed his hand over the horse's nose.

Wearily he rode through the last fragments of jungle without one drop of water to soothe his throat, which was as dry as icing on top of a wedding cake, as he made his way to the base of Elephant Mountain. He took no wonder in the glorious plants and trees that surrounded him and the smell of fresh vegetation that carried in the jungle breeze now made him nauseous, as his stomach rumbled loud from hunger. He tried to eat a hard yellow crab apple that he pulled from a weather beaten old tree that had stubbornly lived too long but spat it out as its bitterness was more disagreeable than his hunger.

After unsaddling his horse and placing the tack in what he imagined was a safe place behind the root of a lime tree he let the horse free to graze on burned grass.

Slowly he began to climb up through the dense vegetation on the side of Elephant Mountain, his head faint from searing heat and pangs of hunger. He imagined a chip shop he was familiar with in Newcastle that was on the narrow road east that lead to Whitley Bay. It was renowned for having the very best fish and chips. The imagined aroma of fresh fish and chips with a little vinegar and a lot of salt from this place tormented him. He even began to speak to the owner,"A fresh cod and chips, Steve. Yes, just one cod and chips. Make that a large chips with tea, no two teas. What's that Steve? Sugar? Yes, why not. I'll have two sugars and a little milk." He repeated the order over and over changing the choice each time and apologising to Steve for the discomfort he was causing. He left Steve's chip shop hungry, with the aroma of strong white vinegar in his nostrils still when he reached the base of the white walls of the maharajah's palace. It stood imperiously overlooking the forest as though it were the heart that pumped the life blood into all it surveyed. Isolated by the dense jungle, its high white impregnable walls reflected the glaring midday sun like an indifferent motorist who chooses not to turn off his head beams. A flagpole soared from a palace tower where a red and yellow flag hung limply with no breeze to display its motif. Arrow slits protected prying eyes on the basement walls and large bow windows with red velvet curtains supplied their rations of light to the floors above. This was the home of an important person who Maximillian thought may be able to assist him in his quest to find the treasure marked on the Scot's man's map.

CHAPTER 4

A gunshot cracked out through the still air and alarmed the peaceful sounds of the jungle. All life panicked and fled frantically deeper into the cover of the undergrowth. Maximillian could hear the terrified screams of a young girl's voice; then silence. He moved cautiously closer to where he thought the sounds originated, keeping behind the cover of the tall thick ferns and treading lightly least a twig crack beneath his step. The craggy mouth of a mountain cave was partially hidden behind thorny bramble briars and Maximillian decided to explore, taking a few handfuls of blackberries from the brambles and devouring them whole. This satisfied his hunger a little but made a black stain around the corners of his mouth. Once inside the cave the cool air was a welcome greeting and he breathed it in deeply. The smell of dampness and the recent presence of animals filled his nostrils but didn't deter him from taking breaths that could blow up a Zeppelin.

"Don't come any closer." A young girl's voice penetrated through the darkness from the furthest corner of the dark cave.

Maximillian stood still, suddenly forgetting the pleasure the cool air was giving him.

"I have a gun so if you come any closer, I will shoot," the girl's voice continued nervously, trembling on occasions with fear.

"I have no wish to harm you. Who are you?" The tone of Maximillian's voice purposely imitated a preacher at a church he used to attend, who was known for his serenity and calming abilities. He adopted this remembered pitch as he didn't wish to be filled with lead and left in this isolated cave where his carcase would certainly nourish the local wildlife.

"I am on my own. Can I help?" He braved one more step forward.

The definitive sound of a pistol hammer cocking

bounced off the walls about him. He froze and listened to the loud beating of his terrified heart as the veins on his temples turned blue from pressure. He wondered macabrely which part of his body would consume the first bullet and gave his chest the once over imagining the red stains that would appear shortly on his shirt.

"I told you not to come any closer. Now move back or you're dead. I mean it." The young girl's voice became determined and in control.

"I am just a treasure hunter. Well, an explorer to be precise who, on occasions doubles as a treasure hunter to keep afloat so to speak. Look I have a treasure map here and he fumbled as he took the old map out of his inner pocket. "It is for…" he continued but was interrupted.

"King Charlemagne's gold mine," the girl's voice spoke calmly as though used to repeating the line in the past. Maximillian took a fresh breath of damp putrid air and swallowed.

"Well as a matter of fact, yes it is. How did you know?" he asked sheepishly fearing the reply.

"You bought it from a gambling one-legged Scotsman in Bombay." The girl's voice continued with a hint of jollity.

"Well as it happens, I did." Maximillian was beginning to feel that yet another of his expeditions was about to hit a dry well.

"Do you know him?" Maximillian heard the hammer of the pistol being released.

"Oh no I don't know him but I have heard about him many times from the idiots who have come to this place to find treasure that doesn't exist. You have been scammed, but don't feel too badly you are not the first and you certainly won't be the last." She laughed briefly as she walked out from the shadows.

She was a very pretty Indian girl about ten years of age with long jet-black hair and piercing ebony coloured eyes. Her head which balanced on top of an exceptionally long elegant neck was kept directed towards Maximillian as she moved with the grace of a panther around the cave. Long elegant fingers held the large pistol in one hand and in the other, close to her breast, she held a small onyx statue of an elephant. Her voice had slight traces of an English accent and Maximillian imagined she possibly had an English-speaking tutor. Even though she was very young she had the demeanour of a much older, worldly person and was in total control of the situation.

Maximillian sat down heavily on a rock as an air of utter dejection overwhelmed him. He now realised that he had wasted the last of his money on a fool's errand and was now broke, penniless, hungry and thirsty, with a steaming hangover and a blackberry-stained mouth.

"Could it get any worse?" he thought to himself and gave a deep sigh.

He stood up slowly; his lifeless movement suggested his legs would not be capable of carrying the weight of his body.

"What is your name?" Maximillian's voice rang of dejection and disinterest.

"Rawinda. There is a path to the palace straight ahead, follow me," she said with confidence.

Just then the faint yet noticeable crackling of dead vegetation on the floor of the cave drew Rawinda and Maximillian's attention and they searched in the shadows for the source of the intrusion. A large, fully grown common krait slid from the dark shadows of the cave, a metre from Rawinda; its mouth open and hissing loudly, ready to strike a deadly blow. Rawinda knew only too well that there was no use in trying to run and stood her ground waiting for her fate. The terror in her eyes focused its attention on Maximillian hoping for his support. Neither of them dared to breath as they watched the snake make its final movements towards her, preparing to launch itself.

Maximillian slowly took a Bowie knife he once bought from a market in Salford Precinct from its sheath and delicately turned the knife around in his hand until he held the tip of the razor sharp blade between his index finger and thumb. Rawinda had a look of resolve on her face as she stared the krait in the eye. It hissed a long fearful sound and drew its head back to strike. Maximillian threw the Bowie knife with precision and it lodged in the snake, inches below its head. It fell, lifeless to the ground. Rawinda drew a large breath and colour gradually began to return to her cheeks. She calmly pulled the knife from the snake and handed it to Maximillian.

"You saved my life. Thank you," she said and smiled at him for the first time.

Maximillian cleaned the knife on his trouser leg and put it safely back into its sheath again.

"We can't have you eaten up by a snake now can we?" he said with a smile.

"Come on follow me." She ran from the cave like an ethereal nymph and disappeared into the undergrowth. A gun shot rang out and Maximillian could hear the bullet buzzing past his head like an angry bee when curiosity brings an intruder too close to its hive. The smells and screams of the front line raced back to the forefront of his memory as he recalled his time spent soldiering in his youth. The remembered fear that the next buzzing sound could have his name firmly tattooed on it made him run, head as low as his gait would allow, all the time following the path Rawinda had taken.

"Almost there, just beyond that brow," Rawinda called back to him as she ran, her voice peppered in fear and her breath measured to allow just that one sentence.

She ran to a small black door in the palace wall and pushed it hard with her delicate shoulder. The door creaked open and they both rushed inside; Rawinda pulling Maximillian in by the arm the final few metres. The door lead into the basement hall with red brick masonry arches and stone walls that were painted with a white lime wash. The floor was grey shiny stone worn from centuries of busy feet and a single lantern burned on the wall to add to the natural day light that squeezed its way in through the narrow

arrow slits. Maximillian could smell the sweet aroma of cooking hit him square in the nostrils and this torment added to his already ravenous pangs of hunger.

"Parth!." Maximillian suddenly saw his old friend from The Valley of the Kings appear with four armed men. He had aged a little, gone grey at the temples but the skin on his face was now pulled tight with worry.

"Rawinda," Parth's voice trembled as he grabbed her and held her tightly. "I heard the shots are you ok?"

"Yes, fine. I am fine. This kind man just saved my life from a krait," Rawinda said and pointed to Maximillian.

In his anxiety Parth had not taken any notice of Maximillian. They looked at each other for a moment and both laughed in a mutual remembrance of experiences shared together in the past. Experiences that didn't need descriptions right now but would always define their friendship.

"Rawinda, this is Maximillian. He once saved my life in The Valley of the Kings in Luxor. I owe him a great deal. Neither of us would be here if it wasn't for his quick actions that day." Parth smiled and left his hand on Maximillian's shoulder. Maximillian rose on his toes in satisfaction at this praise.

"You'd have done the same for me." Maximillian had just about gained his breath back from his dash.

"Ahh that we will never know but I'd like to think I would have," Parth replied.

"And now he just saved my life from a krait. I would have been dead for certain," Rawinda exclaimed.

"It appears that you may just be the saviour of our family," Parth smiled.

"Father, there was someone waiting for me near the cave. They fired shots. But I fired back as well," Rawinda said and held the pistol forward to display it in her hand triumphantly.

"I told you repeatedly not to go to that cave alone but you will not listen. And you took that pistol from my study."

Parth showed a concerned anger and took the pistol away from Rawinda.

"Little girls should not carry these. And I also told you to leave the statue alone. If you keep going to that cave it will no longer be a safe place for us to hide in."

"Yes, I know you are right. I am sorry. It was still hidden safely in the secret alcove in the cave." she handed the onyx statue of the elephant to Parth who held his hands up in a gesture of dismay before taking it from her.

"Why did you bring it here, Rawinda? I told you to leave it where it was." Parth's voice appeared to be tired from repeating the same request many times in the past.

"It is not safe out there anymore father. People know about its location. They must know," Rawinda said and looked at Maximillian for support. Maximillian looked confused and stared at the floor in an effort to avoid inclusion in an argument he knew nothing about. Parth took the onyx statue of the elephant from Rawinda with such reverence that Maximillian suddenly became very alert and imagined that it had to be some priceless object. Parth studied it closely with no facial expression as to give any indication of his feelings.

"Follow me," he said tapping Maximillian gently on the shoulder. Rawinda and Maximillian followed Parth leaving the four armed men in the basement guarding the small black door. Parth climbed a circular stone staircase that was lit only by arrow slits. The door at the top of the staircase led out into a majestic hallway that was covered with overlapping Persian rugs. Rare tapestries depicting famous battles and hunting scenes covered all the walls and long rectangular windows flooded light across the vaulted ceiling that had rich gold decorations in its plaster mouldings. The smell of the lanterns that lit the area mixed with the rich smell of spices from the kitchen to create an intoxicating aroma that almost made Maximillian fall to his knees from its anticipatory effect.

Parth's footsteps slowed and stopped at a door halfway

down the hall and he stood for a moment and looked about him, his eyes narrowing to a squint. He unlocked it with a key that he kept on a gold chain around his neck and he gently pushed the door open. Parth beckoned them inside with a wave of his hand and locked the door behind them once again, anxiously pulling and pushing at the door handle in an over exaggerated and obsessive fashion.

The room had a protective feeling of sanctuary and appeared alien to the turmoil and turbulences of life outside its hallows. This was Parth's private place, an area where his interests and emotions were allowed to roam free from the daily routines of his office and position. The floor was white marble and was peppered here and there with red Persian rugs. A seven-metre-tall white marble chimney piece commanded one end of the room and a set of very large, rare elk horns hung directly above it. The heavy oak shutters on the two long rectangular windows either side of the fireplace were closed tightly and locked. Stray beams of light fought to break through the barricade but their impact did little except to highlight the dust particles in the air. Oil lanterns sat high up on the walls on either side of the marble fireplace. Parth lit them with a wick on the end of a bamboo cane and their light filled the room with a warm golden glow reminiscent of a peaceful Indian sunset. The smell of the paraffin reminded Maximillian of a small nightlight his grandmother kept lit beside her bed as she was very afraid of the dark. For the most fleeting of moments he imagined he caught the aroma of her clove drops and that over sweet old ladies perfume she used liberally.

Maximillian gazed around in awestruck wonder at many glass cabinets that sat neatly dominating the centre of the room. He noticed that they housed many small archaeological artefacts and had a strong desire to race to them and devour the sight of each item but modesty prevailed, and he kept his decorum until given permission.

"This place is known as Parth's haven," Rawinda said with a smile. "It is not very often that strangers see this sanctuary," she continued.

"So, Egypt and all its wonders no longer held any excitement for you my friend?" Parth changed the topic suddenly and Rawinda smiled.

"I gave it my days and there was nothing further for me there anymore. Even the mosquitos had grown tired of my hide by the time I decided to leave." Maximillian gave a shielded stare into one of the display cabinets as he spoke. "You were very lucky that day in the Valley of The Kings. You almost found a burial place for yourself beneath the sands of Luxor." Maximillian eased closer to the display cabinets and Parth smiled as he noticed his coy action.

"It was a close call for sure. But very much worth it in the end." Parth became serious and the skin on his face tightened to show the outline of his skull.

Maximillian's interest grew on seeing his reaction and he moved restlessly from foot to foot in eager expectation of what he assumed he was about to hear. "What did you risk your life for that day? Surely it couldn't have been for that little piece of gold you showed me shortly before you left the hospital in Luxor. Your life for that tiny piece of gold seemed a pretty bad choice then and my opinion hasn't changed since." Maximillian's words goaded a little in an attempt to abstract the details he knew Parth was hiding.

"This is what I risked my life for that day," Parth said and taking the onyx statue of the elephant from Rawinda in both hands he twisted it in a clockwise motion so that it opened into two halves revealing a secret hidden compartment at its core. From this core he took out a small gold object and held it up to the dim light that shone from the wall lanterns.

"What do you think?" Parth said and looked at Maximillian who squinted until his eyes were almost closed to make a better assessment.

"What - is - it?" Each syllable Maximillian spoke was drenched in wonder and he stroked his beard into a point as he leaned forward, his nose almost touching Parth's hand.

"While we were digging in Luxor that day, I saw a piece of gold shining back at me from the limestone at the bottom of the trench. I imagined you all noticed it but it seems none of you did so I scrambled to try and reach it. I thought it was separate from the limestone formation, but it wasn't. It was set into the rock so I took my hammer and tried to break it free from the boulder. Freeing it took much longer than I expected. My frantic efforts disturbed the sand and the trench caved in on top of me. I was sure it was the end for me but I still kept a firm hold on what I found. I had no idea what it was at that time. For some unknown reason I had this strong unstoppable urge to get to this piece of gold. It was as though it were a fulfilment of fate; of some action that I was born to carry out. It was almost as though I had done this before in…you know like a *déjà vu* type of situation. I just couldn't help myself, it drew me to it. I assumed it was part of an Egyptian treasure that somehow got lost outside one of the tombs but later when I examined it further, I realised exactly what I had uncovered. I very carefully removed the rock, millimetre by millimetre from the piece of gold and soon realised that it had actually formed around the gold object multi millions of years ago. As I scraped away the limestone, I realised that there were two independent pieces of gold separated by a thin layer of rock a couple of millimetres thick so in effect they were two separate items encased by limestone that had formed around them millions of years ago. I used radiometric dating to give me a rough guess of the time that would have happened and…" Parth stopped and looked at Maximillian "Guess how old I believe these objects are?" he continued.

"Ermm, well for rock to form around them must be tens of millions of years" Maximillian replied vaguely and continued to lean in towards Parth to get a clearer look at the object.

"300 million years to be as precise as I can be." Parth put the gold object to his lips and breathed on it gently and rubbed the condensation off with the tip of his little finger.

"I have heard about items such as this in the past but I never thought I would ever come in contact with one. I assumed it was all a myth." Maximillian spoke very softly giving extra reverence to the moment.

"All my collection of artefacts stored in these glass cabinets were found embedded in either rock or coal at layer depths that date them all to a time at least 300 million years ago." Parth's lips formed a proud smile as he observed the shocked expression on Maximillian's face.

"The piece I found at Luxor started me off on a quest to collect as many of these objects as I could and presently I own the majority of artefacts of this type in the world." Parth's words resounded with a sense of major achievement and pride. "But this is only part of the story" Parth held the piece of gold he had taken from the onyx statue up to the dim light again to admire it further. "What I have told you defies explanation but what I am about to tell you takes it all to another realm entirely. As I said the two items I found separated by a couple of millimetres of rock were identical images of each other. They were trapped in the rock for 300 million years unable to touch each other." Parth handed the gold object to Maximillian and he took it like he was handed a very delicate rare orchid. He inspected it; his eyes dancing over every millimetre of its surface with excitement and he tenderly brushed his index finger over its surface as though he were stroking the head of a new-born baby.

"Is it some type of wing?" A veil of sweat had formed on Maximillian's face and he roughly opened the top button of his shirt as he studied the object, turning it over and over sensitively in his hands.

"A butterfly's wing." Parth spoke as he opened one of the long rectangular shutters and allowed the sunlight to flood into the spaces the darkness had now lost control of.

"Indeed yes, it is a butterfly's wing." Maximillian didn't take his gaze from the object and moved towards the window to let the natural light illuminate it.

"Where is the second one? Do you still have it?"

Maximillian looked at Parth and then at Rawinda trying to read and second guess their expressions before they had time to speak.

"I keep them separated. One is here in the palace and this one is kept in a safe place in the cave you were in earlier. It is essential that they must be kept separate," Parth said and took the gold butterfly wing from Maximillian and placed it carefully back into the centre of the onyx elephant once again closing the two parts tightly.

"These people who fired shots at Rawinda - do you know who they are? - do they hope to steal your collection?" Maximillian walked around the glass cabinets no longer coyly disguising his interest, now unashamedly allowing his eyes to feast on the contents stored within.

Parth laughed "No, no. They care nothing for these items. They want the butterfly wings."

"Are you going to tell me why? And why do they have to be kept separated?" Maximillian sounded hysterical as though all his words were racing out of his mouth at once.

"How do I know you are not working with the treasure hunters?" Parth had a small degree of concern badly concealed in his voice.

"He is yet another victim of the Scotsman," Rawinda said with a smile.

Parth laughed out loud and tapped his hand on Maximillian's back.

"Not you as well? That Scott's man is a rich fellow by now I imagine, and he never needed to find King Charlemagne's gold mine to amass his fortune either." Parth turned away as he spoke to conceal his desire to break into uncontrollable laughter.

"Ok, ok so I was a fool. That Scotsman is a damned good actor. He should be in Hollywood. He would get an Oscar for his performances." Maximillian looked embarrassed and his cheeks began to turn bright crimson red.

"Why would he go there? They couldn't afford him at

the rates he commands here on the streets of Bombay." Parth could no longer camouflage his merriment and both he and Rawinda broke down in tumultuous laughter leaning on each other for support.

"So, are you going to tell me about the butterfly wings or not?" Apart from his grey horse Maximillian now stood up in all his worldly possessions. And these weren't much to be proud of either, as both his boots had holes in the soles and the tatty old belt that held up his trousers needed just one over enthusiastic tug to break into two halves. So, Maximillian was feeling very vulnerable in his current distressed state now that he had observed the opulent lifestyle of his old partner who had once soldiered with him on equal terms. Parth became very serious suddenly on realising Maximillian's discomfort.

"Ok. I will tell you but no one, and I mean no one must ever know what I am about to say. Do you understand?" Parth became very serious with all traces of previous jollity vanished from his face.

"Of course - you know you can trust me."

Parth gave Maximillian a probing stare to fully convince himself that he could be trusted.

He had kept this burning secret for too long and now needed to tell someone to get a second understanding of a situation that was too terrific to comprehend and too amazing to keep all to himself.

"Once I had all the limestone removed from the butterfly wings, to my surprise, they slotted into each other precisely to form one unit but when they were firmly joined together..." Parth stopped and looked at Rawinda, a flash of trepidation danced across his countenance. He remained silent in contemplation for a few moments; his breath deepening to draw in excessive quantities of cold air as his mind gave him a free hand to trawl through his secret hidden memories.

"What the bloody blazes happened?" Maximillian screamed and began to pull his beard into a point in an unrelenting obsessive fashion; the anticipation now taking control of his reasoning.

"Well, the very second I joined the two butterfly wings together the room suddenly filled to the brim with millions of butterflies. Their mass was so thick I could barely see and the flapping sound of their wings was like the most beautiful music I have ever heard. They seemed to appear from nowhere as if out of thin air." Parth relived the experience again in his imagination and his face developed a look of serenity, as his mind's eye brought him back to that very moment once more.

Maximillian sat down on a cushioned window seat that had a full view of the rose gardens beneath.

"But let me tell you that is not all by a long stretch, Parth said and sat down beside Maximillian who stared intently at Parth, impatient for the next word from his lips.

"A wormhole opened near that gable wall." And he pointed a long, elegant index finger towards the spot. "It was a swirling mass of multi-colour and white vapour. Every so often one particular colour would become more dominant and explode into the room then vanish back to the same intensity as the rest of the colours. It drew me towards its mesmerising presence. I felt a strong desire that I needed to be inside it but I fought the impulse and kept my distance even though the yearning to run into it was so strong," Parth said and his eyes grew wide and wild and his tongue licked his lips as though he held a 99 from the vendor with the three-legged cat. "After a few moments all the butterflies flew back into the wormhole again so I gave into temptation and followed them inside. I could see the butterflies fly towards a very bright light at the end of the wormhole and I followed them as far as the edge but I didn't dare go further. Standing on the edge I looked out into the most amazingly beautiful place I could ever possibly imagine. Endless fields of brilliantly coloured wildflowers stretched far off to distant horizon and swayed gently in a warm breeze that was heavily scented by their aroma.

Countless millions of multi-coloured butterflies fed on the nectar from the wildflowers. Some of the butterflies I imagined had at least fifty metres wingspans and these cast large shadows over the land as they meandered gracefully across the sky. The butterflies I followed through the wormhole flew out into the fields of wildflowers and vanished in an instant amidst the millions of others. As I stood at the very edge of the wormhole and gazed out it seemed that time had no place in the world that lay before me. Everything moved and existed in peace and harmony, so different from the worlds I am familiar with. I so longed to take that final step out into this strange new land as its serenity drew my whole being to its calming presence. Fear of being trapped on the other side and not being able to return to my own time made me leave reluctantly and follow the path I had taken, back through the wormhole and into this room once again." Parth slumped his shoulders down after his delivery and stared at the marble floor.

"This is fascinating Parth. A land of butterflies you say. And you can return there again whenever you wish if you decide to join the butterfly wings together again?" Maximillian spoke, his voice filled with childlike excitement.

"I should say so…" Parth was interrupted:

"No, it is much too dangerous. You must never join the butterfly wings together again." Rawinda spoke with determination and stood in bold defiance before her father.

"Rawinda is right. I can't be sure that if I stood beyond the wormhole if I would ever be able to leave that place again. Would I be trapped in the land of butterflies forever? I just don't know." Parth's words of resolve were unconvincing to Maximillian who could sense that he secretly desired to know more and fully intended to return to the land of butterflies to explore its mystique further when the correct opportunity arose.

Maximillian stayed with Parth for four joyful days. Reminiscing about time lost and battles won.

Sampling his finest red wines and smoking Turkish pipe

tobacco specially blended for him on the Black Sea coast. They both scrutinised each item in the glass display cabinets pondering and wondering over each piece and the life it had lived 300 million years earlier. They made up fantastic stories about these possibilities that got ever more outlandish the more the wine flowed. By each night fall Rawinda could hear them and just about make out their slurred words of mutual gratification over a new even more anomalous possibility that their inebriated imaginations had unveiled. They always stopped just short of joining the two butterfly wings together. Even though the temptation grew stronger as the late wine-soaked hours ticked by on the tall grandfather clock that rang out the time to deaf ears from a shadowy corner of the room.

As a parting gesture Parth gave Maximillian a yellow wax cast of a large pear and thanked him again for saving Rawinda's life. Parth handed over the wax cast of the pear with such ceremony that Maximillian accepted it with a suitable pomp and gratitude. Even bowing his head in reverence as it was handed to him.

"An unusual parting gift. An old wax cast? Very odd," Maximillian thought but having thoroughly enjoyed his four days he didn't wish to seem ungracious.

CHAPTER 5

The Old Rectory, Wales
Time: The present

Chet and Cecily longed for their little private hideaway now overgrown and lost in the undergrowth in their old garden at Robin Hood's Bay. It had taken them a long time to create that perfect place with all their most valuable treasures stored safely together in the perfection of its sanctuary. A world that their imaginations controlled and everything they kept hidden there, be they most humble to the eyes of nonbelievers, were the most important things in the whole world to them.

They called it 'The Woodhouse' even though it had no exterior walls of any sort just the bushes and undergrowth as an imaginary boundary. Each little section of the woodhouse was a very important area in its own right. There was an area to store sweets in a crevice of a beech tree that lay on the east boundary. An area to store weapons in case of attack beneath a misshaped granite rock whose erroneous presence in that place was often the source of debate amongst the adults. Two cutlasses that were made from oddments of wood Maximillian had discarded after he misread his tape measure before putting his saw to work. A sling shot made from an old pair of Maximillian's red braces and perfectly symmetrical balls of clay that were rolled up and stacked like cannon balls waiting for an intruder to dare attack their most special place. A young sapling tree that had been broken in half in a storm and now stood two metres high was their prize weapon. Chet carved the broken top of it into a concave shape that was perfect to house a missile and when the sapling was pulled back sufficiently it could propel the missile some ten metres. This calculation was measured to within a few centimetres so as to know the exact time to unleash the weapon. Thankfully for an intruder's sake none ever arrived so all the weapons lay dormant but in a constant state of waiting. The children would only leave this place when Jilly called out to tell them that it was mealtime.

"Oh I'm not hungry," Chet would always say. "Why does she always call us when I am not hungry?"

But Cecily would convince him that it was for the best and off the two of them would set, back to the real world for a short while, a place they had no control over whatsoever and where they were at the very end of the pecking order.

The raindrops beat down without mercy onto the thin slated roof of the rectory like the arrows from an army of archers in wedge-shaped formation. With just a little more persistence it seemed as though the drops would break right through and flood all before them. Chet and Cecily listened to the rain and were bored. They peered out through the rectory window watching puddles gather like small irregular shaped lakes all around the back yard. They decided there and then that it was time to recreate their "Woodhouse 2" here. It would never be the same as their old one in Robin Hood's Bay of course but they had the master plan in their memories and that was all they needed. From a seat by a window that cried tears of rain they looked out through the drops at the grey landscape around the rectory searching for a suitable place to construct "Woodhouse 2." They deliberated with each other choosing places and then dismissing them for various reasons mostly because a potential area had the likelihood of being disturbed by the presence of unwanted adults. Finally, they both agreed on a spot that had a very tall pine tree at its centre piece in the furthest corner of the garden.

"The pinecones from the tree will fall down into the woodhouse and make ideal missiles," Chet said with glee. The tree sat with its face to the west wind giving a firm guarantee of this. Cecily was never overly bothered by the defensive strategies of the woodhouse but always played along with Chet's ideas for the sake of peace.

"We will have to plant roses and flowers." Cecily's face

lit up like a roman candle as she imagined.

Chet was not overly bothered with this idea but played along with Cecily's suggestions for the sake of peace.

"Grandad has a big pear, you know the one? He never eats it and it's been there for ages," Cecily said.

Chet shrugged his shoulders, "we don't need that," he said with disinterest. "Are you certain that it's real? It looks far too big to be real."

"Yes it is real. Grandad told me it was real and not to touch it but he never ate it like he said he would and that was ages ago. We need food at the woodhouse. If we plant it nearby we will have fresh pears when it sprouts up into a fine pear tree. And we can give grandad some. That will make him happy." Cecily beamed a smile that stretched the freckles on her face delighting at her new idea.

That night they pulled open the curtains and stared out at the full moon that lit their bedroom in milky white shadows. They knew about its strange effect on some people. Maximillian advised them to take care on full moon nights as the bogie man walks the land in search of small children. They pulled their duvets up tight around their faces as they listened for the slightest sound that could herald his arrival. They couldn't sleep for ages thinking about this and their plans for Woodhouse 2. But by the time cuckoo clock on the landing popped out to say ten the whole household was fast asleep and dreaming.

Morning brought a bright wonderful day for Woodhouse 2 construction. The rain had switched off its taps and lakes of water that had formed in the back yard were now a memory. All that remained of them was their dry bed. Chet and Cecily were out surveying their chosen area before breakfast both dressed in their long blue and white striped night shirts.

"What's gotten into them this morning?" Jilly mused as she looked out through the kitchen window at the children walking around the area beneath the tall pine tree.

Maximillian gave a few low grumbles as he got up from his morning paper and looked over his reading spectacles through the kitchen window towards the area at rear of the garden.

"Must have lost something I'd say." He quickly sat back down again to continue reading.

"Call them in will you. They won't listen to me I know. Jilly wiped the white oilcloth table covering with motifs of a deer's head with antlers, as she began to set the breakfast things.

"A man can't have a minute's peace to read the morning papers," he grumbled and got up and walked to the back door holding the paper in his hand. He was in his bare feet and stepped lively as his feet touched the colder stone flags further away from the fireside.

"Breakfast," he shouted "On the double," in his stern voice.

The children heard Maximillian's voice and always obeyed its commands and came running to the house immediately.

"Why won't they do that for me?" Jilly said as she watched them run towards the house, both of them trying to reach the door first and touch it to win the race.

"Well, I remember deep in the outback of Australia many years ago, an aboriginal woman said the same thing to me. I was camped near the Murrumbidgee River…"Maximillian put his morning paper down and straightened himself up in his chair to share this story that Jilly knew would take an age to retell.

"Maybe later grandad," Jilly said and smiled and opened the back door just as the children approached it. They ran right in as if they were expecting it to open by magic.

Maximillian gave his most offended scowl and picked up his morning paper, gave it a right good over extended shake. He hid behind it and began to read again with an occasional indistinguishable grumble going unnoticed by the others.

"We have found our new woodhouse and are going to

fix it up later." Cecily rubbed the nose of one of the deer motifs on the tablecloth as she spoke.

"Wonderful. Maybe grandad will help you?" Jilly replied and looked towards Maximillian still hidden behind his paper.

"Too busy for all that sort of thing." Maximillian's words sulkily drifted from behind his newspaper.

Jilly smiled and mouthed the words," He will help you with it," to the children who looked towards Maximillian and smiled.

INDIA

Time: The present

"Could that handsome prince on his black stallion live in that land beyond the wormhole?" Rawinda thought. "Would he ride up to her in the fields of butterflies, take her up in his arms and win her heart? Would he whisk her away to his castle on a hill that had a wooden drawbridge lying open across a moat just waiting for their arrival?" She imagined sitting in front of him on the saddle with him holding her tightly as they rode across the fields of wildflowers. She fantasised about all sorts of things in the land of butterflies and if she were to admit it these imaginings took up more than a few hours of her time every day. Often she could be seen walking aimlessly and staring with glazed eyes into the unknown her thoughts fixed on all the possibilities that lay waiting for her in the Land of Butterflies.

The cliff top that faced west from Elephant Mountain was a very scenic place with the finest vantage points in the land to overlook Pangong Lake. This was Rawinda's mother Tuliana's favourite place to walk and here she would gather her thoughts in the evenings as the sun began to set. The lake would stretch out in front of her like a simmering gold silk saree to the horizon and the warm breeze that blew in from its vast waters would dance through her hair and return the pink blush to her cheeks. There was one spot near the edge that gave the greatest sensation and it was here that she dared to stand. A grassy ledge filled with the small delicate white flowers of sea campion with an updraft that on stormy days could take your breath. Tuliana had always felt the very slight risk was worth it as a view from this place could easily wash away a thousand problems. It never failed her and would always restore peace once again; quenching any anguish in her soul.

Tuliana had the same jet black hair and ebony coloured eyes as her daughter and even though in her 40th year Tuliana would have passed easily as Rawinda's older sister.

She moved as though time was irrelevant; as though she existed outside its restrictive boundaries. Her movements were as though choreographed for a ballet scene; delicate and empyrean with a serene elegance. But with all the natural blessings she possessed, her greatest beauty was her humility to all and an understanding of the plight of others less fortunate than herself.

Tuliana was loved by all the servants and subjects on their estates. She would regularly make missions of mercy to families who had encountered hardships, offering her kindness and worldly offerings to ease their times of distress. These acts were remembered fondly and broadcast widely giving her a reputation of honour and graciousness amongst all who knew her name.

At Pangong Lake, winter meant severe sub-zero temperatures, ice so thick it looked like it would never melt and a complete freeze over of every living thing. With no touch of human hand, a canvas was painted in white perfection, unaware of any living existence needed to substantiate its magnificence. From Tuliana's view point on top of Elephant Mountain the breath taking winter scene stretched out to a white milky horizon. The lake was a vast motionless white plateaux where occasional icy breezes blew the top layer of snow and ice in whirlwind circles that reached twenty metres high. At its boundary endless forests of white conifer trees decorated with snow and icicles had the appearance of a continuous festive season. In the distance a very pale milky sun, lethargically peered out through off-white clouds that moved with determination over the sleeping landscape.

Tuliana had learned to ice skate at the rink at the Rockefeller Centre in New York during her college years in Julliard where she excelled at the cello. The rink was generally filled with skaters who were self-absorbed in their own image. They fed off and imitated the actions of others to enhance their own. Some true purists were there for the ice only and Tuliana fitted comfortably into this latter category. It was on one of her coveted Christmas breaks back home that she met Parth and fell in love as they both ice skated alone on the vast expanse of Pangong Lake.

It was Christmas Eve and both separately felt a need of a short break away from festive cheer so they felt an hour alone on the ice could be the remedy they needed and have the privacy of its majesty all to themselves. Neither were happy to see the other at first as their plans of complete solitude was shattered. A mutual smile melted the atmosphere and without speaking they skated together for an hour and felt they knew each other's personalities long before they ever shared a syllable. Tuliana fondly remembered those moments every time she stood at her favourite spot overlooking Pangong Lake.

As desperate ruthless outlaws go, Ishmael and Sukey were right up there with the worst of them. Always on the move from area to area in efforts to outsmart the different authorities that were always following hot on their trail, just a short grasp away. On this occasion however they excelled themselves and were in deeper trouble than they had ever been before, with four law authorities now following hot on their heels. They badly needed a safe place to lie low and hideout at least until their ascending stars in the criminal world began to wane and they were no longer desirable to apprehend. They knew that this time it would take longer than either of them cared to imagine.

The deepest jungle was the only option left to them; short of life in a six by eight cell at best or a wet rope on a murky dawn being the most probable outcome; that's if they happened to get caught.

They had plundered and murdered their way across the subcontinent of India leaving a trail of destruction and carnage in their wake. Nothing was sacred to them – men, women and children were all fair game and were dealt with without mercy or apathy. Ishmael rubbed his bony tattooed hands over Sukey's neck.

"Much too beautiful a neck to get snapped by a rope," he leaned over and kissed it, his two protruding front teeth reaching her skin first. Ishmael's long saliva drool ran down the back of Sukey's neck and she reached around repulsed and wiped it off. She shook her hand afterwards as though she had been bitten by a mad rabid dog.

Ishmael's face was a gallery of scars, and he was proud of each and every one. One scar ran from his left half ear to his stubbled chin. He acquired his first scar on his maiden robbery and blamed its presence on the fact that he had been an amateur in his now proficient art. He was a skinny ten year old with a heart as hard as any soldier on the front line and escaped from the orphanage after dousing the matron with boiling hot cabbage water – a life-altering experience for her that some say she rightly deserved. After three nights wandering the treacherous back streets of Delhi where death meant little and life meant less; the aroma of freshly made bread from a street vendor's hand cart was a temptation too strong. Unable to give chase due to the infirmity of age, the old street vendor threw a razor sharp cleaver with precision and struck Ishmael on the side of the face. Now every time the aroma of freshly made bread hit his nostrils, his vivid memory of this event added the taste of his own blood to the experience as it mixed with each mouthful he swallowed that morning.

Another scar ran from his right eye straight through his nose leaving a very noticeable gap on the bridge and ended at the corner of his mouth. The judge considered execution that afternoon but had a very satisfactory lamb shank for lunch and deferred the sentence to life in prison. Bound in chains he was transported in a cage like an animal across blistering open country in midsummer. Lying prostrate on the floor, the sun carved its way into his skin as it thrust in through the open top bars of the cage. His jailers negotiated the ragged horse and cart through a path a foot narrower than it needed to be for safety. The sheer drop to a valley below made even Ishmael avert his eyes. On occasions the wheel of the cart lost its grip and slid over the precipice but was dragged back to safety each time. Ishmael gave out a scream in anguish that rose from the very core of his being and on hearing the sound the horse reared and toppled over the edge falling with the cart to the infinity below. The smell of the decomposing dead horse jolted him back to the land of the living a few days later. He was free from the cage and lying metres from it. He traced the line of his new scar across his face with his thumb.

His two protruding front teeth were the sum total of his dental count and he once had his tongue slit in two by a rival outlaw who took exception to his admiring stares in the direction of his woman. He now could lick each corner of his mouth simultaneously which he did at very regular intervals. On an evening in the not-too-distant past Ishmael was caught shinning down a drainpipe of a house he had just burgled. The homeowner in question was a mule skinner who plied his trade with little care on the front part of Ishmael's scalp leaving him bald on this part of his head. The hair that remained at the back of his head was allowed to grow into an unsightly comb-over that he continuously tried to keep in place with his right hand. He was slightly hunched over from an early onset of rheumatism and dragged his left leg as he walked, this being the result of a sharp undetected bear trap that took no mercy.

Sukey had been an unsuccessful bar hostess and dancer amongst other things. Her mother was British and was, as she flatteringly described herself, a courtesan who shinnied down the drainpipe of her boarding school to work on the streets of Soho. She was soon recruited to service the officers in a barracks in Bombay. It had all sounded exotic to her at the time but as her looks faded with age and gin so did the calibre of her clientele and she died of syphilis on the dusty hay of a carthorse's stall. Sukey was just 14 and finding herself alone in the world, vowed to take revenge on society; mistakenly blaming it for her mother's fall from grace and eventual demise.

In a certain light Sukey could be regarded as pretty with long thick red hair and large green eyes that danced like they were on fire in her head. She had no natural dance rhythm and her abrupt manner ruined her chances in the hostess world. She next tried tattooing and with no artistic ability this career was over as soon as the scars healed on her customers. Spelling wasn't her strong point either and many of her clients ended up with words tattooed to their bodies that didn't relay what they had initially meant to convey. Her legacy from this life choice were two large blue tattooed tear drops under each eye and a green dragon across her forehead. This made her face look perpetually in some form of anguish. She was stick insect thin and her clothes hung on her as though she had just robbed a more rotund lady's clothesline. Ishmael met Sukey at her tattoo parlour and had his back inked. He wanted a leaping tiger but got a big wet mouse with droopy eyes instead. There were no mirrors in Sukey's tattoo parlour on purpose so he never knew what the tattoo turned out like.

Sukey ensured that he kept his shirt on in all company. They decided that they had all the right credentials to go into business together and crime was their only true calling.

They hid deep in the jungle for many weeks on the edge of a tiny stream not daring to make a sound louder than a whisper. But provisions ran out and they had to risk going to the local village for supplies. Neither one trusted the other to return so they went together on the back of the one old grey mule they possessed. The mules' hooves had not been paired for many years and they curled out on all legs some half metre. Ishmael rode behind Sukey on the mule's bony back and every now and again, would make an attempt to kiss her on the back of her neck. Sukey would shout "Cut it out creep," each time and wipe her neck roughly with her sleeve. Ishmael never got offended however but just sat back and waited for another suitable opportunity further down the trail.

The jungle village had one narrow dirt track running

through its length and was overshadowed by tall banyan trees that blocked out most of the sun's rays. Shanty houses were dotted without much thought of symmetry along the length of the narrow path and their rusty galvanised fences gave the place the feel of an abandoned scrap yard. A few thin dogs fought over the dry bone of some unfortunate animal and a long scraggy cat sat on top of one of the shanties watching and waiting for any windfall. A store that had the appearance of many storm repairs had its boardwalk jutting out into the path. The board walk displayed a few items that the owner could clearly see from behind his shabby counter. A tin bathtub and a three metre cross cut were the highlight of the display and would have been difficult to remove without the owner's consent. The place had a peaceful feel about it so they relaxed a little and, after loading the mule with supplies, decided to have one drink in the local tavern which was directly across the path from the store. It was yet another hot day and the tavern had a crowd bigger than the village would suggest.

"Happening spot we have here Sukey my gal," Ishmael said and cockily walked into the bar and up to the counter.

"My gal," Sukey replied in disgust at his disrespectful comment and followed him inside.

The bar was a ramshackle building made up of used timber pallets tied together precariously with dried milkweed plants. The floor was the jungle clay as God created it, with spittoons dug out in the ground here and there for convenience and not for décor. Sukey almost stepped into one of the spittoons that was full to the brim with brown tobacco saliva as she approached the counter which was the remnants of an old horse cart turned upside down with its wheels removed. The axle was still intact and Ishmael walked into it and gave a moan as it embedded itself in his side. Sukey laughed.

"That will be two whiskeys and what are you havin' hun," Ishmael tried to rub the pain away from his side with flat of his hand.

"Smart ass. I will have two as well." She leaned both elbows on to the shaft of the cart and lifted her left leg up to rest on the frame.

The woman behind the bar seemed bored and tired in equal proportions and poured four whiskeys. She pushed them roughly in front of Sukey and Ishmael spilling some as she did so. She wore a tattered green sari with a heavy leather belt around the waist that unsuccessfully attempted to pull her rotund stomach into shape. An old very worn dark brown cowboy hat adorned with a peacock's feather sat in a jaunty fashion to one side on her head.

"Friendly customer service here." Ishmael gritted his teeth as he scrutinized the peacock feather.

"Just drink your drink and let's be getting out of here," Sukey said and swallowed her first whiskey down in one mouthful.

"I am telling you. Laugh at old Zona all you like but Zona no fool, he see what he sees and I sees it with me own two eyes." An old Indian man stood up amongst a table of rowdy drinkers and shouts.

Zona was a craggy old man of indiscriminate age. The sun had tanned his hide and bald head to toughened leather and his face was a cobweb of wrinkles but his eyes were bright and alert and defied the rest of his stricken body. He had one brass earring in his left ear that left a brown stain on his lobe and the side of his neck. A tattoo of a red snake covered his left cheek and one of his eyebrows was missing, burned off with a hot poker many years previous by a man who wore a tailed dress jacket.

"Be sitting down, Zona. Be sitting down. You can't be saying that type of thing about the maharajah," pleaded a very skinny man with a cigarette that dangled from his lips like an extension to his body.

"Millions of butterflies appeared and a big hole opened up and the maharajah went inside and then ran out again and just sat there on the floor," Zona continued his eyes pleading with his audience for their conviction. It wasn't forthcoming and they stared at him with disinterested homogeneity.

Ishmael and Suckey both held their drinks to their mouths in mid swallow as if somebody had pressed the pause button and their ears strained to only hear sounds from the table.

"What this hole, Zona? Tell the truth now or you know what will happen," another seated man who wore an old, tailed dress jacket with no shirt growled a threat.

"Don't know. From nowhere it appeared and the butterflies just vanished into it," Zona continued.

The group at the table all laughed and dismissively waved Zona away with their hands.

"Go home Zona you drunk," the skinny man said as he puffed at his dangling cigarette.

Zona walked towards the door and Ishmael ran and grabbed him by the arm.

"Hey there Zona my man, join us. We need the company," Ishmael said and lead the old man to the shaft of the cart where Sukey was still leaning.

In his haste to hear Zona's story, Ishmael stepped into one of the spittoons that was full to the gills with brown tobacco saliva. He quickly pulled his foot out and began to wave his leg and foot wildly to remove the offending fluid. Sukey laughed so loudly she began to cough and real tears joined ranks with the tattooed ones.

"What will it be old guy; Whiskey?" Sukey asked and nodded her head to the waitress behind the bar to fulfil the order.

Zona nodded in excitement and Sukey lifted him up to sit on the shaft as though he weighed as little as a feather.

"Now tell us your story old guy - we will believe you. Won't we Sukey?"

"I believe you already." Sukey drank down another whiskey carelessly in one swallow.

"Tell truth. Zona only tell truth. Hole opened from nowhere in room after maharajah puts two gold butterfly wings together and butterflies all flew in." The old man took a drink from his whiskey and looked towards the group at the table.

"Where did all this happen old timer?" Ishmael patted him on the shoulder as he manically wiped his shoe on the bare clay floor in a vein effort to remove the remainder of the dripping saliva.

"In Maharajah Parth's palace on top of Elephant Mountain. Me sees it with these eyes and me is never wrong or be telling them lies." Zona spoke in rhyme.

The man in the tailed dress jacket got up from the table and walked over to Zona in a stiff exaggerated fashion that displayed undercurrents of violence.

"Don't be tellin' these stories to strange sahibs Zona. Come back and join us again," the man growled.

Zona suddenly wiped his hand over his missing eyebrow and followed the man back to the table trailing behind him like a pup who has just been scolded for robbing the clothesline.

"Well now what is all this?" Ishmael said with an evil grin of satisfaction.

"I knew we came to this dump for a reason. Karma has led us here. This sounds right up our street.

Let's be off and find this Maharajah and Elephant Mountain." Sukey knocked back her final whiskey in one swallow and walked towards the door. Ishmael poured his two remaining whiskeys into one glass and drank them down in one swallow and for seconds coughed and panted as he tried to catch his breath, his eyes wide to their extremities. Sukey laughed as she watched his performance. With this new-found knowledge they felt they needed a horse to get them safely to Elephant Mountain so they decided to buy one but ended up stealing one instead.

CHAPTER 6

Vishnu was the illegitimate son of an Indian aristocrat. Shunned by his father's family because of the nature of his birth and abandoned by his selfish fun-seeking mother who was one of those wannabe horsey types. One of those overbearing women who moved from being a horse obsessed teenager in the pony club to the domineering gold digging adult who needed her man only for his wealth and position but, given the option, would rather sleep with her horse. He was therefore born loveless, rejected and forgotten. Taken in by Parth's family, his father being the family's distant cousin, he was cared for and loved as one of their own.

From an early age Vishnu excelled in everything he took interest in. He loved to wear shiny black turbans and crisp white linen suits that appeared to have just come out of the tailor's studio. He was never seen in public without his shiny black turban firmly in place. Some said he even slept in it but that may have been an exaggeration. The only thing his horror of a mother and popinjay father gave him was his good looks and as they were elegantly tall, he inherited this gene also. He had the countenance of a Bollywood actor with chiselled features, raven black hair and brilliant white teeth that could easily have been used as a marketing tool for any advancing dentist. But his eyes were perpetually sad. Even when he laughed his eyes never followed in the merriment and stayed distant and melancholy. Vishnu agreed to take responsibility for the wax pear and moved the 7.5 thousand kilometres from Parth's palace in India to England to watch over it as it housed the second butterfly wing concealed deep within. Parth wanted to separate the two butterfly wings by the greatest distance he could to prevent them ever coming into contact with each other again. He feared the giant butterflies could use the wormhole to gain access to his world and possibly take control of humanity. They appeared so peaceful on his first inspection and his fears seemed unfounded but he didn't want to take the chance and be responsible for a cataclysmic event that could not be undone.

Vishnu lived in the shadows of the family throughout the years, protectively watching over the wax pear. On many occasions looking out for the wellbeing of the family even though they were never aware of his existence. Vishnu was very happy in Robin Hood's Bay. He loved its small coffee shops and was a minor celebrity because of his image. He had a job as a night porter in the local hotel: An art deco establishment that owed its avant-garde image to the neglect of previous owners rather than their desire to preserve the era. As he needed very little sleep, he spent his days in observation. He knew Maximillian kept the pear in his garden shed and, on some occasions, when the family were away for a day trip; Vishnu would go into the garden shed and take the wax pear in his hands to check its security. Sometimes he would even hide it more safely in the shed and hope that Maximillian would forget about it completely and leave it in the much safer place he had chosen. Maximillian wouldn't however. He would search and search until he found it again and then leave it in full display once more on a table or on his bookcase where he and everyone else could observe it's Dadaistic presence.

"How did it get there?" Maximillian would always say and take extra-long puffs from his pipe and scratch his head. "Can't remember leaving it there. Must have been the children?" he would say to himself "Chet. Chet come here at once," he would shout and Chet would always get the blame for tampering with its change of position every time.

Vishnu did not like the old mining village in Wales. He much preferred Robin Hood's Bay; especially since he had developed a formally distant but hopeful relationship with the daughter of the landlord of The Red Lion. At the beginning he disliked bitter but as it was the local nectar he sampled it and suitably grimaced. Sandra had very long shiny brown hair that reached to the belt loops of her pale blue denim jeans. Vishnu was more than happy to drink bitter if it meant watching Sandra straining on the pump to pull his pint. She over-exaggerated her actions in doing this as she knew Vishnu observed her every move.

Vishnu made his heart-wrenching move to Wales without telling a soul in the village at Robin Hood's Bay. Sandra waited each evening for the sight of his black turban and bright smile, keeping one eye on her customers' pleasure and the other expectantly on the stained-glass door. She never saw him again.

It was difficult to get night work in the old mining village and after much effort he secured a very lowly paid position as a night watchman in the local shopping centre. The dreary cold shopping centre had seven small shops and a post office. The floors of all the shops and the hallway were laid in 70s black and white plastic tiles that were stained and in places curled up at the ends from wear and neglect. They were a major trip-hazard but customers got used to picking their steps over the danger. The place needed a major revamp and decoration much more than it needed a night watchman. The shopping centre was in the ownership of a crotchety old spinster who was left the property by her entrepreneurial father. She gritted her dark brown dentures tightly together each time she encountered Vishnu, as she secretly fancied him, and wore her best *eau de rose* perfume for him which she'd bought seven Christmases ago at the parish jumble sale. She kept the old bottle, that had long since lost its label, in her lime green plastic handbag and gave herself a few sprays when she felt there was even a slim chance of their meeting. *Eau de rose* was the ideal aroma for her as it had the fragrance of crotchety old spinster combined with a house filled with mangy cats. She kept her fine dry grey hair hidden in a brown hair net which she topped off with a plumb-coloured beret her aunt had bought in Paris in the 50s. Her dark stockings were always bulging around the knees and always seemed like they needed a good big tug skyward. When she felt there may be even a small possibility of meeting Vishnu she painted her lips with a cheap scarlet red lipstick that always gave her a rash. This had the effect of leaving her mouth looking like the entrance to the Mersey Tunnel.

Vishnu tried to avoid her as best he could, but she was more determined than the effort his disinterest would need to undertake.

Acting under orders from Parth, Vishnu purchased the painting at the auction to give the family the funds they desperately needed. The painting was grossly overvalued and now hung in Vishnu's small rented room and masked a damp spot on the wall, thus reverting back to its original function.

Many coincidences that the family questioned in the past were directly attributed to Vishnu's protective presence even though the family were never aware of his existence. Chet and Cecily in particular were constantly being saved from minor perils that without the intervention of Vishnu could have ended in certain catastrophe.

On one occasion a few years previous the danger that was diverted by him was major. Beneath the narrow picturesque streets of Robin Hood's Bay are hidden a maze of subterranean smuggler's passageways that link some of the houses in the village. Some of the passageways travel right to the water's edge. Robin Hood's Bay and the surrounding coastline was a hot bed of smugglers in the 18th century. Brandy, rum, tobacco and tea would make its way from France to the nearby beach to avoid government duty and would be transported through a maze of tunnels to safe houses in the village. The tunnels are now, for the greater part, sealed off but a few still exist and the mysterious hidden presence of these tunnels captured the imagination of Chet and Cecily. For months they explored the coastline looking for the mouth of a smuggler's tunnel, never telling Jilly or Maximillian what they were doing.

"Just collecting shells," Cecily would reply to Jilly questioning on their whereabouts.

"You always seem to be "just collecting shells," but I never see any evidence of shells when you come home," Jilly said as she dried her hands on a white towel after peeling some turnips.

"We have them stored away," Chet interrupted.

"I must see them," Jilly continued with genuine interest.

"Not today we haven't the time. Maybe tomorrow." Cecily smiled innocently and twirled the corners of her hair.

"Ok I will have a look at them tomorrow. There must be a huge amount by now." Jilly opened the oven and put the turnips in to cook.

"Not turnips again," Chet said with disgust.

"Yes, and you be home early to eat them," Jilly said as the back door closed and the children ran off to explore once more.

"We will have to gather some shells and bring them home with us this evening," Chet said as they ran towards the beach.

"Before we go home remember," Cecily added.

Jilly knew that a lifeguard was always present on the beach and that the kitchen windows of many of her friend's houses looked directly out onto the short strand. Also, the eagle eyes of Mrs Pennyfeather, who never missed the drop of a needle on the streets of the village, were always focused in wait of calamity so she could enhance her profile amongst the bingo group. So, Jilly felt safe letting the children out to play in the sand for a few hours knowing that many caring and nosey eyes were watching. But Chet and Cecily didn't go to the short strand; they continued their search for a tunnel entrance along the rocky cliff that meandered its way along the coastline.

Many fossil hunters searched the coastline at low tide as this was dinosaur country known for the ancient relics it cast up on occasions. But today the beach was empty as a high tide was forecast which the children were not aware of. The lifeguard had just taken a five-minute break to make a phone call from the nearby phone box and hadn't noticed the children.

"I have one. I have one. I found a tunnel," Chet screamed and jumped up and down on the sand.

Cecily ran to him, tripping on a bunch of sun-bleached seaweed but quickly regaining her composure again.

"Where is it?" her voice screeched with great excitement.

"Look there it is," Chet hollered in a tone that was synonymous with birthday presents and Christmas mornings and he crawled behind a large unwelcome looking rock that was covered in black wet seaweed which through centuries knew only too well the harshness of the angry waves.

"Eugh, I don't like the look of that place. It is all slippery and slimy and dark," Cecily overly mimicked a heaving action.

"Come on you scaredy cat. I am going on alone. I don't care if you don't come," Chet said and crawled through the slimy black seaweed and into the tunnel.

Cecily stood for a moment looking at her new pink shoes that Maximillian had just bought her. These shoes had sat temptingly in the window of the local shoe shop and Cecily would do a daily pilgrimage to the window to stare at them and covet. They were the latest fashion and so hip. Only two other girls in school had them and they were the two very spoiled brats who always got everything that was in fashion long before anybody else.

After pondering on the probable destruction of her new shoes she decided to follow Chet into the Tunnel; all the time thinking what Maximillian would say if she were to ruin them.

"Wait I am coming. Don't get too far ahead," she said and tried to push the seaweed delicately out of her path with the toe of her precious pink shoe.

"This is major gross," she complained but Chet did not answer.

The tunnel was ice cold, dark and damp inside with the overpowering smell of stale rotting fish. Every sound she made multiplied in volume as it bounced off the green slimy walls. Cecily wasn't pretending now, she really did feel sick but she forged on ahead as she could hear the sound of Chet in the distance; the echoes of the movements he made reaching her ears in a loop. She could see the faint light from his very small torch shining ahead in the lost abandoned tunnel.

"Can you see anything Chet?" panic began to rise in her voice.

"Not yet. Come on; keep moving forward we will be underneath the houses in the town soon." Chet's determined voice was faint to her ears.

"Oh my God if we get trapped no one will ever find us. We will end up like the dinosaur bones people find here. Chet come back," Cecily cried in sudden terror at the thought. Looking behind her all was now pitch black dark. The only light she could see was the faint yellow light from Chet's torch a distance ahead of her which seemed to be fading by the second.

"I think the battery is running out." For the very first-time alarm could be heard in Chet's voice. Cecily screamed. The sound of angry waves crashing against rocks grew louder and the sound raced up the tunnel to their petrified ears like a demon on fire.

"The tide is rising Chet. It's high tide." Cecily began to cry, her new pink shoes now sodden wet and uncomfortably cold.

"Hold on - I am coming back. Stay where you are," Chet replied as calmly as he could and made his way back along the dark tunnel, his torch light now quenched completely as his battery ran out.

He slipped on the slimy rocks on the base of the tunnel's floor and fell over many times in the darkness but didn't cry out in pain, as he didn't want to scare Cecily even further.

"Come on Cecily we have to try and get out before the tide gets any higher. This whole tunnel will fill with water very soon." Chet grabbed Cecily by the arm once he reached her and they moved slowly towards the sound of the loud angry waves that beat against the tunnel walls ahead of them.

Chet had a feeling they were too late and the tide was now too high but he didn't let Cecily know his deduction.

"We are going to die Chet. The water is too high and I can't go any further." Cecily sat down on the cold wet floor of the tunnel and cried.

"We have to try Cecily or we will die for sure," Chet pleaded and tried to pull her to her feet.

"Hey, can you hear me?" Vishnu's voice called out in the darkness and they could just about see the light of a strong torch bobbing up and down as it shone some distance away.

"Yes, yes help us we are trapped," the children screamed as one.

"I am coming. Don't move." The beam of light that reached them from Vishnu's torch grew stronger with each step he made in their direction.

Vishnu kept his identity hidden by shining the light from the torch away from his face once he reached them.

"Follow me - we have to be very quick - the tide is rising fast. We will have to swim the last part as the mouth of the cave is now covered over with 4 metres of water." Vishnu spoke as calmly as he could to try and give the children confidence. He held Cecily by the arm and guided her slowly towards the mouth of the tunnel. They had to stop once the water got to chest high.

"From here we must swim. Cecily, you hold on to me and Chet you hold on to Cecily. Take deep breaths now and then we will go underwater and out through the mouth of this cave. Don't be afraid, we are going to be fine." Even in their terror they wondered who this stranger was and how he knew their names.

"Ok, be getting ready. Breathe in and off we will be going," Vishnu said and waited until the children had taken their deepest breaths and then he led them under the water. The water was black and the current very strong. The children couldn't see anything but they did as Vishnu told them and held on tightly. Gasping for air, the three put their heads above the water on the opposite side of the tunnel and the children screamed with delight. Vishnu pulled a scarf around his face to conceal his identity and lead them to dry land.

"Now go home immediately and do not do anything like this again." Vishnu's voice was commanding and a little angry.

The children stood on the dry sand and watched Vishnu walk back along the beach towards Robin Hood's Bay and vanish.

"Who is he?" Cecily said, still with the sound of fear in her voice.

"I don't know but he saved our lives." Chet helped Cecily to her feet.

"He knew our names Chet. How could he?"

"Don't know. And he had a funny accent as well. I haven't heard anything like that before," Chet replied. "We can't tell Mum or grandad what happened. Say we fell into the sea by accident or something," Chet said and looked at his arm which was bleeding.

"Your arm is cut. Mum will see that." Cecily took a closer look at the wound.

"No she won't see it. I will keep it hidden until it heals."

The children were quiet for the rest of their journey home as they pondered what might have happened except for the intervention of Vishnu. Jilly and Maximillian bumped into each other as they rushed about in panic once they saw the condition the children were in.

"We fell into a shallow rock pool." Chet gave an innocent smile and Cecily tightened her lips to form a narrow line, afraid to utter a syllable.

Maximillian however was suspicious and knew there was more to the story than then children were prepared to reveal.

It was almost dusk in India on the cliff edge at Elephant Mountain where Tuliana rearranged her white straw hat with its exaggerated brim and long pale pink ribbon band and was about to return to the palace. She had taken her evening's share of cool air from her favourite space on the cliff edge and had to forcibly remove her gaze from the Cormorants that skimmed without a care over the pale blue waters of Pangong Lake.

"Right then, sweetie. Tell us all about these butterflies." Ishmael allowed his only two teeth to stick out even further than usual as his head and neck leaned out from his body towards Tuliana's face in an unnatural, ugly angle. Tuliana's lips grew suddenly pale on hearing this unexpected voice and she looked around her for support but none of her servants were near.

"You're the maharajah's missus we believe, so you know all about these butterflies then?" Sukey stood near Tuliana and grinned in a countenance that radiated power and control over the moment.

Tuliana stared at the four teardrop tattoos on Sukey's face and the green dragon that was now crunched up into a far smaller reptile due to the overly exaggerated expression on her face.

"Whatever do you mean?" Tuliana's voice trembled in fear and her eyes searched for an escape but her inquisitors had all routes forward blocked.

"Tell us now or else you will find out for pretty certain that I am not a very nice refined lady like your good self," Sukey shouted close to Tuliana's right ear.

Tuliana held her hand tightly over the offended ear and tried to break through her confines but Ishmael grabbed her roughly by her thin delicate arm and shook her like a snow globe.

"No use runnin' your ladyship - we want to know everything and you are going to tell us everything you know about these butterflies." Ishmael shook Tuliana so fiercely that her hair which was neatly arranged, to its usual perfection in a bun, fell loose about her face.

"Let me go, you are hurting me. I know nothing about any of this. You are mistaken. Let me go."

Tuliana fought to free herself from his vice-like hold. Ishmael loosened his grip on her arm and she stumbled backwards falling over the sheer cliff edge to her death on the sharp black rocks below.

"What have you done you great fool? Now we have done murder again," Sukey quickly moved close to the edge of the cliff trying to follow Tuliana's fateful path with her eyes. The updraft from the edge of the cliff could move a fleet of galleons that day and she stumbled back to the ground.

Ishmael gave a forlorn look towards the cliff edge – a regret for an opportunity lost rather than for a life taken.

"It was an accident I didn't mean to hurt her. She fell back. It wasn't my fault," Ishmael protested and held the palms of his hands out to face towards the sky as if in recompense.

"Every judge in the land will believe you when they hear that explanation. You imbecile." Sukey sprang to her feet and began to run as fast as she could towards the protection of the jungle – distancing herself from the cliff edge with every stride she made through the tall thick ferns.

In the distance Sukey could see a girl dressed in very fine, brightly coloured clothes walking carelessly along the narrow forest path. She squinted her eyes to get a better view and held her hand up to her forehead to block the sunlight. It was Rawinda. She skipped along carelessly, humming a tune and running her hand along the branches of the scented rhododendron bushes, admiring their colourful blossoms on the edge of the path that led to the cliffs.

"Somebody important; obviously not a servant." Sukey licked her lips.

"So, who are you then missy?" Sukey shook Rawinda as though she were shaking the remnants from an almost empty sauce bottle.

Rawinda struggled to free herself and Ishmael, who had caught up once more, took a piece of cord from his pocket and tied her hands together so tightly she felt them go numb as her circulation began to fade.

"My father will flay you both alive for this," Rawinda said as she struggled to get free.

Sukey and Ishmael smiled with the satisfaction of a cat who had just been given left over kippers.

"So you are the bold maharajah's daughter are you?" Sukey ran a knife with a white ivory handle, which she took from her boot, along Rawinda's cheek; not cutting deeply but drawing small beads of blood that sat like red ink dots along her skin.

"No so cocky now - are you missy?" Sukey licked the blood from the blade and tossed it about in her hand always catching the ivory handle as she multiplied the spins to four.

Rawinda became pale as the blood dripped down onto her powder white dress.

"My mother is waiting for me. She will be along this path soon so you had best let me free."

Rawinda's heartbeat fast and loud visibly moving the front of her dress.

Sukey and Ishmael looked at each other for a moment in silence allowing the full effect of her plea to sink in and then they both exploded in a mocking laugh as they pushed her back and forth to each other like a defenceless rag doll.

Sukey brushed the knife a little deeper along Rawinda's cheek. "You wouldn't like a nice big ugly scar across that pretty little face of yours now, I imagine? The boys wouldn't find you very attractive then let me tell you."

Ishmael rubbed his hand along the scars on his own face; tracing them with his fingers and thought for a moment.

"The butterflies. Tell me about them." Ishmael gave an evil smirk and Rawinda could feel and smell his saliva spraying her face as he spoke. She felt faint and nauseous.

"I don't know what you mean." Rawinda closed her eyes tightly in an effort to block out Ishmael's horrific presence.

She could smell his stale body and clothes and foul dead animal-like breath. A large white maggot feasted on an old food stain on the front of his shirt; locked solid to the spot and unaffected by Ishmael's movements.

Sukey flashed the razor edge of her knife across the back of Rawinda's hand leaving a deep gash that immediately began to run blood like a tap down her fingers and onto the forest floor.

"Just to let you know I am a very serious person who always gets what she wants." Sukey greedily licked the blade clean again as though she were feasting on the most delicious hors d'oeuvre.

The dark green vegetation began to turn milky-white to Rawinda, and her breath became shallow as she fell heavily onto the damp earth.

"Why did you cut her?" he asked repeatedly as he jumped about holding his hands on top of his head.

"I wanted to knock some of the cockiness out of the rich spoiled brat." Sukey roughly tied a filthy stained handkerchief around the cut on Rawinda's hand which was now dripping pools of dark red blood onto the floor of the forest. "Best to tie this up case she gets some malady in the jungle heat. Don't want the little bitch to die until we get the information we need." Sukey pulled a diamond and emerald bracelet from Rawinda's neck breaking the clasp and pushed it carelessly into her pocket.

"Carry her." Sukey's eyes were filled with hate.

"No chance. My back would give in." Ishmael rubbed his back and made a facial grimace to demonstrate the possible outcome.

"Useless good-for-nothing. Come on, somebody will come looking for the two of them soon." Sukey roughly picked up Rawinda's feet and Ishmael, complaining, took the heavy end.

Rawinda's cut hand dragged and bled along the jungle floor as they moved deeper into the forest towards their hideout.

Tuliana's friend, who she knew from her Julliard days, arrived promptly at the palace with her violin in a black leather case and was shown to the music room. The walls were papered with images of musical instruments and lofty sopranos who forever held their key to perfection. A fire was always lit in this room winter and summer to keep the many instruments it housed comfortably dampness free.

She was a tall skinny American who had an untamed mop of bright red curls and a pale translucent freckled face. She lived on coffee, Turkish cigarettes and gin so her slender figure never gained a gram since her 15th birthday. Her excessive use of perfume was legendary, and her arrival would always be heralded by the strong lingering aroma of Chanel.

The servants searched to inform Tuliana of her friend's arrival but she was nowhere to be found. After checking the cliff edge, they consulted Parth advising him of her disappearance. Parth was silent as he contemplated as this had never happened before. Tuliana was always completely conventional and her routines were always so precise.

"We will try the base of the cliffs." He found it difficult to imagine this possibility having any validity but it had to be eliminated from his suspicions. The strong wind and sea spray hampered their footsteps as Parth and a group of servants waded through the heavy wet sand at the base of the cliffs in search of what they did not wish to find.

One of the younger servants was the most nimble of foot and discovered her lifeless body crushed on the rocks. Parth gathered what remained of her up in his arms and screamed so loud that even the thundering waves seemed to go more silent in sympathy with his agony.

CHAPTER 7

Fatigue almost having got the better of them, Ishmael and Sukey, red faced and panting, dragged the semiconscious Rawinda with little respect, each holding one of her legs, the final few metres to their hideout. Rawinda's head bumped up and down as it encountered rough terrain, leaving scratches and briar cuts on the rear of her scalp. Her once gleaming black hair was now a mop of grimy entanglement.

"Lucky she is out of it," Sukey laughed as she watched Rawinda's head bump hard against a tree stump.

Ishmael rubbed at the sciatica pain that darted down his left leg and howled like a banshee.

"Rub my back for me – rub it won't you?" he pleaded and pulled his shirt up to reveal the tattoo of the big wet mouse with droopy eyes. Sukey coughed a loud laugh into her sleeve and wiped her nose.

Rawinda's eyes slowly opened as she regained consciousness and tried to lift herself upright. Sukey pushed her back to the ground again roughly with her foot. "We are going to have trouble with this one. Posh bitches are trouble and lots of it." Sukey spat towards Rawinda.

"If you let them," Ishmael grinned.

"Go to the village and see if that old man…what's his name? Remember?" Sukey doled out her commands, her back turned to Ishmael as she stoked the fire.

"Zona."

"Yea; right; Zona or whatever."

Ishmael gave a smug smile, proud of his recollection but Sukey dismissed his achievement. Ishmael's mouth winced in temper.

"Tell that old dude to tell the maharajah that we have his precious daughter and we want to know about butterflies and the treasure or else." She wiped her mouth roughly with the back of her hand and took a long drink from a bottle of whiskey that lay near her tent.

"What treasure? Did she mention treasure?" Ishmael's

face lit up like the Christmas tree on Times Square.

"Why do you suppose we are going to all this bother you idiot. There must be treasure. Butterflies appearing out of nowhere and you don't imagine tons of treasure? You have no imagination that is why you are an idiot. And get whiskey. I would hate to be stuck out here in this desolation with you and that brat if I were sober."

"Orders, orders. I don't know if I can take this much longer," Ishmael grumbled and kicked at a small rock as he made his way out of their hideout.

"And be quick about it."

"Ok, Ok," his timid voice returned like a whisper as he moved out of sight.

Maximillian carried the small bell as though it were nitroglycerine and he was expecting to be shoved. Once inside his shed he wrapped the clapper in some cotton wool he'd taken from a pill bottle so it could not touch the sides and strike a ring. He placed the bell into a small leather pouch that once housed a first class relic of Catherine Laboure. He always regretted losing that relic as he believed it brought him good luck.

"What to do with you?" he let his mind wander. His mind wandered for days and nights until one afternoon when Jilly and the children were out on one of their long-extended walks. He gave his stern cough put the pouch into his pocket alongside his pipe and strode down to the village to think. He always found his thinking process hit the right cog when he walked amongst other folk. Ambling about looking in shop windows but seeing nothing he let his hand touch the leather pouch for inspiration. Neighbours he didn't know yet gave him the first glimpses of their personalities but their individual peculiarities were wasted on him that day. They formed a false opinion of him that they carried back to the idle gossip of their firesides.

"A southern eccentric snob," was by and large the general consensus of those who bid him the time of day.

Their conclusions were furthermost from his mind as he took the leather pouch from the inner sanctum of his jacket and twirled it about in his hand speculating his next action. A heavy downpour struck without warning and washed the streets clean as it raced in fury down the iron grills of storm drains. There weren't many on the streets to begin with but those few darted into shops they had no initial intention of frequenting. Maximillian pushed himself back into the shallow doorway of the butcher's shop and listened to the sound of the rain over the butcher's chopping axe.

"It's in for the day," an old woman said as she roughly pushed by him holding her leg of lamb like a recently won trophy.

"It is?"

"Yeah, sure it is; look at those clouds. Black as my heart." She gave a laugh through pale white gums and walked out into the downpour as though she were strolling down the prom in the fairest sunshine. Maximillian gave a low mumble with words that never formed properly. The butcher kept giving him an uncomfortable stare over his half-moon spectacles and Maximillian tried to ignore it for as long as his dignity prevailed. His modesty began to wear thin after too many encounters with the butcher's eyes and he smiled as he opened the leather pouch; gently removing the cotton wool from the clapper and gave the bell the slightest of rings.

Surrounded by a kaleidoscope of butterflies four metres in circumference who acted as a weather shield protecting him from the rain he walked breezily along the footpath back to the rectory. He laughed, with tears streaming down his cheeks, as he remembered the terror on the butcher's face at the sight of the butterflies swarming over his freshly chopped meat. Frantic eyes pulled curtains closed and shops locked their door as the large round ball of fluttering butterflies moved along the street leaving just the bare sight of Maximillian's feet exposed at their base.

Cecily dug a small hole with her hands, carefully ensuring no unnecessary damage to her nails, and proudly planted Maximillian's wax cast of a pear in some very fertile ground near Woodhouse 2. She used her mum's best gardening compost, acquired from household waste, to fertilise it.

"We will have some lovely pears one day very soon." She proudly admired her perfect work, watering the ground with Jilly's old tin watering can that had been fitted with a new plastic spout, the original tin spout having been lost in one of Chet's failed experiments.

Every evening Maximillian would sit in his shed and smoke his pipe and dream of past and future adventures. Not once did he notice that something very precious to him was missing from his collection.

Maximillian persuaded Chet to lend a hand backfilling the many excavations he'd agreed to deal with but Chet was purposely nowhere to be seen when his time to assist came around.

"It's your summer holidays lad and you need a bit of exercise. I remember back in my youth I would have ten stables cleaned out at the Aga Khan's stable yard by nine in the morning and another ten to do before I got tea. Did I ever tell you the story of the first time they let me ride out in the morning at His Highnesses yard?" Maximillian took his pipe from his mouth and leaned down heavily on his shovel.

"Yes you told me a few times grandad. I know the story off by heart." Having been captured, Chet kept filling a hole but took no pleasure in his work. Because of his current incarceration Chet offered no courtesy in his refusal to listen to the rekindling of Maximillian's cherished memory.

"Oh did I? That's a pity it's a great story. Would you like to hear it again?" Maximillian had an earnest look of eager expectation on his face.

"Maybe we should keep at this job grandad, Maybe tell me later when we are all together at lunchtime. Then everyone can hear the full story again." Chet looked up to the sky in dismay, out of Maximillian's view. Maximillian pondered on this idea for a moment as he stroked his beard into his favoured point and pulled wildly on his pipe.

"Yes, good idea my lad. I will do just that. I am sure everyone will love to hear that story again," and he took to his backfilling once more with extra fervour filling in three shovels to every one of Chet's.

Even though Vishnu was very attentive to the family's every movement he hadn't noticed the disappearance of the pear for two days. Jilly and the children were doing the weekly shop in the village and Maximillian would usually go along with them just for the 99's but of course he never admitted to this.

"Are you coming with us?" Jilly would always ask him and he would give a grumble or two and pretend that he didn't want to go.

"Oh come on grandad. Ice cream!," Cecily would say and smile.

"I knew a dentist once who said that ice cream is by far the worst thing for rotting your teeth."

Maximillian gave a very earnest stare as his lip quivered short of a laugh.

"Oh did he! Are you coming though?" Cecily was unconcerned by this revelation.

"I suppose I will go and get you all an ice cream," he replied acting as though all this frivolity was a terrible imposition on his valuable time.

Jilly and the children would smile knowing that he loved ice cream more than they did.

It was on an occasion such as this that Vishnu noticed the missing pear. He searched every part of Maximillian's shed not leaving the smallest space without the full benefit of his scrutiny.

Blobs of sweat from his exertion appeared around the rim of his perfectly neat black turban and dripped like a distillers tap from his nose. The bathroom window on the first floor was his only method of entry into the house and he climbed the strong branches of the purple laburnum tree knocking off some of Jilly's prized flower heads to reach it. He skinned his slightly protruding belly as he squeezed in through the opening, not designed for human access, and fell onto the green lino on the bathroom floor. His shiny black turban was rumpled and tilted to one side of his head and he immediately looked in the mirror and arranged it properly, giving it a few quick brushes with the palm of his hand to restore its former excellence.

He lifted every loose floorboard and the attic with its millions of large Zebra spiders had to be examined thoroughly but there was no sign of the wax pear.

"Oh Lord of almighty. Whatever will Parth be saying when he hears this news? What will he be saying at all at all," and he gave his head a wobble.

Zona was sound asleep and dreaming; his scraggy old head lying on top of a large pile of empty whiskey bottles that had been drained dry in the nearby pub. Of course, he tried them all before he slept to see if any one of them had a life-saving small drop still left inside to cure his thirst. All were dry as linnets' feathers with just the aroma remaining to tempt and tease him even more. Ishmael kicked him hard on the bum to awaken him and he slowly prised his eyes open to the bright morning sunlight in anguish and rolled his tongue around his dry arid mouth.

"Zona needs a drink." He knelt with a pleading look in his eyes as he held out both his hands in a begging stance that would have had the desired effect on almost everyone except Ishmael.

Ishmael explained his mission and Zona agreed to take the message for two bottles of the local gut rot. One of which he needed there and then to give him courage and to stop the tremors. Ishmael produced a bottle from a tattered old leather bag he carried over his left shoulder. The bag was dark red crocodile skin and was once a very valuable and rare Gucci. Its owner left it on the bare dusty floorboards of a railway station in Delhi as she reached to pay her fare. From that moment to this the bag, plus all its contents were in Ishmael's possession. He gave the expensive Paris makeup and perfume to Sukey but she threw them away. The small derringer pistol he kept for himself and carried it loaded at all times in his boot.

"Now listen here you little lush we need a reply straight away. This girl we have taken will not last long out of her comforts, so tell the maharaja this. And we need to know about the treasure."

"I know nothing of treasure," Zona's voice trembled with alarm.

"There is treasure. Sukey said so," Ishmael replied impatiently.

"But I didn't." Zona nervously tried to move away from Ishmael over the pile of empty bottles.

"Get out of my sight and deliver the message." Ishmael danced a temper from foot to foot and in a flash disappeared into the undergrowth of the forest.

Tuliana's cold lifeless body was kept on a long mahogany hunt table in Parth's Haven for the mourners to file by and pay their last respects. Her gaiety and tenderness; her smile that could bestow that acknowledgement necessary to highlight the most bounteous achievement; her enchantment with nature and those she loved were sentiments all now vanished from her peaceful cadaverous face. She lay there still as though resting – her youthful body taken by death's cold hand, cheating her of experiences in the future that will unfold but will now be beyond her earthly touch.

Parth covered Tuliana's body with a thin white silk sheet but left her face exposed. He sat by her side for three days and nights staring at her body with two streams of tears flowing from his eyes like an eternal spring of grief. Occasionally he would leave the room to enquire if there had been any further news about Rawinda. His servants and all the tenants on his estate were searching for her. Men who knew the terrain and all its hidey holes, but no trace could be found. His addition to the search party would have been of little value so he waited in added torment for reports to come back but none were as he would have wished.

Parth was beyond consolation and hadn't slept or eaten since he found Tuliana's body on the rocks beneath the cliff face. His face was gaunt and unshaven and his appearance uncharacteristically untidy. The house servants began to worry and deliberated amongst each other as to which of them was brave enough to suggest he make preparations for Tuliana's funeral. An old lady bent with age and weary of life was chosen. She had taken care of Parth when he was a child and on many occasions in the past had reasoned with him when all other attempts failed. She entered the room and sat down in silence beside him.

For ages neither of them spoke or acknowledged the presence of each other. Both stared at Tuliana's beautiful serene face that was beginning to turn grey and dark around her eyes.

"I know why you are here." Parth spoke after a long time had lapsed, still keeping his focus on Tuliana's ever changing face of death.

"It is time to let go." The old lady coughed quietly into a handkerchief that was stained with traces of dark red blood.

"I can't," Parth said and buried his head in his hands.

The old lady put her arm around his shoulders.

"You must focus on the living now. Rawinda is alive and she needs you. Tuliana must be laid to rest and her spirit set free. You will meet again. This parting is only temporary." The old lady stood up and coughed quietly into her handkerchief again.

Parth looked at her and nodded in agreement.

"You are right. I must let Tuliana go," he said and walked over to Tuliana's lifeless ivory face and kissed her gently on her ice-cold forehead.

"I must find Rawinda now," he continued and covered Tuliana's face with the thin silk sheet.

A loud thunderous commotion disrupted his final moments with Tuliana's remains as shouting and clamouring associated with the sudden capture of a spritely villain echoed throughout the hallway beyond. Parth beckoned the old lady to stay in the room as he gave an imaginary request with the wave of his index finger. He twisted the crystal glass doorknob and went in search of the cause of the disturbance.

Two burley servants carried Zona, his legs running in mid-air, never quite touching the ground, as his screech all but cracked the glass on the nearby windows.

"This chap knows about Rawinda," the one who had vice like grip of Zona's left arm spoke in a deep tone that resounded like it came from the first fret of a bass guitar.

Parth grabbed Zona by the collar of his shabby green jacket and shook him until it pulled away in his hand and Zona almost fainted.

"They want me to take them to the butterflies. Me don't know. Nothin' else. Your highnesses."

Zona's voice wobbled like a radio inside a washing machine's high spin as Parth continued to shake him.

"You horrible little creature where are they keeping my daughter?" Parth's eyes were bloodshot red with anger and his countenance was that of a man who had lost control of his faculties.

"Met man in village and he tells me story and to tell Your Highnesses. No more from Zona. All Zona knows." Zona collapsed to the floor in a dishevelled heap as Parth let go of his grip.

"What does this man who has taken my daughter look like? Who is he?" Parth looked down at Zona who was now curled up on the floor in a perfect round ball.

"Zona don't know. Zona knows no one," and his muffled voice came from beneath the sleeve of his green jacket as he hid his head in fear under his arm.

"Throw him to the dogs." Parth gave a command and the servants looked at each other with enquiry as Parth did not have a kennel of angry dogs at his disposal.

Zona screamed. "Man with teeth has womans with him" and he cowered even deeper

"A woman did you say? Who is she?" Parth ordered the servants to pick Zona up from the red Persian carpet that now sported a dubious wet stain. Zona was picked up, still in the foetal position with his head covered deep beneath his arm.

"Womans! That's all Zona knows. Womans who drinks whiskey like sahib and no get drunk like sahib." Zona dared to show part of his face from beneath the cover of his arm, revealing one terrified eye that shifted about taking in all before it.

"Where does this woman drink whiskey?"

"In village of Merak near Panagon Lake. Womans and mans with teeth drink whiskey there. I see them one time. They ask Zona to take message and Zona takes message that is all Your Highnesses." Zona pleaded and gradually unfolded himself and stood upright as the servants released their grip on him.

"Let him go, he knows nothing." Parth cast his gaze away from Zona as he spoke, disgusted by the sight of him "tell these people who have my daughter that I will take them to the land of the butterflies if they give Rawinda back to me alive and well," Parth continued, and the servants stood to one side. Zona ran as fast as his old legs would permit, slipping and sliding as he made his way out of the palace back into the sanctuary of the jungle, screeching at the top of his voice as he ran. The animals and birds fled like the parting waves of the Red Sea before him as his shrieks struck terror into everything that could hear.

Vishnu sat lightly on a tubular framed chair that spilled its insides down onto the cold concrete floor. Half a bar of a one bar electric fire was switched on; the half not working was once the previous watchman's cigarette lighter. A calendar of many a yester year displaying the smile and other charms of a scantily dressed biker lady hung like a sun worn trophy over a tea chest that doubled as a table. Vishnu brought his own cup, saucer and silver spoon to his small canteen and they sat in the centre of the tea chest on yesterday's Evening Mail. He was stirring his tea when the old green finger dial phone rang and jolted Vishnu from his anxious thoughts of the missing wax pear.

"Oh, what a to do?" he said as he reached for the phone. His back arched once the voice on the other end reached his ear.

"Yes Parth. Yes. Yes Parth I will bring it back to you straight away. Ermm…yes, it is safe don't worry," and he put the phone down slowly, missing the base on his first attempt. "Poor Rawinda. Oh what to do?"

Vishnu very happily handed in his notice to resign his post to the grumpy old spinster who owned the small shopping complex.

"Knew you'd be a waste of my time" she said and spat on the floor.

Vishnu smiled politely and left.

His pulse raced and his imagination was bouncing as if on the end of a bungee wire as he walked towards the rectory knowing that the wax pear was missing and he had failed his mission.

"Oh Lord of almighty," Vishnu kept saying to himself over and over as he walked along the grassy narrow path that led to the rectory.

"Rawinda's life depends on it and I have let it out of my care. Oh Lord of almighty." Vishnu rubbed his hands frantically over his face as he spoke loudly to himself.

He stopped in his tracks as the rectory came into sight and stood for a moment and thought. He ran many different ideas through his head as to how he should explain to the family who he was and what he needed. None of his ideas seemed rational so he set off again in a very purposeful trot and held his hands towards the sky for a moment in despair.

Chet and Cecily were in their "Woodhouse 2" that by now was beginning to take shape and look even better than their old one in Robin Hood's Bay. It lacked the broken sapling branch however for propelling missiles but Chet installed a mop handle in the ground that worked almost as well providing Jilly didn't notice it missing.

The children were far too busy to see Vishnu as he walked very fast past them towards the rectory.

Maximillian had just received his monthly copy of "Explorer's Updates" magazine and was in his shed reading about a mysterious coloured rock found in the Gansu Province of China where tests had failed to show the exact composition of the material. The only conclusion was that it dated from 300 million BC. Jilly was making lunch and the smell of parsnips and fresh bread filled the air. Vishnu went straight to Maximillian's shed and stood looking down on Maximillian for several seconds before Maximillian, deep in his reading, realised he was there.

"Ah" Maximillian said in shock and jumped to his feet when he saw Vishnu.

"What the…?" he continued and took his pipe from his mouth and dropped his reading material to the floor.

Vishnu smiled "No need to worry sahib - Parth sent me," Vishnu said and patted Maximillian on the arm.

"Parth? Parth? - How the blazes did he know where I was?" Maximillian stooped down and picked up some of the papers he'd dropped.

Vishnu picked up one of the papers, gave it a quick look and handed it to Maximillian.

"Still interested in the 300-million-year-old artefacts." Vishnu smiled.

"Ermm…err," Maximillian coughed nervously "I am. I still read up on it from time to time and how the blazes do you know this?" Maximillian said and pushed his pipe back into his mouth again and began to puff strongly on it, filling the shed with smoke until they could barely see each other.

"I have been watching; well let's say keeping a good eye on you all for years," Vishnu said and opened the door of the shed to allow some of the smoke from Maximillian's pipe to escape.

"Watching us eh?" Maximillian spoke suspiciously from the corner of his mouth.

"As a friend," Vishnu replied, noticing Maximillian's displeasure.

"Well, if that's not the damnedest thing. Why would Parth have you watching over us?"

"To make sure nothing harmful happened to you or the wax pear." Vishnu's voice dropped an octave and became even more serious as the word pear left his lips.

"The what? That old wax pear. What on earth does he care about that old thing for? He gave it to me as a present. I thought bloody odd thing to give a fellow as a parting gift when he handed it to me but I didn't want to seem ungrateful for the gesture so I kept me mouth shut. Considering I helped to save his daughter to boot from that snake - I thought maybe a small handful of diamonds or even a nice little bag of gold would be a far more appropriate parting gesture but I got an old wax pear. And now he wants the bloody thing back." Maximillian's voice raised to a such a pitch that Jilly heard the commotion and ran out of the kitchen and into the garden shed in her slippers; with her yellow rubber gloves dripping water onto the wooden floor.

"Jilly" Vishnu spoke calmly and greeted Jilly as though he knew her as a personal friend.
Jilly and Maximillian looked at each other in confusion.

"Who are you?" Jilly said and walked over to Maximillian and held his arm.

"There is no need at all in this world to fear anything from Vishnu. I am your friend." Vishnu gave his customary head wobble.

"So Parth wants his pear back? Well, he can have the

bloody thing. It is here somewhere let me get it for you." Maximillian turned around mumbling and grumbling under his breath and began to search all the places he remembered having left the pear. "It was here. I could swear it," he continued.

After a while his searching became more frantic, and he began throwing things around the shed as he searched in places he couldn't remember placing or even seeing the pear.

"It's gone." Maximillian straightened his back and looked at Vishnu in distress.

"I know. I searched for it recently and it is not here," Vishnu replied with regret.

"In my shed? You were in my shed and I wasn't here? The damned nerve. A fellow has no privacy,"

Maximillian complained and Jilly held his arm to calm him down as little red circles of frustration appeared on his cheeks.

"So where is it?" Jilly looked very earnestly at Maximillian.

"It's in the house. Must be. The children must have brought it into the house." Maximillian left the shed in a bundle of anxious movements followed closely by Jilly who kept her eyes firmly fixed on Vishnu all the time.

"It must be in here somewhere." Maximillian began to look around the kitchen shelves.

"No it isn't," Vishnu replied calmly.

"How would you know?" Jilly replied with anger welling up in her voice.

"Yes how?" Maximillian stood still for the first time and panted, holding his left hand over his heart.

"Because I have searched the house from top to bottom as well." Vishnu smiled his most innocent smile.

"In my house when I wasn't here?" Jilly screamed and her eyes widened with anger.

Maximillian sat down still holding his hand to his chest and began to breathe irregularly.

"No need to get alarmed Jilly, all I wanted was the wax pear. Nothing else and it is not here so the question now is where is it?" Vishnu said and looked out of the kitchen window towards the woodhouse ignoring Jilly's anger and Maximillian's panic attack.

"We don't have it. I haven't seen it for ages." Jilly left her hand on Maximillian's shoulder and mouthed "Are you all right?" Maximillian nodded in the affirmative.

"Why does Parth want it? Why did he give the blasted thing to me in the first place if he wants it back again? I wouldn't mind if it were something valuable – yes; that I could understand but a wax cast that could only have been modelled by an imbecile with impaired vision." Maximillian got to his feet again and stared Vishnu straight in the eye waiting for a response.

"Parth gave it to you for safekeeping. There is a butterfly wing inside the wax…".

"One of his butterfly wings. Yes, I know about those" Maximillian interrupted Vishnu and his attitude stabilised. Jilly's eyes darted between the two of them craving an understanding.

"He wanted them kept separate and a long distance apart so they would never be joined together again. So, I have been with you all this time and you never noticed me," Vishnu said proudly looking at them to acknowledge a praise he felt he deserved. Neither Maximillian nor Jilly gave him his due right.

"You have been watching that old pear for years?" Jilly said.

Vishnu nodded his head vigorously and smiled proudly. "I have saved you all so many times also and you never knew," Vishnu continued his pride beaming in his face as his countenance lit up at the prospect of finally relaying his many acts of daring do.

"How?" Jilly said unconvinced. She took off her rubber gloves and threw them onto the centre of the table and folder her arms. Maximillian gave her a concerned stare as the gloves were in flight.

"Remember the Christmas morning you found the very large burn on your fireside rug?" Vishnu said.

"Yes," Jilly said sharply, still unconvinced but her interest in his explanation rising.

"I put it out," Vishnu said proudly.

"And the time the wind had blown the electric cable down on the path that led to the children's woodhouse in Robin Hood's Bay and the repair team arrived and you wondered how they could have known," Vishnu said and gave an over exaggerated mysterious look. Maximillian and Jilly gave each other a questioning glance.

"I remember- vividly," Jilly said, alarm at the memory returning to her voice.

"I rang them," Vishnu explained pride making his words flow like molasses in the evening sunshine. "There were many other times that I assisted and you never knew."

"The time that Chet was trapped high up in that tree and the fire brigade mysteriously arrived to take him down to safety?" Jilly said and sat down heavily on a kitchen chair.

"That was me." Vishnu smiled proudly.

"It seems we owe you a great deal. Didn't get your name?" Maximillian held out his hand to Vishnu.

"My name is Vishnu," and he shook Maximillian's hand.

Jilly let all her shortcomings and suspicions of Vishnu vanish and she rose lightly from her seat and gave Vishnu a hug. "Very nice. Some praise at last," Vishnu said, and they all laughed.

"We still have to find that pear." Maximillian spoke as he stared out of the kitchen window in dismay.

"I fear we must find it or Rawinda will die" Vishnu gazed sadly at the floor; all jollity vanished.

Jilly grabbed Maximillian, digging her nails into the sleeve of his jacket. "Whatever do you mean?"

Vishnu relayed the full story of Rawinda's perilous predicament and there was a thoughtful silence as they racked their brains wondering where the pear could be.

Maximillian continued to stare out through the window towards the children's Woodhouse wiping the condensation on the glass into the shape of Australia. Tasmania ran down undistinguishably in a wide horizontal line.

Just then Cecily decided that her flowers and the buried pear needed some watering as she felt the summer sun was drying up the ground faster than usual. She filled the old tin watering can with the plastic spout at the tap near Maximillian's shed and walked over to her flower bed just outside the entrance to the woodhouse.

"Ha ha, that is it," Maximillian shouted and ran as fast as he could to the kitchen door and out into the yard. Jilly shrugged her shoulders in a questioning fashion and both she and Vishnu followed him. Maximillian ran in an awkward gait towards the woodhouse as he was wearing old slippers with thin worn soles that didn't keep out stone bruises. He gave the occasional "Ohh," and "Ahh," as he ran and stood on an offending object. Cecily had just finished her watering and looked at Maximillian in shock as she was not accustomed to seeing him move any faster than snail's pace.

"What is wrong grandad?" she dropped the watering can in shock.

"Listen Cecily I don't mind, honestly but do you have the wax pear?" Maximillian asked as calmly as his panting voice would allow.

A guilty expression covered Cecily's face like a cheap Halloween mask and she looked at Jilly, tears forming in the corners of her eyes.

"Have you got it darling?" Jilly put her arm around Cecily's shoulder.

"We don't mind if you have. We won't get annoyed." Maximillian let his hand rest gently on Cecily's head.

Chet appeared from the woodhouse on hearing all the commotion.

"It is buried there. I knew it was a stupid idea. That it would never grow into anything. I told her," Chet said and pointed to the flower bed that Cecily had just watered.

Vishnu fell on his knees in his crisp white linen trousers and began to dig frantically with his hands in the wet clay, like a greyhound burying a bone, until he uncovered the wax pear and a large beaming smile covered his face.

CHAPTER 8

Rawinda's temperature rose during the night and a feverish sweat covered her face like a death mask. Her drenched, fully clothed body was sprawled out on the ferns as though she had just been dragged from a river. Loud semiconscious moans of her agony awoke Sukey.

"You should have noticed her hand dragging in the clay; you big fool," Sukey screamed at Ishmael as she fixed her stare on Rawinda's worsening condition.

"What! You have some nerve to blame me. Why did you slash her in the first place?" Ishmael defended his position and also kept his gaze firmly fixed on Rawinda's half open eyes. Her eyeballs rolled about as though she were following the meandering flight path of a bee gathering nectar.

"Oh, there is no point mentioning that now," Sukey said and took another look at Rawinda's hand which by this point was beginning to turn blue.

"Of course, there is no point when you are to blame. I can only imagine what you would be saying if I had slashed her." Ishmael also took a look at her hand and jumped back sharply.

"It smells," he rubbed his nose and jumped up and down on the spot in agitation.

"Of course it does. It is badly infected. Whatever bug she picked up it has acted on her very fast. This doesn't look good at all. Could be gangrene. We will have to get her to the palace, or she will croak it for certain." Sukey roughly grabbed Rawinda's feet.

"It couldn't be gangrene – surely that would take longer to take hold," Ishmael said and leaned down to inspect her wounded hand. "I think you are right," he said after his assessment "Why had this to happen. Why can't we get a break just once?" Ishmael continued and stomped his foot into the earth in a childlike tantrum.

"Get her arms now. There is no time to waste. She could drop off any minute." Sukey gave off a stare that came from the minus side of the barometer and Ishmael did as he was told.

They struggled out of their hideout and along the path that led back to the palace.

"You have no concern for my aching back."

Sukey didn't answer. Ishmael continued to grumble to himself. On occasions they had to let Rawinda lie on the ground as she looked as though she might die if they continued further. Her face was a pale blue and her breathing wasn't strong enough to cloud a mirror. Each time her strength rallied a little they set off again. Carrying her until just before nightfall they reached the boundary of the palace gardens. They left Rawinda in full view on the main path that led to the palace. Ishmael fired a few shots into the air from the derringer he kept in his boot and the cracking sound disturbed the peacocks who screamed and flew about in frantic circles.

"We will never find the treasure now." Ishmael ran cutting vegetation angrily out of their paths with a machete as though he were attacking his imaginary bad luck.

"I have every intention of finding that treasure. It is mine. I want it. I must have it no matter what happens." Sukey spat the words out with a steely determination.

"We have nothing to bargain with now. So, what do we do?" Ishmael stopped and leaned down holding his hands on his knees while panting long gasps of breath.

Sukey ignored his pause and ran past without a reply. Ishmael chopped into an innocent tree with his machete to relieve some of his frustration and screamed at the sky with his mouth stretched to its periphery. Sukey reached their hideout and drew her knife - waving it in front of her with menace as she noticed a figure lurking in the shadows.

"Someone's here," she whispered quietly to Ishmael as he reached her side panting from exhaustion.

Ishmael took the derringer from his boot and looked about sharply; every sense he possessed in full alert.

"Behind that tree," Sukey pointed with the tip of her

knife.

Ishmael cocked the delicate trigger of the derringer. "Who's there? Come out now." He held the gun steadily with both hands and pointed towards the tree.

Zona held his hands over his head and meekly emerged from the shadows taking baby steps on the dried leaves that could be heard to snap beneath his feet in the tense silence. Ishmael put the derringer back into his boot with a scoff.

"How did you find this place. Sukey put her knife away.

"Zona knows everything and Zona knows nothing," he said with a smile and gave a little dance.

"Did you give the maharajah the message?" Ishmael growled his question as he watched the dust rising in a cloud from beneath Zona's feet.

"What does that matter now?" Sukey opened a fresh bottle of whiskey and took a long drink as though she were drinking fresh cool water from a mountain spring.

Zona's eyes lit up and he licked his arid dry lips when he saw the bottle.

"Zona tell all when he gets whiskey," a drool of saliva began to trickle from the corner of his open mouth as he stared motionless at the bottle. Ishmael begrudgingly pulled a fresh bottle from their stash and threw it to Zona who grabbed it as if his life depended on catching it securely. He pulled the cork out with his teeth; spat it carelessly to the ground and held the bottle on his head allowing the liquid to hit the back of his throat like a firehose until he'd finished half.

"Thirsty today." Sukey was impressed

"Zona thirsty every day," he grinned "Zona give message and maharaja very angry with Zona and very angry with you two sahibs," he replied and his countenance became very serious.

"What did you tell him about us?"

"No, no Zona says nothing of you kind peoples. Nothing comes from Zona's mouth," he stared at Sukey's hand as it reached for her knife.

Sukey removed her hand from inside her jacket keeping her steely gaze on Zona who took another long drink from his bottle and panted as though he were greedily taking in the last morsels of the jungle air.

"You had best not tell anybody anything about us or where we are. 'Cause if you do," Sukey made a gesture with her hand, mimicking an action of cutting his throat.

Zona took a long swallow. "I know more," he said.

"What do you know?" Ishmael lay on the ground beneath a tall oak tree and held his arm over his eyes to block out the piercing hot sun.

"More bottles for Zona?" Zona made a nervous attempt to bargain.

"If the information is worth it. Sukey dumped vegetables that looked past their date onto the ground near the stone fire circle and began to strike damp matches.

"Something arriving from England soon. I overheard them mentioning a second butterfly wing." Zona allowed a glimmer of authority to dictate his tone as he was proud of his new information.

Ishmael and Sukey became statuesque, only their eyes moved towards Zona.

"Zona hears from palace servants that it is coming from England soon. He needs it to rescue Rawinda." Zona smiled with self-satisfaction and took an exaggerated look at his almost empty whiskey bottle.

Ishmael threw him a fresh bottle. Zona smiled broadly and caught it in one hand.

"So, he doesn't have both butterfly wings here. Ermm," Sukey pondered as she finally found a match that struck a light.

"Where Rawinda?" Zona looked about him.

They did not bother to reply to his question.

"Who is this person in England that has the second butterfly wing?" Ishmael stretched himself as though trying to ease the pain in his back.

Zona shrugged his shoulders and gave his very best

vacant stare. "Zona knows nothing," he replied, his words slightly slurred from alcohol.

"We will be waiting. And this time we will get it right. I want that treasure. No more Mr. Nice Guy from us do you hear," Sukey said and gritted her teeth.

Zona took a deep swallow and fell back into the thick ferns where he lay motionless.

Vishnu holding the wax pear close to his chest like he was cradling his first born led the procession towards the rectory with the family following close behind him. They all entered through the back door and Vishnu placed the wax pear carefully on a towel he draped across the kitchen table.

Maximillian locked the door banging the top and bottom bolts closed with his fist; Vishnu smiled.

"May I use this knife?" Vishnu picked up what appeared to be Jilly's best kitchen knife and, after getting a slightly reluctant nod of approval from Jilly, began to cut gently into the wax.

He cut layer after layer of wax from the pear like thin wafers of Parma ham afraid to damage the treasure hidden at its core until finally the outline of the onyx elephant could be seen. Once the wax was completely removed Vishnu held the onyx elephant in both hands and twisted it delicately in a clockwise motion. It separated into two halves revealing the gold butterfly wing lying majestically inside on a bed of the finest red silk. Vishnu held his breath and took the butterfly wing from its sanctuary. He held it above his head for the others to admire.

"Craftwork beyond perfection." Maximillian put his best reading glasses on to observe it more closely.

"Parth hoped the butterfly wings would never be joined together again. He fears this strange inexplicable land of butterflies that exists beyond the wormhole. This is why he wanted you to take it far away so that even in moments of his own curiosity, the temptation to join the two butterfly wings together could never be fulfilled." Vishnu spoke very solemnly.

"Now they are to be reunited again and the mysteries of the land of butterflies will be revealed. Fascinating just fascinating." Maximillian put his best reading glasses safely back in their case. He gave the shiny new case a small wipe on his trouser leg to remove any possible stains it might have incurred. There was no need.

"I must act with all haste and get this back to India immediately. Rawinda's life is at stake." Vishnu placed the butterfly wing carefully back onto its silk bed inside the onyx elephant once more and securely twisted the two halves closed again. He placed it with extreme reverence into the inside pocket of his jacket.

"I bid you all farewell." Vishnu smiled as he walked with haste to the back door and began to pull the unwilling bolts open.

"I must say it has been fun watching over you for the past few years. I will miss you all." Vishnu gave a sentimental solemn smile as he finally persuaded the bolts that he needed to leave.

Maximillian straightened himself up; stood proudly on his toes and gave a deep cough to clear his throat. This was a look that Jilly knew only too well. A look she feared whenever it flashed across Maximillian's face. A look that didn't appear very often but when it did almost always meant turmoil.

"Oh no. Whatever is the matter with you now?" Jilly looked at Maximillian with trepidation and wrung her hands like she were tightly ringing a tea towel dry.

"I am going with you." Maximillian spoke with determination to Vishnu ignoring his daughter's question.

Jilly looked towards the ceiling and held her hands up in the air in despair.

"I knew it and you are most certainly not going," she said "A man of your age traipsing off to God knows where. India of all places. Look at you. You get lost going to the village for the morning paper."

Jilly's voice lilted in despair and she looked to the children for support in her argument. The support she felt she deserved wasn't forthcoming so she sat down heavily on a kitchen chair and rested her head in her hands – her hair fell about her face making it almost invisible.

"Jilly is maybe right sahib. It could get dangerous. I am not sure what to be expecting. You will be better off to stay here with your family." Vishnu tried to reject Maximillian's offer as kindly as he could.

Maximillian looked very offended.

"I will tell you my good man that I have crisscrossed the entire landmass of India many times and know it better than anybody. And I did it long before you were born too I might add." Maximillian straightened his back even further until it almost formed an arch in an on-parade type military stance.

"Yes, yes sahib but that was long times ago and like you correctly say you were a younger man."

Vishnu dismissed the offence sent like a rocket in his direction and continued to smile.

Jilly agreed with Vishnu's interpretation of the situation by nodding her head frantically in the affirmative, her blond hair dancing uncontrollably about her face as she stared with dagger looks towards Maximillian. He noticed her stare but looked suddenly away from it. The children delighted in all of this commotion and laughed at Maximillian's serious expressions as for once he was being scolded like a child and told what to do.

"Yes grandad you have to stay at home. You are too old," Chet said and tried not to laugh.

Maximillian ignored his comment with a stern cough and Chet and Cecily laughed out loud.

"Well, I am going to my friend Parth's assistance in this his hour of need whether you like it or not."

Maximillian's words seemed final as he shared his solemn sentiment equally with Vishnu and Jilly. Vishnu looked perplexed and Jilly hid her face in her hands again. The children laughed and danced around the floor.

"We are coming too. We are coming too," they chanted as they danced. "We are going to India," they repeated over and over as they danced.

"How long will all this take?" Jilly looked at Vishnu earnestly.

Vishnu shrugged his shoulders with an expression of genuine uncertainty.

"Two weeks? Three?" Jilly continued, her voice weak with the imagination of it all.

"You must stay here of course and take care of the children." Maximillian suddenly realised the purpose of her questioning. "I am an old hand at all this. Once you ride a bike you never lose it. You know it makes sense that I am better off on my own. Footloose and fancy free as they say."

Maximillian bounced up and down on his toes a couple of times and sucked his stomach in to give himself a temporarily fleeting virile appearance.

Jilly completely ignored him and he looked miffed at her utter dismissal of his imagined command of the situation.

"I don't know Jilly. Maybe days maybe weeks I can't tell but Parth has a private jet waiting for me right now, at Biggin Hill Airport so I must make my haste. I don't have the luxury of time right now so I must insist on all of your cooperation." Vishnu looked confused as his eyes pleaded with Maximillian to change his mind but his pleading stare was wasted and Maximillian once more retrieved his best reading glasses and put them securely into his pocket.

"Fine that settles it. I am coming with you. I travel light when I am on expeditions."

Maximillian quickly gathered extra tobacco that he kept airtight in a shiny brass World War 1 chocolate tin that had been given to his uncle Tom who was buried in some unknown place in Ypres that even his headstone in Poelcapelle couldn't determine. Not wishing to waste any further time arguing the point which he realised would be futile, Vishnu nodded in agreement but did not look at all happy with the arrangement.

"Hold it for one minute. We are coming with you. I can't let you off out there into God knows where on your own," Jilly objected obstinately and folded her arms in stubborn defiance. Anyway, it is time we used those new passports I got last year at your insistence. Remember you promised that you were going to take us all on a trip to Valencia to see your cousin the mayor. Maximillian coughed nervously and emptied a pocket that was used to house objects he might find useful during his everyday life. A small, tightly rolled ball of electric cable, two staples for fencing, six four-inch nails, a cap end for a six-inch water pipe, a partly used roll of red sticky tape, a dried out roll of putty and a compass. He looked at them hesitantly for a moment as they sat on the kitchen work top and debated with himself the merits of keeping some of them but the tobacco won the debate and he pushed the extra pouches into the vacated pocket. He gave it a reassuring tap with his hand.

"Lucky I insisted on passports in that case," and concealing a smile he turned away from everyone's view.

"We are going to India, we are going to India," they repeated over and over as they danced about the kitchen.

"Oh this is not good memsahib. Not good at all, at all." Vishnu sat down heavily at the kitchen table and held his head in his hands moaning utterances in Hindi.

Parth sent two of his most loyal servants ahead to the Ganges River 2000 km away to make preparations for Tuliana's cremation. They were sent to Varanasi one of the oldest cities in the world, a place of human habitation for 5000 years. Everyday hundreds of funeral pyres are lit on the banks of the river and amid the sound of bells and extreme heat the ashes of the dead are then scattered out to the murky dark waters of the Ganges hoping to reach Moksha where the soul of the deceased will finally be transported to heaven and escape the Hindu cycle of death and rebirth. Back at the palace, screams and pandemonium bounced off the walls and tapestries in the main hall as a group of servants rushed in carrying Rawinda's limp frame. Tears flowed like rivers of grief leaving traces of their meanderings viable on their dusty faces. Parth fell to his knees and a wail of grief that sprung from the very depths of his tormented soul echoed to every dark corner of the palace.

Parth cradled Rawinda in his arms; his head fell down and rested on her lifeless shoulder. Some of the servant women gently took Rawanda from him and carried her to her bedroom. Parth followed and could tell by the sombre expressions on the faces of the women that Rawinda was gravely ill. They laid her with reverence onto her bed of pale pink sheets as if knowing this posture was to be her last earthly position. The low chanting of anxious prayers were heard and cut through the silence of the room. The heavy lined curtains were pulled tightly closed on the golden glow of the sun leaving the bedroom in an eerie darkness. Oil lanterns and candles were lit and the smell of wax and paraffin filled the air. The servant women worked with very little communication as they treated Rawinda as best they could before the arrival of the doctors. Parth stood helplessly at the side of her bed in a state of death like grief with all colour and expression vanished from his countenance. A small blue butterfly glided peacefully through the air with purpose in its flight and landed on Rawinda's ice pale cheek.

It was Chet and Cecily's first time in an airport and their eyes were wide with wonder. Their new surroundings were like a melting pot of humanity with so many differing nationalities all represented in one area. They were fascinated by a group of elegant African women who wore multi-coloured traditional dress and who smiled at the children as they noticed them stare in awe.

"Wow. I would love clothes like that," Cecily said as she stared.

"Yeh so cool," Chet replied.

They watched attentive faces gazing at departure screens before rushing off in differing directions.

"They rush about a lot here," Cecily said as she sat back further into her seat to observe.

"Much busier than the village," Chet laughed.

They sat by a large window with dull lifeless glass in the departure lounge and stared at the plane they were about to embark. They visually checked its every detail particularly searching for cracks in the metalwork. Chet prompted Cecily to examine each part just be sure as the pilot and the crew could have easily overlooked a crack or two.

The tyres looked like a major accident worry to Cecily. They looked so tiny in comparison to the massive size of the plane and she wondered could they explode just as they took off. "Can you see any tread on those tyres?" Chet squinted as he put his nose up to the window and stared out at the white and blue jet that flexed its imaginary muscles of dominance.

"No, none at all," Cecily whispered in terror.

"That's what I thought. Old tyres. They must blow when we take off," he said with a knowledgeable nod of his head.

"Do you think so, Chet?" Cecily grabbed his arm. "Do you really think so?" she continued.

"Bet you that gold piece that makes my hands go green that grandad gave me. They will blow for sure."

"Oh no Chet." Cecily squinted to get a better look at the tyres.

"We are gonners I'd say. We won't make the end of the runway," Chet said with certainty and he looked out through the window to the runway and pointed to the place he predicted the tyres to give way. Cecily looked towards the long runway that had a heat mist rising over its surface and imagined her impending fate flashing before her inner eye.

"A ball of flame is how we will go. Big ball of flame." Chet opened a bar of chocolate that Vishnu had bought him earlier and offered half of it to Cecily. She declined his offer as she was too afraid to eat.

"A ball of flame," she said timidly and looked towards the end of the runway again "That's how we will go?" she hushed nervously.

Vishnu had been in touch with the relevant authorities and booked the extra passengers onto the jet and took care of all the necessary paperwork with a sophistication and ease that came naturally to him.

They sat together on the plane with Jilly on the aisle seat. Vishnu and Maximillian sat just opposite and chatted constantly.

"We are off now," Jilly said with a false and rather nervous smile to the children as she wiped her sweaty palms on her tartan dress. The engines revved up to maximum ready for take-off and Jilly's nails dug deep into the arm rest of her seat.

"Should we tell mum about the tyres?" Cecily said in a panic and grabbed Chet's arm.

"Too late now we are gonners," Chet replied and closed his eyes as if waiting for the impact.

"Oh no, a big ball of flame," Cecily said out loud and Jilly gave her a stare.

The plane charged the runway and everyone held their breaths. Maximillian and Vishnu were deep in conversation but very aware of the take off.

"What do you make of it all?" Maximillian enquired but looked straight ahead as the plane took off imagining over and over in his head that he was on the 347 train from Manchester to Liverpool.

"Parth mentioned the wormhole that opened up when the two butterfly wings were put together and the
that lay beyond, but what does it all mean?" Maximillian relaxed his grip on his arm rest as the jet levelled off and the slight turbulence subsided.

"In ancient beliefs the butterfly is the personification of a person's soul. It was thought that when someone died their soul became a butterfly and visited relations to reassure them that all was fine. In some cultures it was thought that a new human soul was created each time a butterfly emerged from its cocoon. The Greek word for butterfly is psyche which translates as soul and that they believed that dreams were the result of the soul-butterflies wandering through other worlds. A native tribe called Nagas who lived in Manipur in the Indian state of Nagaland, an area near where I grew up, believed that they were descended from the butterflies. Their tradition states that there was a land where the butterflies were the rulers and that humans were their subjects. It was from this time and place that they believed the tribe originated and they believe that this place still exists in some form of a parallel dimension." Vishnu spoke with a passion that suggested he had the subject well researched.

"This is the land that Parth fears? He fears these soul butterflies could escape into our time and control the human race in our current dimension?" Maximillian queried.

"It appears so sahib. It appears so." Vishnu held his hand tightly on the pocket where he kept the butterfly wing as if he was blocking his life's blood from draining from his heart.

The tyres didn't burst on take-off as Chet imagined and there was no ball of fire to consume Cecily.

Instead, it was the smoothest eight hour flight Vishnu or Maximillian had ever remembered, with some sleep added in for good measure.

Zona's source of information was accurate as always. He was able to tell Sukey and Ishmael in great detail about the pending arrival of Vishnu and the family's flight from England. Vishnu had phoned ahead to the palace to expect the extra arrivals and make preparations for them. So knowledge of the family's arrival was known amongst all the servants. For this information Sukey doubled Zona's ration and gave him two bottles of pale, badly distilled gut rot.

"We must get that butterfly wing. I want that treasure now. I have waited my whole life for it and it shall be mine." Sukey's frustration rose to such heights that she was almost hysterical and fluffed her hair with both hands into an unkempt ball of madness.

Ishmael nodded his head in agreement and gave Zona an extra-large pat on the back just as Zona was taking a drink. Zona gasped and coughed as the whiskey went down his gullet the wrong way.

His eyes ran with tears flowing like rain down his leathery cheeks and he gasped for air.

"You're a top man Zona. You will have a steady supply of whiskey for life if we manage to pull this one off" Ishmael said and was about to give Zona another large appreciatory pat on the back but he noticed its advance and quickly moved to one side to avoid the contact of praise. Ishmael wasn't impressed at Zona's avoidance of his gesture.

"Whiskey for life for Zona," and he danced his little dance around the campfire taking an occasional drink from the bottle as he repeated his chant loudly.

"If he doesn't shut up I swear I will swing for him," Sukey screamed and Zona suddenly stood statuesque.

"The flight is coming in this evening so we will be there to give them a welcoming reception." Sukey sharpened her knife on a whetstone with long slow purposeful movements of her hand spitting on the blade every now and again and giving outbursts of laughter that only she appreciated.

The jet was welcomed to the runway by a beautiful hazy Indian evening and moist tarmac. The sky was blood red and a sense of exotic adventure seemed to lie just beyond the cabin windows.

Chet and Cecily missed most of the flight as they fell asleep. Their eyes grew heavy and they tried everything they could summon to stay awake so as not to miss one moment of this amazing adventure but it was not to be. The sound of the jet's wheels caressing India with a smooth welcoming touch jolted them back to cognizance and they yawned and felt cheated of all the precious moments they had lost forever.

"You were supposed to wake me up." Chet needed to lay blame and Cecily was available.

"No you said you would keep me awake remember," she replied angrily.

They both made a solemn pact by hooking their pinkie fingers that this would be the last occasion they would miss important moments on this adventure.

"We must not let this happen again. We will have plenty of time to sleep when we get back home," Chet said angrily and wiped his eyes.

"No more sleeping. We have too much to see," Cecily agreed and wiped her eyes as well.

The children had witnessed large crowds before of course. Occasionally Maximillian took them to watch Sheffield United play at Bramall Lane. Cecily went along for the ice cream as she didn't like soccer very much and hated the deafening chanting noises especially when a goal was scored. The children imagined the crowds at these football matches had to be the largest crowds in the world.

Their opinions changed dramatically however when they witnessed the myriad and infinity of the crowds in India. Cecily grabbed Jilly's arm as they walked towards the baggage reclaim area. It was a free for all type of airport. No special quarter was given to passengers coming off private jets. Everyone had to rough it to the open baggage area here but this lack of luxury didn't bother any of them. Maximillian held Chet's hand even though Chet complained and struggled to break free at every opportunity. He hated the indignity of being treated like a child especially in front of young girls his own age who were allowed to walk freely and looked at his incarceration with amusement.

"Let go grandad," he would say and struggle to loosen Maximillian's grip.

"The bogeyman will have you if I let you go," Maximillian replied without the smile he would love to have shown.

"Bogeyman?" Chet replied in contempt and continued

to struggle.

Sukey and Ishmael were dressed in stolen airport cleaners matching yellow overalls and stood hiding in the shadows scanning each person in the crowd who disembarked from all English flights. Ishmael had his hands leaning lazily on a large plastic rubbish bin on wheels. They both stood out like an apple in a bag of potatoes from the rest of the airport staff.

"You're new?" an overfriendly cleaner spoke to Sukey and smiled politely.

"Buzz off with yourself," Sukey growled and the cleaner disappeared quickly into a rest room.

"Here they are," Ishmael pointed anxiously to a family of two adults and three young girls. "You are such an absolute fool. An old man, a young woman, two children and an Indian man with a black turban. Can you not remember what Zona told us. You complete idiot," Sukey replied never taking her gaze from the passengers as the crowd made their way towards a conveyor belt that churned out suitcases of every colour like a monster regurgitating its suitcase dinner.

"There had best be some amazing treasures in this land of butterflies," Ishmael grumbled as he took yet another disapproving look at the yellow overalls he was wearing and shifted them about his person to make them appear more appealing.

"I don't look so bad in these. Do I? I think I look great," he said and stared at Sukey waiting for a compliment.

Sukey didn't look towards him or reply. Ishmael scowled.

"Here look, dope," she snapped after a few further minutes.

"It's them," Ishmael replied as they hungrily watched Maximillian arrive at the conveyor belt holding a tight grip on Chet's struggling little hand. Jilly and Cecily walked behind them and Vishnu followed at the rear observing everything like a black panther above a corral of cattle.

"We have to get our hands on one of those children." Sukey began to panic as she scanned the scene for a suitable opportunity; mulling possibilities over in her brain like an advanced computer on a performance enhancement.

"I will create a diversion and then you grab the boy. Did you bring the chloroform?" Sukey doubtfully looked Ishmael up and down.

"Of course I did. Do you think I am an idiot?" Ishmael produced the bottle from the pocket of his yellow overalls and wiggled it about in his hand in a teasing fashion in front of her eyes.

"I will come back to you when I have the diversion set and we can both hide him in the bin. Get as close to them as you can and wait for my say so. Do not do anything until I am with you," Sukey commanded sternly and marched off into the crowd pulling her oversized overalls up with her hand.

"Till I am with you. As if I am not capable on my own," Ishmael grumbled and mimicked her voice.

Sukey placed a roll of firecrackers into a bin near the baggage conveyor belt and lit the fuse. She always carried these with her on missions as they had in the past produced her very best diversions. The firecrackers began to ignite like excessively eager guns on a pheasant shoot and the fact that they were inside the bin increased the volume of their detonation by multiples.

"Get down everyone there is a crazed gun man over there. I see him. He is going to kill us all," an overweight lady with cherry red cheeks and a highly strung temperament screamed and fell to the floor and covered her head with her hands. She kicked and screamed as she lay on the cold marble floor and began to pull frantically at her hair which had previously been arranged very neatly in a tall beehive hairstyle. It now fell down around her shoulders in a crazy tangled mess.

Jilly, Cecily, Maximillian and Vishnu dived to the floor

but Chet didn't get a chance. With military precision Sukey and Ishmael put a cloth soaked with chloroform around Chet's mouth and nose then they both bundled him into the bin without anybody noticing. They wheeled the bin away fast as the firecrackers continued to ignite sounding as though heralding the doom of all those who lay prostrate on the floor, afraid to move even a facial muscle.

"It is all ok folks. It was just some little ole firecrackers in that bin over yonder there," a tall Indian security guard with hunched shoulders and a Mexican style moustache said in fake American cowboy accent. He beckoned calmly to the crowd with an exaggerated sweep of his hand to rise to their feet again. Everyone dragged themselves up slowly, some crying hysterically, others deathly pale from the shock of it all.

"Chet, Chet," Maximillian screamed as he looked about him, his eyes squinting as they searched through the frantic crowd.

"Where is Chet? Where is he?" Jilly screamed in terror and grabbed Cecily by the arm.

Vishnu jumped up onto the side of the baggage conveyor belt to get a better look through the vast uneasy crowd.

"He's gone," Cecily screamed.

Sukey and Ishmael drove the small yellow refuse truck slowly out through airport security and screamed with laughter as they turned the vehicle out onto the main road to Pangong Lake.

Cool summer breezes blew the long delicate curtains in slow rhythmic dance and fanned the smells of spices and incense to every corner of the palace. It was another beautiful Indian morning where the early sunlight cast its yawing gaze of illumination onto the petals in the garden beneath Rawinda's window. The shutters were closed and bolted in that dark room where the stale smell of sickness hung heavy in the air. A small tiffany lamp that was once a birthday present from Tuliana gave off a pale orange light that faded into darkness a few metres from her bed. It sat on a crowded bedside locker that also housed many random bottles of clinically aromatic medication. So far none of it was having any effect even though the best doctors in the land were at Rawinda's disposal and kept vigil over her constantly, day and night. The servants lit sage incense near the door which produced long trails of white fragrant smoke to ward off negative energy and placed bright radiant crystals in the corners of the room and around her bed.

The doctors conferred amongst each other in quiet melancholic tones and agreed that there was no possible hope for Rawinda's recovery. The infection had taken too strong a hold on her body and there was nothing further they could do except pray, which some of them did.

Rawinda had been in a deep coma, her eyes closed as though in peaceful sleep, since she was found abandoned on the jungle path. It was the medical opinion that she would not regain consciousness again. Parth could sense this from their grim expressions but did not want to believe it. The servants cried bitterly out of Parth's view as they wanted to give him whatever last few moments of hope remained. He sat by her bed holding her delicate white hand tightly and stared at her with tears that dripped onto her raven black hair. It seemed like the saddest place on earth.

Airport security in dark blue uniforms and thick leather soled shoes scampered about and searched the airport for Chet but without success. Some of the passengers on the English flight assisted, calling out his name in differing strong accents but no trace of Chet could be found. Jilly and Cecily sat together on a shabby aluminium bench that was covered with graffiti, executed by a talent challenged artist but they did not notice this. They cried constantly and were comforted by some of the women from the British flight.

"This is terrible love. You poor lovie," a lady with a

broad Mancunian accent tried to console Jilly but she too began to cry, making the scene even more dramatic. In the end Jilly had to put her arm around the Mancunian lady in efforts to console her.

"I fears it is not good memsahib Jilly," Vishnu said gravely. "The devils have him whoever they are. It must be a ransom and they must know who we are so our best plan is to go to Parth's palace and wait for them to get in touch with us," Vishnu continued.

"Do you think it is related to the butterfly wing?" Maximillian spoke in a low subdued voice to Vishnu as he was now feeling guilty at having been responsible for bringing the family to India and for not taking better care of Chet. He couldn't believe that he could have let Chet's hand go when the firecrackers ignited. He thought it an act of cowardice that he couldn't imagine himself capable of and felt very ashamed.

"This is what I am thinking sahib. I am almost certain they are after the butterfly wing and they know who we are so we had best get to the palace as soon as we can. Parth will know what to do." Vishnu spoke with confidence and helped Jilly to her feet.

They all thanked and bid their goodbyes to the kind folk from the British flight who assisted in the search. Jilly gave a particular thank you to the lady from Manchester whose tears had by now dried up completely as she sat unconcerned happily eating a mandarin.

"Small pale sick looking boy drink whiskey?" Zona offered a bottle to Chet.

Chet didn't answer and looked away, feeling ill after the chloroform and disguising his terror with great effect.

"Make him big and strong like Zona. Look Zona has no pale face; so he will drink alone," Zona gave a loud manic laugh and twirled in circles around the fire kicking up dust that rose in a cloud over his head.

"Take a message to the palace booze-hound," Sukey

spoke in a tone so cold it made Chet shiver and she gave Zona a hard kick on the bum with her boot. Zona jumped and rubbed the assaulted area with his free hand. Chet laughed quietly to himself making sure they didn't notice.

"Zona don't like being on the end of memsahib's boot," he said angrily.

"And I just don't care what Zona likes or don't like." Sukey took out her knife in a flash of her hand and waved it in front of Zona's sun peeled skinny nose. He suddenly became silent, his rebellious outburst well and truly over and he smiled meekly.

"Tell the maharajah we have this brat and if we don't get those butterfly wings he is…," and she made a gesture with the knife which mimicked cutting Chet's throat.

"Poor small boy. And such a thin neck too." Zona gave Chet a sympathetic stare.

"Never you mind the boy. We want those butterfly wings delivered here tomorrow morning at the latest. Tell him we mean business and no tricks or else." Sukey threw her knife with precision and pinned a large tarantula spider to the trunk of the tree just above Chet's head.

"Did you hear her? Get a move on." Ishmael made a false threatening run at Zona who fled, his knees almost touching his chin as he scampered from the camp.

Chet had never encountered anything like Sukey and Ishmael in his short life. He imagined all the most despicable evil villains in the children's books he had read and the ghost stories Maximillian told but nothing compared to these two he thought. The tarantula that was pinned by the point of Sukey's knife just above his head was truly dead and decomposing in the heat. Chet realised that this would be his fate if they didn't get all their demands met.

Chet fancied himself as an escapologist. He liked the word even before he knew its meaning and after hearing stories about The Great Houdini from Maximillian, he read a very short book on the subject.

He would ask Cecily to tie his hands and feet as tightly

as she could, then turn away and count to ten. But because Cecily was really quite hopeless at tying knots, Chet could always easily undo the bindings and stand to attention, proudly displaying the loose ropes in hand long before she made it to ten. He felt he could give Houdini a run for his money.

"You are very clever Chet," Cecily would say, and Chet would believe it. On this occasion however Ishmael was very good at tying knots and Chet could not get the bindings on his hands and feet to budge one centimetre and his face displayed a sadness for the loss of his dreams rather than his fettered condition.

In his grief Parth's hair hung down over his furrowed brow and touched his four-day stubble. His stomach rumbled loudly but he didn't feel the pangs of hunger even though he only ate one biscuit in a time that only his digestion remembered. Having suitable transport made available to collect Vishnu and his party from the airport were far from his thoughts so they had to make do with whatever was available in the taxi rank of scrapyard wrecks.

Their chosen lime green minibus decorated with hundreds of badly drawn eyes all staring psychotically, pulled up to a sudden halt at the palace having travelled at breakneck speed through the jungle. With white bloodless fingers the occupants all released their strained grips from seats or any object that for the duration of the journey from the airport gave them any stability.

"That was certainly an experience," Jilly said sarcastically to the driver who was dressed in a scruffy full a length purple Indian tunic. He smiled innocently through a mouth with intermittent missing teeth and was delighted at having reached his destination intact for once. Maximillian had to be helped off the bus by Vishnu and Cecily and he disembarked awkwardly banging his knee on the door pillar.

"The bloody man is crazy. Look at him," Maximillian said and stood looking eye to eye with the ever smiling driver. "You are mad you know, completely mad. You shouldn't be in charge of a wheelbarrow much less a taxi," Maximillian continued, his eyes wild with terror and anger and gave his knee a rub to ease the pain. The driver assumed he was being praised and joined his hands together in front of his face, angelically nodding in delight and patted his minibus like it was his favourite pet.

"Bloody lunatic," Maximillian said and limped towards the palace.

Vishnu paid the driver without any complaint and followed Maximillian, Jilly and Cecily into the palace. It was yet another beautiful Indian evening and the palace looked magnificent in the amber setting sun with the sounds of nightjars smoothing out the silence but none of them noticed. Their minds were fully engaged and busy elsewhere.

Parth forced himself away from Rawinda's bedside leaving his hand in hers up until the very last second. He greeted them in the main hall. They were all shocked by his appearance, especially Vishnu who began to fear the worst.

"It is good to see you looking so well my old friend. It's been a while." Parth tapped Maximillian lightly on the arm.

"How is Rawinda?" Vishnu spoke fearing the answer.

"Not good my friends, she is very ill." He kept his emotions together to let the words escape in a whisper from his lips.

Vishnu took the onyx elephant from his inside jacket pocket and carefully twisted it to open. He took the butterfly wing out delicately with two fingers and handed it to Parth who gave a smile of gratitude to Vishnu. He in return nodded his appreciation; their mutual feelings conveyed in silence and understood without words.

"Thank you, Maximillian, for keeping it safe for me all these years."

"Ermm well ermm that's ok Parth," Maximillian said happily taking the unworthy praise and meekly looked at Vishnu who shrugged his shoulders and smiled back in return.

Parth beckoned Vishnu and Maximillian to Rawinda's room, and they followed him with sombre faces.

"Can the others come as well?" Maximillian asked timidly, not wishing to be separated from the others.

"Of course. Why not? All prayers are needed now." Parth let his words fall softly as he continued towards Rawinda's bedside.

"Tell him about Chet." Jilly grabbed Vishnu's arm jolting back from his forward gait.

"Of course, Jilly I will. Let us see Rawinda first. There is nothing we can do for Chet until the kidnappers get in touch with us first which they will do before long. Do not worry yourself, they will not harm him. They need the butterfly wings and will certainly hand him over safely to get them."

Vishnu's masquerade of tranquillity attempted to console Jilly.

"But what if Parth won't agree to hand the butterfly wings over to the kidnappers?" Jilly said trying to hide the terror in her voice as it began to rise in crescendo above its previous whisper.

"All will be fine. Trust me." Vishnu gave a knowing smile and patted Jilly gently on the arm to reassure her. His reassurance didn't have the desired effect as Jilly's eyes danced about her head darting looks of trepidation like spears to all who engaged them.

Once inside the dark hopelessness of Rawinda's bedroom everyone fell silent and watched as some of the servant women kneeling at the side of her bed began to wail loud cries of grief. Parth rushed to Rawinda knowing she was now close to death. Her face was ashen grey and her breathing so weak and crackling that it heralded death's pending arrival. He screamed so loudly that Jilly could feel a cold shiver engulf her body and she grabbed Cecily's hand. Vishnu started to cry and Maximillian left his hand on Vishnu's shoulder in an effort to console him.

Parth pulled the covers from Rawinda's bed leaving her

slight, motionless body exposed and threw them violently across the room. Some of the women tried to stop him but he screamed at them to leave him be. Everyone stood back in wistful dismay and watched as Parth leaned over Rawinda and picked her up tightly in his arms as though love had an action to describe itself. They all made way as he quickly carried her out of the bedroom in long purposeful strides and down the long hallway towards Parth's haven.

"His mind has gone," one of the women cried and blessed herself repeatedly in a loop of compulsion.

Parth held Rawinda's face tightly to his chest and after swiftly entering the room he walked to the area where the wormhole had once appeared. The others followed in silence not daring to breath any more than was necessary.

"Vishnu, the second butterfly wing - please." Parth pointed to one of the glass cabinets.

Vishnu rushed to the cabinet and, without fumbling, opened it. He gently took the second butterfly wing from its resting place on a bed of red silk and handed it delicately to Parth. Parth glanced at Rawinda for the briefest sad moment and turned to the others giving them the despondent stare of a man who has reached the end of his rope with nothing more to lose. Jilly held Cecily's hand tightly.

Maximillian stood beside Vishnu and the servants. They all watched in fearful apprehension as Parth nervously pressed the butterfly wings tightly together.

The servants moved nervously into a tight group, pale faced they chanted ritualistic lilts of precautionary blessing and pleaded with Parth to stop. But it was too late. When he ignored their pleas they fled the room in terror. The instant the butterfly wings were securely fixed together the room suddenly filled with the full orchestral sound of flapping butterfly wings as millions of brightly coloured butterflies mysteriously began to appear from nowhere. They ranged in size from small delicate barely visible dots of colour to large sturdy unfamiliar creatures with half metre wing spans.

Their flight was in no way threatening and they flew, oblivious to the group who stood in awe of their presence. The quantity of butterflies steadily began to increase, invading the personal space of the group until wings began to gently caress their faces, impeding their vision of each other. The butterflies radiated an aura of peace and harmony that almost anesthetised the assembly. Cecily spun around in wonder as she watched and tried to catch one of them in her hands but was unsuccessful at each attempt.

A small dot appeared in the atmosphere two metres from the white marble floor and began to grow and expand mysteriously. It was pale yellow to begin with but as it grew it changed into a multi-coloured swirling circle that grew larger by the second until its presence dominated the entire gable wall of the room. Maximillian gently pushed Jilly and Cecily back to safety with his hand as they all stared in wonder at the kaleidoscopic whirlpool that enticed them all to draw near. The sound of fluttering butterfly wings grew louder as if in anticipation of a forth coming event. The swirling colours suddenly vanished in a cloud of white mist and a wormhole opened up that covered and completely dominated the east gable wall.

A fresh cool breeze that carried the most beautiful fragrance of wildflowers and honeysuckle raced from the wormhole and flooded the room. The mesmeric aroma hit the back of their nostrils like a runaway steam train and their faces were all at once consumed by the serenest of expressions. No eye blinked, no head moved on its shoulders; all vision was focused on the wormhole. All senses were at its disposal as though waiting for its permission to move. A crystal bright light so white it made their faces appear transparent, glowed from the unknown and consumed the room, highlighting even the smallest blemish. If the brilliant perfection of nature could have a unified sound then it was this resonance that caressed their ears and heightened their eagerness to explore its source deeper inside this preternatural domain.

Parth carried Rawinda as though he were holding the most delicate precious flower and followed the breeze in a trance like gait into the wormhole. The butterflies calmly created an arch over his head as they flew towards the mouth of the wormhole and disappeared inside in a long trail of shimmering silky red wings. The others looked on for a moment in wonder and then moving as one they all followed him, their breathing shallow and their eyes focused straight ahead like headlights shining on a long flat road. The heavenly bouquet grew stronger with each step they took and their eagerness to uncover its source increased. Parth watched the butterflies fly out from the exit of the wormhole into endless fields of multi-coloured wildflowers and honeysuckle which the scented breeze gently caressed in order to create its aroma. They danced lightly across the colourful landscape feeding peacefully from the nectar on what could only have been a beautiful midsummer's day. An abnormally large sun sat high in the pale periwinkle blue sky and dropped its incandescent rays onto all it surveyed.

The fields of wildflowers stretched out in all directions as far as the eye could see, to distant heat hazed horizons. Oak trees whose diameters could cover the floor area of a few standard houses stood three hundred metres high and were dotted sparingly in the landscape like monstrous ladders to the heavens. Butterflies with wingspans of many hundred metres mingled with others in a descending order of scale. The smallest in the chain of proportion landed peacefully on the back of Parth's hand and quivered its wings peacefully without agenda as if it were sent as the ambassador to welcome him to the land of butterflies. The contradiction in scale of the trees and the butterflies to the ones he was familiar with made Parth very uneasy.

Vishnu followed Parth and took his first nervous step out into this strange new world holding his hands over his eyes to gain a better view. Maximillian followed, tightly linking Jilly's arm. Cecily broke free from Jilly's relaxed grip and ran out into the midst of the wildflowers. She fell among them laughing with delight as she rolled about. They all experienced the same disturbing feeling of macropsia. Jilly felt faint as her brain tried to rationalise the surreal comparisons of what she was familiar with to what she was now experiencing. Maximillian took out his pipe and lit it quickly, clenching the shaft tightly between his teeth as he scrutinized his new surroundings. His brain flicked through every past experience to make a comparison but nothing remotely similar was in his catalogue of memories. He muttered to himself in unrecognisable words, occasionally scratching his head and checking the size of the trees with pencil proportions.

"Bahh. Can't be," he mumbled a few times as he checked and strained his eyes to a mammoth butterfly that hovered at their highest pinnacle casting a brief shadow over the group as it sailed casually through the air. Vishnu ran his hand gently over Rawinda's ice-cold cheek, ignoring the fantastic scene before him. Small groups of pretty yellow houses stood beneath the tall oak trees and used their high canopy for shade. They all had green thatched roofs and all their front doors were painted dark blue. Each house had two windows either side of the front door with transoms and mullions but no glass. The paths that connected the houses in each group together were topped with fire engine red gravel. At the furthest horizon Vishnu could see a large white butterfly that had a wingspan of what he imagined to be at least four metres.

"Look," Maximillian exclaimed to the group and pointed nervously towards the massive butterfly.

It fluttered its massive wings calmly and followed the meandering path of a standard sized butterfly rising up to great heights and then changing course gently for no apparent reason before descending towards land once more. It continued this deviating pattern as it gently made its way through the clear blue sky; each rippling flutter moving it closer to the apprehensive faces.

"Oh my God, is it dangerous do you suppose?" Jilly

screamed and grabbed Cecily who was still rolling happily amongst the wildflowers forgetting all, preferring to enjoy the company of the petals.

No one answered her question. Parth left Rawinda gently amongst the wildflowers, like a petal that fell from their delicate stems. Her breathing by now was so faint her chest made no movement to demonstrate the existence of life. Vishnu leaned over her and brushed a stray strand of her raven black hair from her icy white motionless cheek.

"You had to try." Vishnu tried to console Parth, his assessment of her condition concluding that all hope was now gone.

"I don't know what I expected." Parth sat down heavily on the ground beside Rawinda, his head leaning so low it almost touched his belt buckle. "It is just fields of wildflowers and butterflies and I expected a miracle." His voice was weak from disappointment and a grief that made his face age as though he had been transported many years forward in a time machine.

"But what a lovely place to die," Maximillian said innocently then held his breath realising that his words were very inappropriate.

Jilly gave him a disapproving daggers stare and shook her head in annoyance at his insensitivity.

Parth looked at Maximillian for a moment with a shocked expression, as the statement temporarily jolted him out of his melancholic trance.

"Yes, I suppose you are right Maximillian. It is a beautiful place to die. We have done all we can. Now we must leave her in God's hands." Parth stared at Rawinda. Even though the moment was very sombre; the fragrance, the beauty and the peace of the surroundings strangely made Rawinda's pending death seem that much easier to bear. They all knew that her final moments of life were now drawing to a close, but their sixth senses could feel that death's finality didn't have the same impact here as it did back in their own dimension. They all sat around her in the wildflowers as her beauty and youth expired. Cecily made a chain from red and yellow daisies and placed it on Rawinda's head like a miniature crown. The others smiled. Parth and Vishnu held her white fragile hands as they all prayed silently.

The melody of Mozart, the mystery of Tchaikovsky, the energy of Stravinsky and the ethereal beauty of Debussy and Prokofiev were all consolidated into one sound that danced lightly over the fields of wildflowers and accompanied the large white butterfly they had admired moments earlier. All except Parth rose quickly to their feet and stood waiting in fear. He gave the large butterfly one disinterested look and lay down in the wildflowers beside Rawinda. The music got louder and even more beautiful as the large butterfly approached and an air of peace that escorted its arrival descended on them all. The butterfly hovered over their heads for a moment casting its massive shadow over Rawinda. Cecily tried to shoo it away, but Jilly pulled her close to her for protection. Slowly the butterfly descended, fluttering its gigantic wings and with its long thin forelegs gently picked Rawinda up from the ground. Parth jumped to his feet waving his arms and shouting words that never formed properly. Both he and Vishnu tried frantically to hold on to Rawinda's hands but the butterfly was too strong. It pulled away from them with grace and swiftly took her high into the air; gently flying back on the path from which it came. They all ran headlong after it, field after field shouting and pleading but eventually the distance between them became unfathomable. Their weary legs grew heavy and tired and they finally gave in. They watched it hopelessly; their faces flushed and exhausted as it took Rawinda higher into the sky and further away towards the distant hazed horizon. Parth lay on the ground and cried, banging his fists hard into the clay. "I couldn't even have her last moments in peace," he cried.

The nearest small settlement of yellow houses at the base of one of the giant oak trees was a short walking distance from them and Maximillian and Vishnu decided to see if they could get some explanations. Jilly sat beside Parth but her comforting words did little to console him. Cecily kept looking into the sky in the direction the large white butterfly had taken Rawinda and her mind raced with magical wonderment. As Maximillian and Vishnu neared the yellow houses they could see some people in a perfectly manicured garden peacefully arranging seed beds with the utmost care and attention. All the people were dressed in long white tunics that had a yellow ribbon belt tied neatly around the waist. None of them wore shoes but had yellow gaiters that stretched from their ankles to their knees. Vishnu walked slightly ahead of Maximillian and was first to make an encounter with the people. He thought they were by far the most elegant and beautiful specimens of humanity he had ever seen. The men were all over six feet tall and the women all over five feet ten. They had long elegant slender necks and faces with differing features but each face was a perfection of beauty and white, blond hair that was kept neatly in a similar bob style by both the men and the women. Their eyes were their most striking feature, for each of them had large placid and tranquil eyes of the bluest blue Vishnu had ever seen. The people never looked up at him or acknowledged his presence. They just continued quietly with their work as if he and Maximillian didn't exist.

"Hello there," Maximillian cleared his throat and spoke in his most eloquent tone as he nosily observed what they were doing.

"Ahh seed beds," he continued "Vegetables or fruit?" He happily walked over to one of the beds that was surrounded by an oak timber frame that measured forty metres by twenty. Nobody answered him. He counted the seed beds and there were fifty of them lying eastward to the sun.

"I don't think they speak English," Maximillian spoke with the troubled expression of a man who has just been jilted at the alter and looked at Vishnu for his assessment.

"नमस्ते। हम आपको नुकसान पहुचानेका मतलब नहींहै। यह जगह कहां है?"

("HELLO. WE DO NOT MEAN TO INCONVENIENCE YOU. WHERE IS THIS PLACE?").

Vishnu spoke in Hindi and smiled politely waiting for a reply, but none was forthcoming.

"What did you say? I don't think they understood. Something about "place" was it?"

"I asked them where we were," Vishnu replied.

"Maybe they don't hear us. Could be they are all deaf," Maximillian began to clap his hands loudly as though he had just beheld the finest entertainer to see if that would attract their attention. Vishnu imitated Maximillian and began to clap his hands so loudly he felt pain.

"Please be quiet." One of the women with blond hair put her finger to her lips to hush them. "You will frighten away the bees and we need the bees," she continued, and her other companions nodded their heads silently in agreement but never once acknowledged their presence.

"So, you speak English?" Maximillian perked up with a sudden delight.

"In the land of butterflies all communication is understood as if only one language exists. So your English as you call it is just another communication sound that we can process and reply to in our own tongue but you hear the reply in your English" she said and stood up from her work and looked at him for the first time.

"Ermm, oh I see." Maximillian was confused and mulled the idea over in his brain.

"Where are we, memsahib?" Vishnu gave her a broad innocent smile.

She looked at both of them in a confused manner.

"Where is this place?" Maximillian spoke with determination and straightened his back in an attempt to show his authority over the situation.

"Where else but the Land of Butterflies," she said and then bent down and continued with her work once again. Vishnu and Maximillian focused on each other with confused expressions. They were astounded by the tranquillity of the people who continued to work calmly as if nothing had happened and no one had interrupted them.

"A large white butterfly just took one of our group," Maximillian spoke with authority "and we want her back again; as soon as possible," his words grew with more dominance as he finished his request but none of the people looked up from their work or made any reply.

Maximillian gave Vishnu a worried stare and pulled his beard into a point in a nervous fashion.

"Memsahib," Vishnu said appealing to the blond-haired woman. "Where did the large white butterfly take our girl please, memsahib?" Vishnu's polite calm tone was the elixir needed to get a response. The blond-haired woman cleaned her hands on a piece of cloth and straightened her back to look at Vishnu.

"She has been taken to the Hall Of The Butterflies for assessment," the woman replied and then continued once more with her work making small holes in the clay with a special pointed stick before inserting a small delicate seedling with care and precision.

Jilly and Cecily linked the dejected looking Parth; who dragged his feet, as though he might fall at any moment, towards Maximillian. A group of children dressed in white tunics with yellow ribbon waist bands were sitting on the ground near the seed beds. Their white, blond hair cut to the same style as their elders glistened in the sunlight. They were packing seeds into containers made from bamboo leaves and never looked up from their task. Cecily stared at them with wonder and would love to have joined them but Jilly kept a firm grip on her hand.

"The white butterfly took Rawinda to the hall of the butterflies," Vishnu spoke to Parth.

"Where is the hall of the butterflies?" Parth shouted his

face red with fear and temper.

"That doesn't work here. Be calm and they may respond," Vishnu spoke quietly into Parth's ear.

"Quiet be damned," Parth screamed and ran over to one of the men who was stooped working on a seed bed and grabbed him roughly by the arm. The man calmly stood up and stared at Parth. A force of energy was released like a laser from the man's piercing blue eyes that knocked Parth back five metres to the ground. The man stooped down again and calmly continued with his work not in the slightest bit perturbed by the encounter. None of the other people looked up during the incident and they all acted as if nothing had happened.

Vishnu picked Parth up from the ground, "better to be polite to them," Vishnu said "they don't respond very well to aggression or superior attitudes. Maximillian has unsuccessfully tried that."

"What! Ermm. What was that? I wasn't, was I?" Maximillian asked with genuine surprise.

"Just a little sahib," Vishnu replied with a smile.

"I have to find my Rawinda." Parth began to cry bitterly into his hands.

On seeing his emotion, the people all stopped working and gathered round him silently; wiping their hands of the clay they had gathered and arranging their tunics to uniform perfection. Vishnu, Jilly and Maximillian feared the worst, imagining a sudden attack was imminent, and began to take cautious steps backwards away from the emerging people. Jilly grabbed Cecily's hand even tighter and she winced in pain. "Mum that hurts," Cecily said but Jilly took no notice of her complaint.

The people began to chant in unison and picked Parth up and carried him shoulder high to one of the yellow houses. Vishnu, Jilly, Cecily and Maximillian followed cautiously as the group carried Parth, who appeared to be in a trance, inside; his eyes were closed and his facial expressions changed constantly as though he were experiencing activities that were displaying themselves continuously before his inner eye. He sat cross legged on the floor in the centre of the group who gathered tightly around him chanting quietly.

"Oh dear God what is happening?" Jilly made a movement to run from the place with Cecily but Vishnu gently held her hand.

"No wait. Don't run away, memsahib. They mean him no harm. If they wanted to harm him they would have done so by now," Vishnu said and Maximillian nodded in agreement.

Parth opened his eyes and in a transfixed state began to view a scene that was not of his present reality. He began to smile happily as he watched the scene, that was only visible to him, unfold in his imagination.

"What does he see?" Jilly asked as she watched Parth's face change expressions reacting to visions that were only known to him.

"It looks like a form of transcendental meditation. His mind is in a different place. He is experiencing a diverse setting. I have seen this type of thing before," Maximillian spoke quietly as his intensity in observation grew.

"So have I, sahib. But this is much more profound," Vishnu replied.

"Yes, look at his face. He is living in a moment in a different realm," Jilly's voice trembled in wonder.

The chanting stopped suddenly and the people left the building quietly in an orderly row and walked serenely back in single file to the seed beds to continue with their work. Parth opened his eyes and smiled a very broad satisfied smile.

"What happened? What did you see?" Vishnu said.

"I saw Rawinda. I spoke to her," Parth said calmly and smiled. He had the appearance of a person who had just awoken from a long restful sleep with all traces of his previous anxiety completely vanished. His face was serene and his breathing calm and regular.

"How could that be?" Jilly said in a very matter of fact tone and folded her arms.

"She is fine now and feeling better all the time," Parth said in delight and looked at the others eagerly awaiting their positive response.

The others were in silent contemplation. Each of them imagining differing bizarre scenarios.

"She is in the hall of the butterflies. A beautiful voice spoke to me. It appears to be in control of everything that happens in that place. It was a voice filled with love and peace and instilled in me a belief that all will eventually be fine. I could not see any bodily form for the voice, but it echoed all around me with a comforting warm feeling of love and security. It knew and understood the most hidden secrets of my soul and I felt like an innocent child in its presence eagerly awaiting its direction and consolation."

Parth's speech was more elated than either Maximillian or Vishnu had ever remembered in past conversations with him.

"Did you ask about the hall of the butterflies? How we can get to it?" Vishnu leaned forward eager to hear the reply.

Parth shook his head negatively and looked at the ground. "I am afraid that I do not know."

"It must be near here. Can't be too far away. The large white butterfly only took her less than an hour ago. They don't fly that fast and you were with her a few minutes ago," Cecily said innocently and the others smiled in admiration of her perception.

"Very true and well deduced young Cecily. We must search for it right now." Maximillian rubbed the top of Cecily's head with his hand. She generally hated him doing this especially after fixing her hair to her favourite style but on this occasion she didn't mind and smiled as she looked at him relishing his praise.

"The people felt sympathy for you when they saw you cry." Jilly rubbed her hand gently on Parth's shoulder.

"I don't remember being moved into this building. I was

overcome with emotion and then I was with Rawinda. Talking to her. Laughing with her as we used to. She was still unwell but in an amazing state of accelerated recovery. It all happened as simply as that."

"I will ask the blond-haired lady again where the hall of butterflies is." Vishnu rubbed his hand over his black turban, closed the two buttons on his white linen jacket and walked out of the building.

"It was such a magnificent place. The vaulted ceiling in the room where they kept Rawinda had to be 200 hundred metres high. It was so immense. Beautiful multi-coloured murals of butterflies adorned every surface of the ceiling. The murals were gigantic. Each butterfly painted on the ceiling had to be 20 metres wide at least and they were so many colours, so many dazzling colours I just had to look away from their brilliance. Rawinda lay in a large golden bed in the centre of this vast room."

"Her bed was gold?" Maximillian suddenly imagined that this could finally be the place of treasures he had searched for all his life but never got close to finding.

"Yes solid gold and ornate beyond belief. The craftwork was like nothing I have ever seen. In the centre of the headboard I could see what had to be the largest diamond ever imagined. It must have been two feet square and it was flawless. The glow from it lit Rawinda's face so that she looked like the most beautiful heavenly angel. The bed clothes were made from Muga silk and decorated with hundreds of images of Adonis Blue butterflies on a background of pale violet. Rawinda's pillow was white Banarasi silk and her gleaming black hair lay restfully across it." Parth's expression became serene as he relived the moments again in his imagination.

"Could this place really exist outside of your imagination?" Maximillian excitement was in hyper-zone and a twitch he hadn't experienced for many years in his left eye remerged.

"It was all so vivid it has to be real. My imagination was

never good. This was real. I know it. There was a stained-glass window on the furthest gable wall that must have been at least one hundred metres square. I think it was a Queen Alexandra birdwing butterfly that embellished it and it was fifty metres wide or more. The light shone through the butterfly's iridescent bluish green coloured glass and gave the room its unique soothing ambience. I felt that this was a room of rehabilitation. A room of healing. There was someone nursing and caring for Rawinda just out of my direct view. It's shadows were always in my peripheral vision. Feeling its presence near I called out to it a few times hoping to attract its attention but there was no reply. Rawinda wouldn't discuss it when I questioned her about it even though she seemed to know more. I found that very disturbing I have to say. Whatever it was, it was restoring Rawinda back to health again," Parth concluded in a quiet thoughtful tone and silently left the building with the others, staring blankly ahead of him in quiet reflection.

Vishnu took short steps in his polished patent shoes on the red path that led back to the area with the seed beds as he gathered his thoughts. He debated within himself the best approach he should take to uncover the answers they so desperately needed. The blond-haired woman kept her head down as she continued to plant seedlings with a purposeful rhythm.

"We need to find Rawinda. Will you help us?" were the only words Vishnu could conjure up after his intensive inner inquisition but the blond-haired woman made no reaction. He felt like screaming but did what his grandmother taught him long ago and counted to ten and back. He was at seven on his count when Jilly stood beside him and stared at the red dots of frustration that had built up on his normally pale cheeks.

"Are you ok?"

"Maybe not. I am thinking." Vishnu gave a forlorn stare towards the blond-haired woman.

"Listen we must find Rawinda. My son has been

kidnapped and is in danger. We must get back to our own time do you understand?" Jilly tried to control her growing anger which was making her voice quiver in a high-pitched tone. Small red and yellow butterflies landed on Jilly's shoulders as they appeared to detect her anguish. They fluttered their wings as if in solidarity with her plight and one of them brushed itself against her cheeks in a dignified homogeneity.

Vishnu could detect Jilly's rising mood and gave her a signal with his lips to remain quiet knowing that an arrogant approach would gain nothing but yet another unhelpful silence.

"Are you hungry?" the blond-haired woman enquired without making any eye contact. They looked perplexed by the question, shocked by her sudden atypical benevolence.

The others arrived on the scene on cue to witness Jilly's open mouthed shocked expression.

"Yes, we are, memsahib. Very." Vishnu gave his most subordinate nod of acceptance and out of sight of the blond woman beckoned to the others with the slightest wave of his hand to remain calm.

The blond-haired woman straightened her back, wiped her hands delicately on a piece of white cloth that appeared to be cut for the purpose from one of her old tunics. Without giving the group one glance she walked towards one of the yellow houses. Her other comrades all stopped working on hearing her voice, wiped their hands as she did and followed her quietly. Vishnu, Jilly, Cecily, Parth and Maximillian (I will refer to this group for the purpose of convenience from this point forward as the Indian party) watched them all march silently in single file following the blond woman into the yellow house. None of them gave even a passing glance towards the Indian party. They all remained expressionless and silent; functioning out of habit and moving as if controlled by a single brain.

Vishnu ushered the Indian party to follow quietly in single file to witness an experience they all were very apprehensive about.

CHAPTER 9

Mosquitos were in full swarm that evening and hungry for blood. They didn't much mind whose vital fluid they stole. Saint or sinner was all the same to them. They hovered over Sukey and Ishmael's hideout and attacked at will. Some died in their attempts, crushed beneath a fast-moving flat palm and some successfully sneaked a bite and flew with a full belly back to the ranks to boast of their easy pickings.

Sukey was getting very irritable as a reply to their ransom demands was not as swift as she had imagined, plus she had been bitten by mosquitos so many times she lost count. Her face was a pin cushion of bites and red blotches. One eye lid was swollen so large from a bite that it covered over the pupil giving her limited vision from it.

"Are they disrespecting us on purpose; do you suppose? I think they are. Let's send them an ear. A blood-soaked ear usually sparks the attention." Ishmael picked up a rusty old knife they used to chop their meat into manageable portions. He spat on the blade and rubbed it on his filthy trouser leg. Sukey looked at Chet's left ear and pondered. "Such a small ear; It will probably wither up into nothing in this heat if we cut it off. Would they even know what it was by the time it makes the palace? I doubt it would look anything like an ear by then. It would look like a cat's tongue at best," Sukey said regretfully and pulled Chet's ear forward with two fingers to finalise her opinion.

"Yeh, I see what you mean. How about a foot. A foot wouldn't wither up that much. It would still look something like a foot by the time it reached the palace," Ishmael said and frantically rubbed the blade of the knife on his trouser leg in eager anticipation of some action.

Sukey thought for a while. "I see where you are coming from with that idea. Good one. But the brat will die if we cut off his foot. Remember the trouble we had with the last brat, and we only just cut across the hand," Sukey said and grimaced in remembrance. "Best leave him intact - for the moment anyway," Sukey continued and gave Chet a cruel stare.

Chet, having listened to their plotting began to shake uncontrollably as he stared at his feet and held his hands over his ears; he needed all his four parts and couldn't decide which one he should let go if that time arrived and he were given the right to choose.

Ishmael and Sukey sat together by a raging campfire that shot red hot sparks like rockets high into the evening sky and spoke so quietly Chet couldn't hear. They stared in his direction from time to time with plots that housed menace but try as hard as he could to listen not one further word reached his ever-attentive ears. After many waterless whiskeys they fell back in the dirt and drifted off into a drunken slumber.

During the night when the campfire was a memory and the cold chill took hold of old bones, Chet made a very loud screeching noise, one that could frighten the very whiskers off the grim reaper.

Sukey and Ishmael awoke suddenly and sprang to their feet. Chet pretended to be fast asleep and appeared to be a very competent actor. They both stooped down over him and stared furiously.

"He did it. It must be that brat." Ishmael screeched in a tired tormented voice that demanded sympathy and was almost tearful from fatigue.

"Maybe but he looks fast asleep to me." Sukey took a closer look at Chet, her stale whiskey breath covering his face in a damp sour mask of noxious aroma.

"If he is not asleep then he is a bloody good actor," she continued in a crabby attitude synonymous with fading ale.

After some time, silence covered the camp again. In the sanctuary of darkness bugs and insects felt that everything was safe to explore once more. All that could be heard above the occasional hoot from a nearby night owl was the relaxed snoring sounds from Sukey and Ishmael which drifted up to the canopy of the forest. This was the opportunity Chet waited for and he let off an enormous eerie screech that shocked the night owl from its nocturnal perch. Sukey and Ishmael sprang to their feet once more, guns drawn and looked about them in shock, their hearts beating out of control.

"You are right. It's that bloody brat. "Sukey gave Chet a kick with her purple Dr Martin boot. Chet screamed and innocently pretended to have just awoken.

"That was you? Wasn't it? I know it was you. You horrible little urchin." Sukey grabbed Chet and began to shake him like he was an exotic cocktail in the making.

"What do you mean? I was asleep. I did nothing." Chet acted his part to perfection.

"Don't injure this one. Remember last time? We need to keep this one sound… well soundish,"

Ishmael said and gave Chet a hard kick with his cowboy boot.

Chet screamed. Sukey and Ishmael dragged their weary feet back to their sleeping areas and fell down like they had been shot by a sniper. Just at that moment when sleep was about to steal their consciousness, Chet gave an almighty roar and the two awoke startled once more.

"Ignore him. There is nothing we can do. He is determined to keep us awake," Sukey said and covered her head with a dark brown moth-eaten blanket that made her limit her intake of breath due to the strong smell of dampness it radiated like a rugby team's locker room.

If a look could kill, then Ishmael's in Chet's direction would have done its duty. Ishmael covered his head with a filthy numnah that had absorbed the sweat of a dozen horses and a one humped camel.

Chet's screeching ritual continued throughout the night until the morning sun lit the forest and remnants of embers still flickered amidst the ash in the campfire. Sukey arose to a kneeling position, her head held low. Her face was pale grey, like the colour that sits on top of a bucket of sour milk and her eyes dropped so deep that pink lines sat beneath her eyeballs. Strands of her hair pointed in all directions and she gave them an unconcerned brush back with her hand. She rubbed her face with frantic movements to remove traces of sleep and then kicked Ishmael hard on the bum. The sweaty numnah fell from his face and he gulped in the fresh morning air in large greedy mouthfuls.

"You horrible little swine. No breakfast for you today I can tell you and no dinner either." Sukey lit the fire, delighting in the fact that all of the heavy white smoke was blowing in Chet's direction. Chet returned her icy stare with a look of complete innocence and even though he tried not to; coughed.

"If only I had my good broken sapling branch from the woodhouse in Robin Hood's Bay, I would fire a missile and hit her right between the eyes," Chet thought and stared at his desired target.

Sukey noticed him stare and wiped her eyes with her ashy hand as she imagined he must have noticed something lurking there.

"You will be sorry yet my lad let me tell you. When your belly is rolling with hunger; you will be sorry you messed with me." Sukey laughed. Chet was silent.

Ishmael got to his knees and remained on all fours for minutes with his forehead touching the ground as he tried to gather himself together. He groaned a loud exhausted groan similar to the sound a large tree makes as it succumbs to the woodcutters' axe and falls helplessly to the ground.

He stared at Chet as he painfully rose to his feet and threw the sweaty numnah as far away from him as his strength allowed.

"No mercy for you from here on you horrible little brat," Ishmael growled. "Ransom or no ransom there will be no mercy."

Chet was very afraid but cloaked it well behind a brave innocent smile.

The sharp sound of twigs breaking in the undergrowth mingled with the cracking of the campfire but only Chet noticed. Zona darted from shadows and danced his little dance around the campfire occasionally rubbing Chet's head roughly as he passed him by. Chet tried to extend himself away from Zona's hand each time but his tethers were tight and restricted him so he was forced to accept Zona's intrusion most of the time.

"Zona has the news. Zona knows all." Zona danced with his hands held high in the air as if he was trying to grasp a coveted, obscure object just beyond his reach.

"What do you know? You annoying little horror of a man." Sukey looked him up and down with distain and spat from her dry mouth onto the emerging flames of the campfire.

"Zona very thirsty. Two bottles thirsty me is thinking on this fine morning." He smiled broadly and continued with his dance never making eye contact with either Ishmael or Sukey.

"Give him what he wants. I can't take this today."

Ishmael very reluctantly took a bottle from their stash and wiped his hand over it lovingly before throwing it to Zona; who caught it perfectly.

"Zona two bottles thirsty; remember?" Zona stood still and gave a nervous smile his red tongue sticking out from his sun blistered dry lips in anticipation.

Ishmael let his two front teeth protrude over his bottom lip and gave a stare that might turn Zona inside out if it that were medically possible. Ishmael threw a second bottle with extra velocity as though he were a baseball player throwing a beanball. Zona caught it with precision in one hand and then danced with delight around the campfire. He opened one of the bottles with his teeth and spat the cork into the fire.

"Won't be needing that again. Zona's breakfast," he said with glee and drank down half the bottle in one swallow. Sukey concealed her admiration of his prowess at downing whiskey as she gave him a shrouded glance.

"Now what is this great news and it had better be good."

Sukey rubbed her finger lightly along the blade of her knife to see if it needed its daily sharpening just yet.

Zona looked at the knife and gave an extended swallow.

"They have all gone," he spoke as though his mouth was on fire and all his words were trying to leave through his lips at the same time.

"Who's gone you little lush?" Sukey brandished the knife in front of Zona's face.

"All gone with the butterflies. Maharaja and the British. All gone me told. All gone. None left. None at all," Zona said in terror and kept his gaze firmly fixed on the glistening blade that dallied in front of his eyes.

Sukey stared at Ishmael suddenly and a look of nervous panic danced about her face like a firework that wasn't anchored properly and didn't know which direction to fly.

"I heard it. I know they all went with the butterflies. All gone." Zona looked sheepishly at Sukey and rubbed his fingers over his missing eyebrow.

"Blast, blast, blast it all," Sukey screamed and grabbed the bottle from Zona and took a long drink herself. Zona looked aggrieved as his eyes measured the exact amount that flowed down her gullet.

"Maybe we can follow them? Can we?" Ishmael's eyes danced between Zona and Sukey waiting for a reply.

"You could be right for once. Maybe we can." Sukey smiled at this thought "you come in useful sometimes."

Ishmael absorbed the praise with a self-satisfied smirk as compliments rarely came his way.

"Can we follow them?" Sukey stared at Zona.

"They left from room they call Parth's haven and all afraid to go in there now." Zona sat down at the campfire on the opposite side to Chet, his head beginning to spin a little from the lack of food, an abundance of whiskey, too much dancing in circles and the sight of Sukey's knife.

"Ok. Get ready we are going to this room right now. Untie that urchin and we will take him with us for security." Sukey gave Chet's ear then his foot a stare of regret.

"Zona gives great news always. You can always rely on Zona for the greatest of all newses," Zona held one hand to the temple of his dizzy head.

"You are coming with us," Sukey gave a sudden determined glare at Zona.

"No, oh no, Zona only goes in the jungle. No, no, can't be done," Zona's revolt was short lived.

Sukey produced her knife and Zona fell and then staggered as he tried to get to his feet quickly. Sukey caught him by the collar of his shabby green jacket which tore as she gripped it. She held the sharp knife under his throat drawing just a little blood which trailed down the front of his neck.

"What was that you said again about not coming with us?" Sukey gritted her teeth.

"Zona said he is going with the memsahib wherever she wants to go. Oh yes, he loves to go with the memsahib even at the risk of his own…" Zona gave a sudden gulp "death."

The palace was very quiet and appeared abandoned as Sukey pushed Zona in through the open front door with the point of her knife sticking in his skinny rib cage. Ishmael followed closely behind with a very tight grip on Chet's jacket. He gave him a rough shake every now and again in repayment for lost sleep. There were no servants to be seen anywhere; no aromatic aromas of spices cooking in the kitchen and the eerie silence raised Sukey's senses to a heightened alert like a hungry mountain lion ready to pounce.

"Where is this Parth's haven?" Sukey pushed Zona in the rib cage again, this time the knife penetrated his skin and drew blood. He gave out a loud scream. Ishmael laughed.

"Here. In here," Zona pointed to the door of the room that housed the display cabinets. The door was slightly ajar and pieces of broken pottery and a few items of clothing lay on the threshold.

"Someone was in a hurry". Ishmael picked up one of the garments and held it against himself to examine its suitability to wear.

Zona meekly put his foot inside the room and Sukey pushed him hard in the back, his slight frame crumbling like the body of a dead rabbit before the force. He fell with a bang onto the white marble floor and curled up into a tight ball covering his head under his arm. Ishmael gave him a look of contempt as he walked past dragging Chet along in tow.

The wormhole was still open on the gable wall and swirled around at fantastic speed in a fusion of magnificent multicolours. Sukey and Ishmael stared at it in trepidation as they did the colours changed to a white foggy mist that also vanished in seconds leaving just the mouth of the wormhole open and inviting; tempting investigation. Sukey and Ishmael, still with a tight grip on Chet's arm, stared nervously into it squinting their eyes for the best possible vision but didn't dare go further.

The buzzing sound of millions of angry wasps raced from inside the wormhole growing louder and more menacing by each blink of their eyes.

"What's happening?" Sukey screamed her question towards Zona who peered out at her from underneath his arm with one eye as he remained in a tightly curled up foetal position on the floor.

A gigantic swarm of angry wasps flew swiftly through the wormhole and filled the room to bursting point in seconds with a malicious throng. Sukey and Ishmael screeched like suckling piglets, waving their hands about and jumping up and down in frantic vain efforts to frighten off the attacking wasps who left stings on every inch of Sukey and Ishmael's exposed skin.

Chet watched as millions of butterflies flew peacefully into the room from the wormhole, making the most enchanting fluttering sounds he had ever heard. Sukey, Ishmael and Zona could not see the butterflies and Chet could not see the wasps.

Sukey and Ishmael noticed that Chet was not affected by

the wasps and couldn't fathom the serene and enchanted expression on his face. Chet laughed in merriment as he jumped up and down happily trying to catch one in his hand but failing by what he imagined must be just a millimetre each time.

"Look he is trying to catch a wasp in his hand. Knew that kid wasn't right." Ishmael watched Chet's actions whilst fending off the attack.

"There is definitely something the matter with him. I knew it." Sukey lashed out with her knife at the legions of wasps that flew in attack towards her, missing Ishmael's face with the razor-sharp blade on more occasions than he preferred.

No longer able to endure the stings and pain; Ishmael and Sukey raced together into the wormhole leaving Chet behind to play elatedly with the butterflies. They clambered and fell as they made their way through the misty nihility of the wormhole; not caring what fate awaited them on the other side. The hoard of angry wasps followed them diving in groups to attack any visible areas of naked skin. Chet laughed until tears fell from his eyes as he couldn't understand why Sukey and Ishmael were reacting like this as all he could see were legions of beautiful butterflies.

"They are afraid of butterflies. Not so tough after all," he laughed and jumped as high as he could once again to see if he could catch one in his hand but he couldn't.

Zona slowly unravelled himself on the cold marble floor and watched the last of the wasps fly back through the open mouth of the wormhole. His bald head was red and swollen from the numerous stings he'd received as he lay motionless but made no reaction to the pain and consumed the countless stings in quiet agony. Once the last wasp had vanished, he ran as fast as his old legs could manage deeper and deeper into the protection of the jungle, ripping off his clothes as he ran to rid himself of the last of the wasps. His howling could be heard on the shore of Panagon Lake.

Once the last of the butterflies had vanished back from

whence they came, the mist returned to the mouth of the wormhole once more and the swirling mass of colours returned, spinning frantically as they covered the entrance on the gable wall once more. Chet sat on the floor and watched all the colours with amazement. They reminded him of old Miss Coleran's colour chart in art class; the one she made on a cardboard wheel that she occasionally spun around fast so the colours almost merged into one. "She'd like to see this," Chet thought. "Beat her colour wheel hands down."

The guns and knives in Sukey and Ishmael's pockets began to turn to hot liquid metal once they entered the wormhole scalding the parts of their skin the wasps hadn't feasted on. They both threw the rapidly dissolving weapons onto the floor of the wormhole where they melted and disappeared in seconds in pools of boiling hot ore.

Sukey and Ishmael screamed in many agonies as they ran headlong in front of the wasps and into the land of dark shadows.

CHAPTER 10

An icy cold wind blew without mercy across a deserted wasteland of sheer rock and black wet sand. No flower, tree or vegetation of any type could be seen. A bleak forbidding sun sat unwelcoming in black clouds and cast exaggerated shadows of the rocky surface clear out to the distant wintery horizon. This was a merciless place where a body could freeze into a block of ice rapidly without proper shelter. The wind was not strong but it was constant and reached right into the bones.

Carcases of dead animals and birds were dotted here and there in the landscape, preserved almost intact by the icy cold. Their cause and time of death unknown. A violent river carried its top layer of ice with it as it flowed aggressively as if heading to fight a foe it hated. It never gave the ice a chance to form a sold mass on its surface. A cold spray from pockets of water that were exposed in places between the ice, shot high into the air and fell back to the river again as icicles. This wasn't a hospitable place for life of any kind. No tree or vegetation could or would wish to survive here.

Sporadic showers of large hailstones fell like missiles without warning. This lasted for minutes then stopped suddenly as though someone had mercifully turned off a tap.

Sukey and Ishmael fled the wormhole into this abyss and shivered as they wrapped their very light summer coats, which were better designed for hot Indian weather, as tight to their bodies as they could. It made little difference. Their body temperature plummeted, and their lips began to turn a sombre colour of Klein blue. As icicles began to form on their eyelashes and hair, they made an attempt to run back into the wormhole but it vanished into a white mist, disappearing suddenly as they approached it.

"Ahh no!! It has vanished. We are trapped," Ishmael screamed as he ran vainly around in circles searching for the entrance to the wormhole like an old dog chasing its tail.

"No use fool, it's gone." Sukey walked to some large cold rock boulders that partially blocked the frosty east wind that was already turning their hard hearts to ice. She crouched low beneath them for shelter. Ishmael gave up searching for the wormhole and kicked out viciously at some small rocks that lay in his path, before joining her. They both sat crouched and frozen together, lamenting their ill-fated decision to leave the jungle and blaming each other for the predicament they were in.

"We are trapped here forever," Ishmael said and stuck out his two front teeth in panic. Saliva on the tips of them turned to solid ice making it very difficult for him to pronounce his words properly.

Sukey coughed as the cold wind raced down her gullet. "This was all your fault. I regret the day I met you. But for you fool, I would be back in the warm jungle right now, robbing some deserving soul of their worldly possessions; sun tanning my face and feeling good all over. I am ending our pathetic partnership here and now. I am going it on my own from here on. I couldn't do much worse. You are an idiot and a major liability." Sukey slapped Ishmael hard on the back of the head with the palm of her hand.

"What?" Ishmael said in a loud voice "What?" he repeated even louder with a sarcastic tone added to the second "what" for effect.

Sukey sulked with a pout that gave her a double chin and made no more comments. Ishmael rubbed the back of his head to relieve the sting and glared a look of downright disapproval.

"Where did all those damned wasps go to? They are not out here in this freezing cold like us," Sukey said after a long period of uncomfortable silence where both contemplated being free from each other. One thought of this freedom in terms of releasing rough iron shackles from their ankles; the other thought of it in dreamy pink clouds.

"Right. Very good point. Where are they indeed?"

Ishmael was happy the silence was broken as he sat pondering on life without Sukey. He didn't fancy the idea of losing her even though she didn't appear to bother in the slightest about parting company with him. Both stood together and scanned the bleak frozen landscape but they couldn't see any trace of the wasps.

"Wasps can't live in this cold anyway. Can they?" Ishmael said and crouched down behind the rock again.

"I wouldn't have thought so. But they are here somewhere." Sukey kept upright and continued to look out into the cold wind for an answer. She shielded her eyes with her hand, occasionally wiping away tears that the icy wind created. In the distance she imagined she could see something large move in the shadows and she squinted her eyes to a tight slit to get a better perspective.

"There's something out there. I can just about make it out," she shouted above the sound of the wind as it blew her hair in all directions and tangles across her blue numb face. Her nose had begun to run earlier but now unknown to her a frozen shard of ice pointed down from it like a crystal spear.

"What is it? Is it the maharajah?" Ishmael screamed his reply to her but still stayed crouched low behind the shelter of the rocks. He rolled himself as compactly as he could into a tight round ball in an effort to fend off the cold but it had no impact except to leave an area of his bare back exposed between his belt and shirt tails.

"No. It's - it's - it's," she kept repeating her words over and over again in shock.

"It's what? For God's sake? It's what?" Ishmael angrily got to his feet to have a look for himself.

"It looks like a very large monstrous sized wasp," she replied and an uncustomary quiver of fear entered her voice.

Ishmael didn't reply but squinted in the direction Sukey was frantically pointing. On seeing the terrifying vision for himself, Ishmael dived back behind the rock again. He crouched as low as he could this time in fear rather than to avoid the blistering wind. Sukey plunged behind the rock also and in panic hugged Ishmael. Ishmael forgot about his fear and tried to kiss her on the neck but his two front teeth covered with ice met her skin first. Sukey pulled back suddenly and slapped him hard on the face. Ishmael smiled in satisfaction feeling that the searing pain was worth his brief moment of ecstasy.

An abnormally large, weirdly shaped shadow developed on the ground in front of them - growing in stature by the second. They both stared at the shadow shimmering awkwardly and expanding on the dark wet sand before them. Sukey reached for her knife - an act she always did in any crisis but remembered its fate. Ishmael reached to his boot for the derringer, but it was lying in a pool of hot liquid metal on the floor of the wormhole. They sat trembling awaiting their fate as the shadow grew so large it was incomprehensible. Their breaths seized up and stopped in fear.

"It must be that wasp." Sukey grabbed Ishmael's hand for comfort. Ishmael gave a leery grin; forgetting all his previous woes and pending peril he kissed her hand with a tenderness his countenance didn't seem capable of generating. Sukey pulled her hand away suddenly and wiped the area he had kissed on her sleeve in a manic, frantic action. Ishmael looked despondent and abruptly turned away from her, allowing a small whimper to break free from his blue lips, like that of a tiny puppy. Sukey was completely indifferent to his attitude and oblivious to his mood and spat on the area he had kissed before wiping it again in the wet dark sand. Ishmael badly subdued a second whimper.

A wasp twenty metres tall walked casually around the rocks and stood glaring down at Sukey and Ishmael. It had massive transparent wings that buzzed at a crazy rate per second and multiplied the cold chill. Its black compound eyes focused on them as did its several simple eyes but Sukey couldn't detect any way of understanding its emotions from their stare. Two antennae moved about at random as if feeling and assessing the cold air above their heads for answers. Its thorax and abdomen were coloured in the brightest yellow like sunlight on a field of ripe wheat and a black so dark that it even looked unnerving in this woeful landscape. Sukey and Ishmael both grabbed on to each other in a vice like hug. This time Ishmael didn't feel the urge to kiss Sukey's neck.

"So, what do we have here now?" the wasp said and stooped its head down to get a better look.

They didn't answer but kept their eyes closed and shivered with fear waiting their fate.

"Not dressed for this weather either," the wasp laughed. What do you want here in the land of dark shadows? You have come for our queen haven't you? Don't deny it. I have seen your sort before. But you never last very long out here in the cold. A few more hours should see you both off by the looks of you. You are both turning a nice shade of blue already. Soon your weak little hearts will stop beating and kaboom – you're dead. Two more carcases to blot the landscape." The wasp bellowed a sarcastic laugh as a large blob of saliva from its mouth hit Sukey and Ishmael directly in their faces. They tried frantically to wipe the thick white sticky mucus away with their sleeves. And spat out the fragments that had gained uninvited entry to their mouths, but they only managed to remove a portion of it.

"No, no we don't mean any harm we have come for for…..." Ishmael's mind froze on his reply.

"Treasure. We have come for treasure." Sukey dared to give the wasp a quick sheepish grin.

"Treasure in the land of dark shadows," the wasp laughed "I still believe the butterflies sent you here to kill our queen. Kill our queen! That's what you want to do. Kill our queen," the wasp's voice thundered out with agitation and aggression. It bounced up and down on the spot in anger causing the nearby rocks to move with the vibration.

"We thought we were going to find butterflies and treasure." Ishmael sheepishly looked at Sukey for support of any kind as he felt these were his final pleas in this life.

"Are there no butterflies here in the land of dark shadows?" Sukey's smooth performance of her innocent act even made Ishmael give her a second look.

The wasp laughed and shook all over. Its wings buzzed like crazy and it cleaned its face manically with its two forelegs. "No. We don't have butterflies here," it managed to bellow the words out through its wild laughter, as more saliva from its mouth hit Sukey and Ishmael in their faces and ran down their cheeks in large sticky gooey blobs that smelt like a freshly opened dung pit.

"I feel sick," Ishmael said as he tried to wipe the saliva away with his sleeve again but his sleeve was now dripping wet from the last saliva attack.

"We were told about butterflies and treasure so it seems we have been grossly mislead," Sukey said politely and made an attempt to rise to her feet in an attitude that should in most circumstances have peacefully wound up the debate.

The wasp buzzed its wings furiously and she was blown back heavily to the dark sand again.

"So, you haven't come to kill our Queen," the wasp said and his head crouched even lower to observe more closely any possibility of guilt in their expressions.

Both Sukey and Ishmael shook their saliva sodden heads vehemently denying any grievous intentions and produced large innocent smiles to seal the purpose of their objectives. After giving them a careful intense scrutiny, the wasp believed them and straightened itself up to its full height.

"Ok I believe you - but if you are telling me lies you couldn't believe in your wildest imaginings what will happen to you both. Get up and follow me. You may be useful in the future," the wasp commanded and turned its huge bulk slowly and began to walk ahead of them, its massive stinging tail wiggling back and forth before their eyes as it moved. Sukey and Ishmael walked cautiously behind it. Both of them quietly imagined what it must be like being on the receiving end of one of its massive stings.

The wasp walked for a mile or more through the cold desolate rocky landscape occasionally buzzing its wings, which made a deafening sound, and giving out a shriek of glass shattering laughter for no apparent purpose. Sukey and Ishmael quickly put their hands to their ears each time they anticipated it doing this. It walked alongside the fast-flowing river for part of the way as its icicles fell onto the already frozen Sukey and Ishmael - compounding their discomfort. Here and there the frozen remains of massive dead butterflies lay intact. Their wings vertically closed together like hands joined in prayer and pointing to the black clouds in a state of dignified defiance. The wasp slowed its gait momentarily at each dead butterfly and gave a loud scoffing laugh. It stopped suddenly as it reached a high mountain of rock that the damp climate had turned black, with pockets of slimy green algae. It was sheer straight to the sky; impossible to climb and its austere appearance made the surroundings look even more bland and foreboding. Looking about it with caution as if expecting danger, the wasp buzzed its loudest buzz to date. Even with their hands pressed tightly against their ears Sukey and Ishmael fell to their knees in agony as the thunderous sound fried their brains numb.

A rock over one hundred metres high in the side of the mountain moved to one side as though it had the mass of a delicate feather. The wasp awkwardly meandered his way in through the opening followed nervously by Sucky who pushed Ishmael hard in the back, ahead of her. The area opened up into a dimly lit cave about a mile long and half a mile high. In the centre of the cave a platform made of luminescent gold rose up two hundred metres from the ground and in the centre of the platform, a throne made of the reddest rubies Sucky had ever seen, glowed regally. A wasp forty metres tall sat pompously on the ruby throne and surveyed all that was happening before her with an air of opulent boredom.

"That must be the queen." Ishmael pointed towards the

ruby throne.

Sukey slapped Ishmael's pointing hand down with her tightly clenched fist.

"Don't point at her you great fool or they will think we are here to kill her for certain." Sukey stared with a gluttonous gaze at the riches before her as a small drool of saliva ran down to the point of her chin and balanced there in a small bubble.

Millions upon millions of wasps from standard size to some forty metres high hovered and walked on every inch of the vast cave so in affect the only place to stand was the actual place they were already standing on. The cave stank heavily of rotting fish that had been left out in the hot sun so long even a hungry cat wouldn't entertain. The heat from the bodies of the wasps was intense and foul. It hit the back of Sukey and Ishmael's noses like the brain freeze that comes from too large a bite of extra cold ice cream on a hot summer's day. Sukey and Ishmael waved hordes of frenzied wasps away with their hands. They were not successful and sting began to sit upon sting in a ladder of pain.

"Stop; listen to me brothers," the large wasp shouted out a command to the attacking wasps "These two I found wandering outside in the land of dark shadows. Who knows - they may be useful to us yet in our glory days to come, so nobody sting either of these two," he paused, "just yet," and it laughed a bellowing laugh that made it buzz its wings and shake all over. His command was greeted with the angry buzzing of millions of wasps' wings that created a din similar to the propellers from an ocean liner in full throttle.

"We won't Sleipnir... Yet," one of the twenty-metre-high wasps said with a deep angry tone.

"What does he mean - yet?" Ishmael whispered to Sukey and gave the huge wasp with the deep voice a fake innocent smile.

"Useful in the glory days to come; alarms me even more," Sukey replied and began to squeeze a painful sting from the centre of her chin.

Once inside the long yellow house the Indian party stood near a glassless window and watched the people set about preparing food with a military precision that was formed from their familiarity with each other and the tasks they performed. Cecily looked down through the cracks in the floorboards to a narrow stream that flowed beneath the house where abnormally large fish swam in straight purposeful lines, dead set on their journeys to some sea or other she imagined.

Each person knew their own responsibility and dutifully carried out their chore in peace without any effort or tribulation. A large oven occupied a position in the wall two feet above an open fire that appeared to have been kept kindled throughout the day. The comforting smell of the oak firewood reminded Maximillian of his favourite seat by the fire in the rectory in Wales and he reached inside his jacket for his pipe. Jilly gave him a stern stare and he sulkily put the pipe back into his pocket again. There were seven couples in total. Each couple worked closely together but independently of the others and harmony reigned amidst it all. A fish three metres long was taken from the oven and carried by two of the couples to a plain oak table that stretched almost the full length of the yellow house. Thirty sturdy oak chairs surrounded the table, all with large images of a monarch butterfly carved into the backrest. The children, fourteen in all, entered the house a little later than the adults, without having to be summoned and sat in designated places around the table. Two children sat beside each other and left two vacant spaces for two adults. Jilly imagined correctly that each couple had two children and the individual family unit sat together at mealtimes. The rest of the Indian party didn't notice this detail however as they all stared at the large beautifully cooked fish, their mouths salivating as they breathed in its aromatic fresh smell.

"Are you hungry?" the blond-haired woman enquired emotionless as she looked at Cecily.

"Yes, very hungry." Cecily's face lit up at the prospect of

tasting what her sense of smell had already experienced.

The blond woman quietly took five oak plates and served out a large helping of fish onto each and handed them to the Indian party. There were no knives or forks and following the example of the blond woman they all began to eat with their fingers. The blond-haired woman sat down in her family group and they communicated without speaking; smiling occasionally at a mutual pleasantry that was being relayed amongst each other. None of the other couples acknowledged the presence of The Indian party and acted as if they didn't exist. They walked by and around them without making any eye contact. Just once they heard the blond woman's husband speak and call her Atia.

"Atia is her name," Jilly whispered to Vishnu.

"Yes, I heard. Maybe she will respond better to us if we use her name?" Vishnu shrugged his shoulders in an unsure questioning fashion.

Each family unit interacted with each other in the same way Atia's did and appeared to exchange stories and pleasantries without any outward sign of communication. This fascinated Maximillian more than the others as he had heard in the past about an ancient civilization with communication skills such as this on his eastern travels long ago. Some of Parth's artefacts from a forgotten time 300 million years ago had images of human like creatures but with no mouths or ears and he now wondered if this could be a symbol for the people he was witnessing here in the land of butterflies.

Mealtime concluded as calmly as it had begun and the room was left pristinely clean and tidy before the people and their children all walked peacefully out of the long yellow house in single file and back to the seedbeds once more.

Atia was last to leave and gently ushered the Indian party out in front of her without words but with a formal gesture of her hand.

"Atia," Vishnu said in his most calm voice "We appreciate your kindness."

Atia made no reply and began to walk towards the seedbeds.

"Will you help us?" Jilly's pleading voice was close to tears.

To the Indian party's amazement Atia stopped and turned around and faced them. She looked at Jilly for a moment and as she did Jilly's facial expression changed as her mind was transported to Chet as he sat on the white marble floor of Parth's haven. Jilly could see him playing happily with a battalion of lead soldiers whose shiny uniforms were painted red and white. He was eagerly lining them up ready for battle and was happily engrossed in play, lost in his imaginations. Earlier Chet had found the toy soldiers hidden in an old metal box in the darkest corner of the room. The box was just about visible under the weight of an abundance of old long forgotten but once important sun-bleached paper documents but Chet noticed it.

Tears of happiness ran down Jilly's cheeks and her face radiated a smile that deserved to be immortalised by an artist's brush. The others realised that she was having a similar out of body experience to the one Parth had had earlier. Cecily grabbed Jilly's hand when she noticed her tears and as she did Jilly suddenly returned from her trance. The experience only lasted a few moments then Atia looked Jilly firmly in the eyes and Jilly was suddenly filled with a reassuring feeling of peace.

"Chet is fine. I could see him playing. He was safe and happy," Jilly said as she picked Cecily up in her arms and spun around in joyous circles. The others smiled in delight at her release from concern.

Atia made no reaction and in long purposeful strides meant to win back lost time, returned to the seedbeds.

"They are cultivating wildflowers," Maximillian observed with a knowledgeable nod of his head.

The seedbeds were meticulously well maintained and perfectly formed rows of young plants sprouted their heads lazily for the first time to take in their first rays of warm sun and witness a whole new world.

"They are mostly milkweed plants," Maximillian said with an erudite expression "Milkweed are the larva food source for monarch and most other butterflies. Bet none of you knew that?" The others shook their heads negatively and for once Maximillian had an attentive audience.

"The other wildflower varieties they have in the seedbeds produce nectar which is the main dietary requirement of the adult butterfly. I am not just a pretty face you know." Maximillian lit his pipe and puffed out large clouds of aromatic smoke which drifted high into the clear crisp virginal air.

Atia straightened her back from her work and looked straight into Maximillian's eyes without expression. Maximillian returned her stare with scrutiny and kept puffing out larger streams of white smoke that sat like a large white feather pillow over the Indian party's heads. His mind was suddenly transported into the lower lobe of his left lung and he watched in horror as the smoke from his pipe turned the walls of his lung a sticky dark brown colour. He could see the smoke badly irritate his alveolar wall and he screamed "Stop, stop," as loud as he could. He ran around his left lung, his feet sticking to the thick mucus, examining the damage that had been done by his years of excessive pipe smoking. He touched the alveolar wall with his hand, and it stuck to the slimy residue like wood glue. As though touching a stinging nettle he pulled his hand away and the slimy brown gunk dripped from his hand and onto the polished toes of his brown shoes. He returned to reality without prompting and with eyes as wide as a young doe he stared at Atia. He swiftly dragged the pipe from his mouth and threw it as far away as the strength his right arm could muster. It hit the gable wall of one of the yellow houses and smashed into a thousand white shards. The others looked at him in shock, especially Jilly and Cecily who knew that particular pipe was like an extension of Maximillian's body.

"What happened?" Jilly grabbed him by the arm in an

attempt to calm his frustration.

Maximillian was panting like a horse that had just won a four-mile chase; almost in panic attack mode. His face was bright red and his eyes were stretched open to their maximum extremities.

"I was just walking around inside one of my lungs and it was not a pretty sight let me tell you."

Maximillian began to over exaggerate coughs, trying his very best to exhale as much of the smoke he had just inhaled. He panted and coughed, bent over with his hands resting on his knees for support. He gave a large phlegmy spit onto the ground which Atia noticed and Cecily squirmed her face at in disgust.

"Oh gross grandad," Cecily said and scrunched her face into a look of utter displeasure.

Vishnu and Parth laughed.

"It was anything but funny. I will never smoke again and that is an absolute fact," Maximillian said with determination and meant every word. Atia made no reaction and returned to her work once the phlegmy spit she stared at had dried up suddenly and mysteriously into dust.

CHAPTER 11

A dark black cloud sailed quickly into the crystal blue sky at the nearest horizon and made its way towards them. Unlike clouds the Indian party were used to, this cloud moved with intent as if having an understanding all of its own. It had the presence of menace and foreboding about it and partly formed into a hideously evil face that became clearly visible for moments before fading into an indistinguishable misshape and then repeating the process in a loop. The people all straightened up from their work and a united expression of horror filled their faces. They gathered tightly together in a group without speaking and held hands in a circle with their eyes closed.

A group of mammoth blue butterflies appeared from the opposite horizon and flew towards the black cloud flapping their gigantic wings with intensity as if in a state of war. The cloud allowed its evil face to fully form and it made hideous grimaces and spitting actions with its fiendish mouth. The wind the butterflies' wings created blew the black cloud back across the horizon and it disintegrated and vanished. The people once again calmly resumed their work without celebration.

"It came from the land of dark shadows," Atia said without looking at the Indian party "the wasps sent it," she continued.

The Indian party looked at each other confused; delighted she acknowledged their presence but were troubled by her revelation.

"Who are the wasps, memsahib? And why would they attack you?" Vishnu spoke meekly wishing to draw every syllable of explanation he could from Atia.

"The wasps control The Land of Dark Shadows some distance beyond that horizon." Atia stood up and pointed in the direction from where they had just seen the black cloud disappear. "The boundaries between our kingdoms were set many years ago after the first great battle between the butterflies and the wasps. The butterflies were victorious and drove the wasps across the Putorana Plateau to that desolate waste land called The Land of Dark Shadows. The wasps need the nectar from our wildflowers to survive as nothing grows in The Land of Dark Shadows. We fight a constant battle with them over our nectar. The wasps can travel to the Land of Butterflies to pillage our nectar and ruin our wildflowers but the butterflies can't follow them across their border to the Land of Dark Shadows as the butterflies are ectothermic. Butterfly wings need a high temperature so that they can fly. Their wings will not work in The Land of Dark Shadows. There will be another major war soon. I can sense it." Atia tutted morosely and continued with her work again.

The turbulence created by the gigantic blue butterfly's wings unsettled a partly broken branch high up in a massive oak tree. The Indian party heard the cracking sound of the breaking branch and watched it fall heavily down through the air like it were made from lead. Its flight path was directly over the area where the children were working packing seeds into the containers made from bamboo leaves. The branch hit the ground with a thunderous roar lifting leaves and dust high into the air. It made direct contact with one small girl whose frail body lay helplessly trapped beneath its cumbersome weight.

The Indian party headed by Vishnu raced with lightning speed to free the little girl from beneath the branch but the people ignored the incident and continued working without even looking once in the little girls' direction. Parth, Vishnu and Maximillian lifted the branch with great difficulty and would have appreciated the assistance of the people. Jilly and Cecily pulled the little girl's ragdoll body free to a safe area and left her to lie motionless amongst the wildflowers.

"I am afraid she is dead," Vishnu said solemnly as he tried unsuccessfully to find a pulse at the side of her slight neck.

"She is Atia's daughter," Jilly screamed in horror and

gave Atia a cold stare that with any mass would have delivered a fatal shot.

Atia continued about her tasks unconcerned as if nothing had happened. Cecily started to cry and Maximillian put his arm around her and walked her a distance away from the little girl's dead body.

"It's your daughter you heartless creature," Jilly screamed in rage as she stared at the oblivious Atia.

A large black butterfly with a wing span of around thirty metres glided gracefully over the top of the tall oak trees and descended with gradual fluttering of its colossal wings to where the body of the little girl lay. The Indian party moved in one formation away from the descending butterfly and grouped tightly together holding on to each other for comfort and stability in their shock. Fear kept their vocal chords free of any sound. The black butterfly hovered over the little girl as if assessing her injuries and then took some clay from the place where she died and put it carefully into a sac on its leg. It picked the little girl up lovingly as though she were its own and flew high over the top of the tall oak trees and vanished with her into the mist of the distant horizon.

Jilly was irate at Atia's reaction to the death of her daughter and fumed tight lipped, tossing her hair high into a new bun as if ready to fight. Vishnu intervened and held her arm.

"No memsahib Jilly. This is none of our business. They have their own culture and we must leave them to it. We came here for Rawinda and when we find her, we will leave this place and these strange people and go find Chet." Vishnu spoke with a calmness he had learned to summon quickly, from his good friend and teacher all things peaceful - Thich Nhat Hanh. Jilly calmed down a little and grudgingly nodded in agreement, her lips pressed tightly together in repressed anger.

"I am not heartless," Atia spoke from a distance never looking at Jilly or Vishnu as she continued with her work.

"So how would you describe yourself? Your daughter is dead, and you couldn't care less. All you care about are your precious seeds. You are a sad pathetic person," Jilly said coolly, unable to restrain her anger this time.

"My daughter is not dead as you call it. She will return to us." Atia dismissed Jilly's attack on her personality with a gracious calmness.

"She was dead, memsahib Atia. I am a paramedic," Vishnu said earnestly and gave a head wobble.

"Not dead. No death in The Land of Butterflies," Atia replied and gave the briefest calm smile. "Only wasps die here. That is how I know about the word death and dying," Atia continued "the butterflies protect us from death and all disease. My little girl has been taken to the Place Of Renewal and she will remain there for a few days and then she will return to us in perfect health again. The black butterfly brought her soul in the clay it took with it and her soul will be reunited with her body again soon." Atia was unaffected by all that had happened. Even her voice was as calm as the first time the Indian party heard it.

"Where is the Place Of Renewal?" Maximillian moved towards Atia, dragging his heals in the clay in a sheepish gait as he remembered his excursion to his lung and didn't wish for another involuntary galivant.

"You want to find your son?" Atia replied coolly.

The Indian party held their breaths and stared at Atia in disbelief.

"Is that possible?" Maximillian said and moved even closer to Atia. "How could that be. Surely his body died in our time, so you are saying that his soul came here?"

"Souls who are deemed worthy and are in a state of purification bypass what you are familiar with as the boundaries of time. Special souls from times millions of years before you and from millions of years after you must serve their purgatory in The Place Of Renewal. The soul butterflies - these are the very large butterflies you see here - can access this area of renewal as they can move freely through a vortex that exists between worlds and time. So, you see everything is possible in The Land of Butterflies," Atia replied and gave Maximillian a sudden penetrating stare.

Maximillian's consciousness was transported to the edge of a stagnant still lake in late summer. The water was grey and lifeless without even a ripple to give it a soul. Dead vegetation and rotting branches sat motionless on its surface as if captured in an old sun-bleached photograph. A smell of death hung in the air and dominated every experience the senses were exploring. Bees and flies hovered over the dead water and a group of cranes were feeding on the bank, picking their long legs elegantly out of the murky water as they trolled the area for worms and snails. Weeping copper beach trees completely surrounded the lake, their dark red branches dipping into the water. The sky was eerily grey, and the sun was hidden behind its murky mask of sorrow. Maximillian could see row upon row of expressionless people sitting motionless on the grass and staring forlornly out across the lake as if waiting and hoping to be rescued. Their appearance was destitute and their faces all radiated utter abandonment.

There was no sound other than the uneasy buzzing of bees and flies. Even the cranes were silent as were the staid old branches of the copper beach trees. Maximillian walked slowly amongst the rows of pale faced people who seemed to be abandoned by everything they held dear. All the energy of living was drained from them, and their limbs were like appendages that had no purpose. Each person stared at him with gaunt hollow eyes in a fearful anticipating look. A look born from a dereliction of the soul that could only be resolved by the intervention of a celestial saviour. From over the top of the trees Maximillian could see the large black butterfly carrying the body of a young girl. Its wings fluttered calmly through the still, putrid atmosphere as it flew over the lake and over the heads of the rows of people sitting by the water's edge. The butterfly disappeared out of sight behind the trees to a place beyond the lake and the rows of people never gave it a passing glance.

Maximillian tried to interact with the people but none of them would reply to his persistent questions. They remained motionless and observed him with anguished stares that could only originate from the darkest recesses of their tormented souls.

"Dad, Dad," a familiar voice called out and Maximillian searched the sea of despondent faces to find the source of the voice he knew so well.

The wasp's hot sticky cave was a place of utter pandemonium and chaos. The only thing that appeared to be serene was the weighty, fat Queen. The large red glistening rubies on her throne that gave off the wealthy aura of a Tiffanies window display were very tantalising to Sukey and Ishmael as they surveyed their splendour from a distance with greedy, avaricious eyes.

"Just the smallest corner off one of those rubies will set me...... us up for life, Sukey said as they watched the queen shuffle her large bum around on the ruby thrown trying in vain to make herself more comfortable.

"Just look at those rubies," Sukey continued in near desperation and then stared at the chasm of ferocious wasps that sat between them and the riches that could fulfil all her heart's desires.

"There has to be a way." Ishmael rubbed his chin, avoiding sting marks as he tried to think up a plan.

"I would very much like to hear that one." Sukey rubbed her hand over some very sore stings on her forehead and cheeks that were turning so red from infection she should have carried a warning flag.

Sleipnir noticed them staring at the Queen's throne and wiggled his way through the multitudes of wasps and stood before them and stretched himself to his full height.

"You are observing our queen. Don't deny it, I was

watching. You are here to kill her? Aren't you? You are," he bellowed in a tone that made all the wasps for fifty metres around stop dead in their tracks waiting anxiously for a reply with their wings buzzing and their stings primed in anticipation of an incorrect response.

"We were just admiring your queen's magnificent throne that is all," Sukey replied innocently and smiled, twirling the toe of her shoe onto the grey stone floor like a bashful child.

"We have never seen so many rubies and such large ones," Ishmaels said and gave Sleipnir an honest, guiltless smile.

"Nice teeth" the wasp said and stooped down low to take a closer look at Ishmael's two teeth.

"Why; thank you," Ishmael replied with genuine bashfulness and rubbed his slit tongue over them.

"I will remove those first if you go within a hundred metres of that throne," Sleipnir shouted and swung around knocking Sukey and Ishmael to the ground with his large stinging bum. His shout covered them both from head to toe again in thick saliva. They tried to scrape it off with their hands as best they could and threw it into a pool of sticky goo on the ground. But most of it stuck fast.

"We don't have rubies other than the ones in our Queen's throne here in The Land of Dark Shadows. You are wasting your time searching for treasure here. The riches you crave and much more, in abundance will be found in The Land of Butterflies. The rubies in our queen's throne were captured many years ago from the hall of the butterflies in the first great war. A war we lost but almost won. Almost won." The tone of his voice dropped in lament and reminiscence. "This time we will show no mercy and attack with such a force they could never imagine. We are strong now and our numbers have grown. The Land of Butterflies will be ours this time. If you want riches beyond your imaginings then I promise you will have them. Follow us into battle against the butterflies and the rubies in our queen's throne are just mere trinkets compared to what you will find beyond the Putorana Plateau in The Land of Butterflies. Until then keep your greedy eyes off our queen and prepare yourselves for battle. This will be a war to end all wars. We have languished here in The Land of Dark Shadows for far too long. We will exterminate all those dainty horrible butterflies with their pretty little coloured wings and those perfect little shiny people with their gold sashes. We will kill every last one of them. No mercy," Sleipnir screamed manically and the surrounding wasps buzzed their wings like crazy on hearing his rousing call to arms. He wiggled his way forward through the myriad of wasps and disappeared into their clammy, rancid midst.

"Prepare for battle?" Ishmael imitated Sleipnir's voice quietly to Sukey "I don't like the sound of this. I only fight for myself…and you of course my beauty," Ishmael continued.

Sukey gave a disinterested scoffing laugh "Yeah whatever. But we must go along with their plans. We have no choice. But once we get a chance to find treasure then we will lose these freaked out wasps in a heartbeat," Sukey said and spat onto the ground in contempt. Ishmael copied her action and tried to spit as well but his saliva got entangled in his two front teeth and dripped disgustingly in a long phlegmy line from their tips. Sukey winced and looked away in disgust.

"Wait and you will see. I always knew our partnership would hit the big time." Ishmael smiled in self-satisfaction and rubbed the saliva from his mouth with the back of his bony hand.

"Yeah sure. Whatever," Sukey replied indifferently.

The queen rose from her throne with a spoiled lazy action and stretched herself to her full height, looking regally down on the wasps who all became silent on seeing her rise to address them.

They waited, staring up at her hauteur. Not one wing among millions made the slightest movement.

Ishmael could hear himself wheeze and he gave a small

cough that didn't clear his phlegm. Sukey kicked him hard on the leg. He winced in pain and made a gesture that it wasn't his fault. Thousands of nearby wasps stared at them with their wings buzzing and the stings in their tails showing, just itching for action. Ishmael noticed this and took a deep breath and smiled nervously at the enraged wasps. They shook their tails back and forth menacingly and faced him, primed and eager for a sudden attack.

"I, your queen will now address you," the queen began to speak in a tone of contemptuous interest.

Ishmael stared at the thousands of angry wasps who faced him down and pointed to the queen in an attempt to redirect their grievous attention to her forthcoming speech.

"Listen to your queen." Ishmael folded his arms pretending to be attentive to her every word, attempting to shift their attitude from their current ominous threatening behaviour.

"You wasps of the order of Hymenoptera listen to your beautiful charming and ever youthful queen. She who needs no mirrors to know she is beautiful beyond all beauty and elegant beyond all elegance. I your queen who is the bravest and most intelligent wasp who has ever lived, rules here from this humble uncomfortable throne. I asked for diamonds, but I accepted these paltry rubies to show how humble and unpretentious I am. I sit a mere two hundred metres above you but that doesn't mean I feel two hundred metres above you. Actually, I feel far higher above you than that but I have humiliated my royal presence to sit at this meagre height of two hundred metres. Each day I must endure your proletarian behaviour and having to observe your utter commonness makes me feel good about myself and shows me just how superior I am to you all in every way possible." The queen smiled and gave a regal wave with her foreleg. The wasps grew into a frenzy, buzzing their wings in delight and flew in pandemonium around the vast cave, crashing head on into each other on more occasions than not. The larger wasps bumped themselves off the rocky ceiling and made thunderous booming noises that echoed through every corner of the vast cave. Sukey and Ishmael put their hands tightly to their ears to block out the rambunctious noise, but it made little difference.

"She is mad. The queen is mad," Ishmael shouted to Sukey but she couldn't hear him and he clapped his hand wildly in mock appreciation of her sentiments.

"She is completely insane," Sukey shouted to Ishmael, but he couldn't hear Sukey either.

"We can no longer survive in this cave in The Land of Dark Shadows. We need nectar, sunlight and fresh air and we need it right now." The queen's voice resounded throughout the cave and the wasps frenzy grew even more violently energetic. "We need the wildflowers from The Land of Butterflies. No longer can you fly across their border at night to steal nectar like the despicable common thieves I know you really are. We must stand upright and fight to the end and to victory."

And the queen stood up and reached her two forelegs as high into the air as she could. "This cold climate is killing your gorgeous and magnificent queen. My face is dropping from having to live here in this frozen wintry land with you utter trolls." The queen pulled the fur on her face back with her two forelegs to stretch out the wrinkles and with a third leg held a very small mirror up to her face expectantly to examine the contrast that action may have made "It is time to fight the butterflies to the death and take control of the hall of the butterflies. It is a place worthy of my regal person and I want it now. The Land of Butterflies will be mine. I want it all now. And also, I shall be better capable to tolerate your deplorable presence in its splendour." The queen completed her speech and sat down giving an over exaggerated and refined, regal wave as she did so. She wiggled her large bum about, uncomfortable in the ruby throne. The hysterical buzzing of wasp wings and their frenzied actions almost caused the roof of the cave to crack open but the bumping of the larger wasps' bodies against it pushed the rocks back into shape again in a restorative fashion they were completely unaware of.

"These wasps are completely crazy. They are delighted to be insulted by this crazy queen," Ishmael said in disbelief.

"I couldn't care less. I want the treasure. I want it all as well. Let's see what the beautiful charming queen will do about that," Sukey replied and gave a fake beaming smile in the direction of the queen who at no time noticed or recognised her presence.

Maximillian's eyes frantically searched through the ocean of helpless faces that stared at him, to find the voice he recognised. A melody that didn't follow the structure of harmony and that jumped key in no standard time, changing the tempo at random and moving from sharps to flats irregularly, droned across the lake constantly in a loop. It heightened the sense of hopeless abandonment of the setting and added to the anxiety of the people who sat in the rows by the shoreline. Above this menacing sound Maximillian heard the voice once again.

"Dad, dad," the voice continued, and Maximillian began to run through the rows of despondent people examining each face as he ran.

"I am here," he shouted as he ran, stumbling on occasions and falling in his haste. None of the people sitting by the lake offered to help him to his feet each time he stumbled. They looked on indifferently as he feebly lifted himself upright each time.

"Over here," the voice called again, and Maximillian ran in the direction of the sound.

Actions he was familiar with since Rutherford's very first step as a child manifested themselves and Maximillian stopped dead in his tracks as he saw his son running in his distinct gait through the crowd. They stood face to face and for seconds just stared at each other in amazement then held each other tightly without speaking for moments only their hearts could count.

"Rutherford let me look at you." Maximillian stood back from his son as his eyes absorbed every inch of his image, repeating those moments when he first saw him as a newborn baby.

"Dad how have you come to this terrible place?" Rutherford said still holding on tightly to Maximillian's hands as though he were afraid he would vanish if he let go of his grip.

"I am not altogether sure. I am here by some form of telepathy or quantum superposition - I think. Where are we?" Maximillian said.

"This is the place of renewal." Rutherford's voice sounded the admittance of a deep lament that had all but consumed him.

"Have you tried to escape?" Maximillian looked about him sharply for a possible liberation plan.

"There is no escape from the place renewal. We have all tried numerous times. We can get to the boundary of the lake just beyond the weeping copper beach trees but once we put one foot beyond their perimeter line we are automatically transformed back to the edge of this lake again. We often see the black butterfly fly over our heads as it brings people to a separate region beyond the trees, where souls are reunited to their bodies but none of us can get to this place either. Some of the people here have sat by the lake for thousands of years waiting their time of renewal and they claim the reuniting of the soul to the body in this area is the phenomenon we know in our time as a near death experience. Remember you used to tell me about that when I was young? They also say that the black butterflies fly through a time vortex beyond the trees to get to this place and the region doesn't exist in our time." Rutherford's words were inanimate and dripped from his tongue like a dying breath.

"Yes of course I remember. It happened to me once, that time my oxygen tank got trapped in rocks when I was diving for pearls in Bahrain. I was a gonner for certain. Dead they say for ten minutes or maybe more. They pulled me up to the diving platform and but for that French boxer with his big fists pounding on my chest… well… it would have been the end I am sure." Maximillian became morosely reminiscent.

"But you told me you remembered a place of peace and an abundance of love consumed you. You said you wanted to stay there and never come back," Rutherford coaxed a reply.

"Yes, that is true. I was filled with a feeling of immense love and peace like nothing I have ever experienced and would have happily stayed there," Maximillian replied with a fond reminiscence.

"Did you see the soul butterfly? Did it bring you to the area of renewal?" Rutherford's voice became anxious and expectant.

"I remember the brightest white light I have ever seen. Powder white, brighter than the first cover of snowflakes on the ground. I kept drifting towards it. I needed to be inside the light somehow and it wanted me there. I felt that it was where I belonged. And yes, there was a butterfly come to think of it, I can remember it now. It was there, but until this moment I didn't pay much attention to its presence. Funny how its memory was lost to me until now." Maximillian smiled fondly at his recollection: his cheeks going pink with the contentment the memory gave him.

"So, you came here to this place back at that time. You obviously don't remember but a soul butterfly must have brought you beyond the vortex for renewal and then transported you back to your own time once more." Rutherford left his hand delicately on Maximillian's shoulder.

Maximillian could plainly see the long scar on Rutherford's head from his fatal accident and he rubbed his hand gently over it.

"I made one foolish mistake. I didn't look where I was going that day. If only I had, I would be at home now with my Jilly, Chet and Cecily," Rutherford said with words that originated from the saddest place in his heart, and held back tears that were one more sad breath away from exploding like a fountain. "How are they? I hope they are not overly upset by my death?" he continued and looked mournfully towards the water's edge.

"They miss you very much of course but they are fine. Chet and Cecily have grown so tall in a short while. And Jilly is still baking beautiful pies," Maximillian said and rubbed his portly belly. They both laughed but it was a laugh of convenience rather than a spontaneous display of joviality.

"They have grown? How I miss them. How I miss Jilly and you of course Dad. Will I ever meet them again I wonder?" Rutherford said and held on to Maximillian tightly once more.

A butterfly's wing brushed Maximillian's face gently and his consciousness returned. He stood at the side of the seedbeds once more and looked at Aita. She returned his gaze for a moment and without further reaction returned to her work.

"I have just been speaking to Rutherford. He is fine and looks well. He misses you all," Maximillian said and shook with excitement as he stared wide eyed at Jilly and Cecily.

Jilly's face went pale, and she leaned against Vishnu for support.

"Are you ok, memsahib Jilly?" Vishnu held her upright with both hands.

"Was it like my vision? Did you see Rawinda?" Parth rushed to Maximillian his face broadening with a smile from the anticipated answer.

"I was in the place of renewal and I saw Rutherford there. I didn't see Rawinda as she is still alive," Maximillian replied and left his hand on Parth's shoulder.

"You saw dad?" Cecily said and began to cry. Jilly comforted her with words the rest couldn't hear.

"What is this place of renewal Sahib?" Vishnu said.

Maximillian relayed his experiences and the conversation

he had with Rutherford, to his eagerly attentive audience who, for once waited on his every word.

"Tuliana died before her time. She must be in the place of renewal. Did you see her? Was she there?" Parth grabbed Maximillian's arm so tightly that his nails dug into his skin and Maximillian winced from the pain.

"She is probably there as well my friend, but I didn't see her. There is an infinity of souls in the place of renewal. It would be a feat beyond any living persons' capabilities to see all of them.

Maximillian's voice faded to a hush.

"My Tuliana is alive. She is alive." Parth's voice reached to the very top of the tall oak trees.

"Atia knows where they all are. She knows where the hall of the butterflies is and she knows where the place of renewal is as well. Why won't she tell us? I must go to Rutherford. I must see him." Jilly's voice became irate, and her mood was now beyond reason. Temper filled her like a pressure cooker about to explode.

Parth agreed and, making a solemn pact together, they decided they needed answers immediately.

He accompanied Jilly as they marched with steadfast gaits towards the seedbeds. Atia and her people made no reaction to their sudden arrogant approach and dismissed their presence as though they didn't exist.

"You will tell us where my husband is now Atia," Jilly screamed. I want to see no more visions. No more hocus pocus I want to go to the place of renewal right now," she demanded, her face purple with anger and her eyes so wide they almost stretched to her ears.

"And I want to go to the hall of the butterflies to find my daughter," Parth interrupted with equal anger and agitation. His usual sleek well-groomed black hair was tossed and unruly; and he wrung his hands so tightly they began to turn blue.

Atia and her people took no notice of their anger or demands and remained composed and completely indifferent to their presence. Jilly jumped out into the middle of one of the seedbeds and began to rip up the new fledgling plants with her hands, throwing them high into the sky. The leaves fell like rain drops covering her with limp dead foliage. As her anger grew her destructive performance picked up momentum and she ripped up a large section of the seedbed right at Atia's feet. Parth followed Jilly's example even though Vishnu tried to stop him. He got on his hands and knees to give his ruinous actions better propulsion and went along the rows pulling up milkweed plants faster than any traction engine. The people stopped working and stood together in a group holding hands. At once Jilly and Parth rose gently into the air above the seed beds their legs and arms rotating frantically as thought they were in freefall. They were removed without any visible means to the clear ground alongside the rest of the Indian party. The milkweed plants all reformed themselves again and floated back to their original places in the seedbeds, perfect and intact. The people continued to silently hold hands after Jilly and Parth had composed themselves and the Indian party looked at each other, fearing that retribution for this ruinous act would shortly take place.

"This doesn't look good for us if I am a judge of mutton." Maximillian put his arm protectively around Cecily.

"Maybe the memsahib should try more amicable methods in future. Just maybe?" Vishnu said and allowed a very nervous smile to sit on his lips for a millisecond.

"They are about to do something sinister I can feel it." Parth looked downcast with regret and the feeling of embarrassment and shame flowed through his tone.

Vishnu looked at Parth without sympathy and, giving a loud "tut tut," wobbled his head.

The Indian party grouped closely together and put their arms around each other expecting the worst.

"This maybe a time to pray if you are a praying person," Vishnu said and began to chant in Hindi.

The people broke rank and calmly walked back to their work once more. Atia walked with relaxed composure towards the Indian party and stood before them.

"We have decided to bring you to the hall of the butterflies," she said and without further ado, set off walking towards the distant horizon on the path the black butterfly had taken. Atia didn't look around to see if they were following her. She moved ahead treading gently on the wildflowers who all bowed down under her weight and then lifted back to full height once she had passed. The Indian party eagerly followed her, breathing in the exotic aromas of the wildflowers as they moved in her wake. Countless millions of butterflies of every variety dined on the nectar from the wildflowers and rose delicately into the air in front of Atia, forming a tunnel of butterflies five metres high in front of her as she glided through. Once the Indian party had followed Atia through the ephemeral tunnel, the butterflies all gently descended back to feed again and the tunnel dissolved behind them like a tall wave whose scattered energy evaporates into a sandy beach. In the distance they could see mammoth fields of gigantic soul butterflies dining on the nectar of wildflowers that were at least thirty metres tall. The blooms of these wildflowers were ten metres wide and the gigantic soul butterflies, some with wing spans of twenty metres, hovered gracefully beside the blooms to feed. Many of the wildflower varieties were unknown to Maximillian and he concluded to the others that most were species unheard of back in their own time beyond the wormhole. He gave a running commentary on his vast knowledge of wildflowers as they followed Atia. This grew very tiresome after the third vast field they crossed but they couldn't help but listen. Many of the wildflowers had varying coloured blossoms extending from a single stem; blossoms of red, blue and purple all growing from a single shoot. They stood in admiration for moments but charged off quickly again, as Atia relentlessly glided ahead and began to gain ground distancing herself from them. If not constantly observed she could easily have vanished midst the taller flowers in the expansive fields they passed through.

"Keep your eyes on her, Vishnu," Parth commanded as he stumbled forward breathing heavily.

Maximillian rubbed the back of his tightening calf muscles and was also beginning to feel the strain but soldiered on feigning vigour. In other circumstances he would love to have lain face down in the flowers and rested from his exhaustion but that wasn't to be. They passed through so many fields Cecily became bored and gave up counting.

"How much further?" Parth gasped the exhausted tone of one who is ready to throw in the towel.

Atia didn't reply or make any response. She showed no concern for his fatigue as she floated ahead of them looking as though she had just taken her first step on this arduous journey.

Vishnu grabbed Parth's arm and assisted him to move forward. Jilly did the same for Maximillian even though he insisted it was completely unnecessary. A tall lush green mountain range lay ahead of them. It was in contrast to the manicured flat fields of wildflowers as its terrain was wild and unkempt and had lain just as God created it, untouched by human endeavour. Its vegetation was the culmination of the law of the survival of the fittest where nothing needing sustenance prevailed. It was the tail end of the Himalayas with no snow or ice on its pinnacle just yellow firs and briars and occasional weather hardened tree that lay at an angle to accommodate the north wind. Atia marched up a narrow animal path that appeared very familiar to her and disappeared behind undergrowth that blotted out the path after a few hundred metres.

"No. I can't go on any further." Jilly sat down heavily, and Cecily foundered like a house of cards, with her head across Jilly's lap. Parth collapsed face down on the ground, his arms and legs splayed out like a fallen scarecrow in the stubble. Maximillian eased himself down to the ground as though this were to be his last seated position in life. Vishnu stood over them "We must follow Atia," he pleaded.

"Not one more step. We will catch up with her when we get some rest. Look at Maximillian he is almost dead," Jilly complained and pointed to Maximillian as he panted, his cheeks bright purple.

"Errm… I'm not so bad really," he lied and coughed. Vishnu sat down and nodded his head in acceptance of their decisions. "So be it." His voice sounded defeated.

Atia was long gone out of their view by now and they all felt their position was hopeless.

On the very pinnacle of the mountain where the path meandered through a devil's bit, Vishnu noticed a small dot move as it beckoned down to them.

"It's Atia." Vishnu pointed towards the small white dot way up high amongst the distant heather.

They all stared in a slow fatigued fashion, moving their necks slowly, their heads barely able to follow their brains' command.

"She is calling us," Vishnu said in alarm "We must follow her now. Please. Let us try," he continued his voice almost in tears and he tried to lift the unmovable Maximillian to his feet.

The others were unable to give a willing response and stared at the ground and made no eye contact with him.

Maximillian took the leather pouch that contained the small silver bell from the pocket of his safari jacket, opened it and delicately removed the bell. He removed the cotton wool from around the clapper and, under the weary scrutiny of the others, gave it the slightest ring. As he did so the large white butterfly descended from behind one of the sky's sparsely populated milky white clouds and floated down to hover just above them. It gently gathered them into a tight group with its forelegs and lifted them high into the sky and fluttered its giant wings gently to the top of the mountain and placed them on a small stony plateau beside Atia. The white butterfly lifted into the sky again and disappeared, without trace, behind the stationary pale cloud once more. The marvel that stretched out before them from the pinnacle of the hill gave them no time to wonder or question Maximillian's bell or the sudden miraculous appearance of the white butterfly. They stood in silent astonishment, mouths open like young thrushes in a nest and eyes wide open.

The hall of the butterflies lay in a valley of wildflowers beyond the mountain and was so vast it defied logic. It stretched as far as eyes could see to two opposite horizons. Gigantic towers sitting every half mile on its extremity wall, reached thousands of metres into the iridescent blue sky.

Flags two hundred metres square embossed with the images of many different varieties of multi-coloured butterflies blew gently in the breeze and were attached to quarter mile long flagpoles that were fixed to each tower. Their billowing sound in unison heightened the sense of immense grandeur. The granite stone entrance was carved in the shape of two towering butterfly wings and sat in the centre of the structure. Its tips pointed hundreds of metres into the air. It was accessed by a flight of five hundred stone steps that lead to a balcony plateau of many acres that was covered with grey polished stone flags. Colossal statues of once famous soul butterflies dotted the park landscape in front of the hall. They perched captured, frozen for ever in differing poses of flight on top of mammoth hand chiselled stone pedestals and were enamelled in full brilliant colour. They glistened majestically in the evening sun as if protectively watching over the hall.

"The hall of the butterflies," Atia graciously made a sweeping gesture with her hand towards the building and without emotion or further comment turned away from them and retraced her steps back down the narrow mountain path. They watched her go and were strangely lonesome as they witnessed her grow smaller and smaller on the horizon. The butterflies formed a tunnel ahead of her again as she drifted back through the fields; her dot vanished completely into the hazy mist of the hot summer's evening as she made her way back to her village of yellow houses.

A animal path, rough with rocks and stubborn briars meandered its way down the opposite side of the mountain. The descent was a cake walk to them after their previous march. They didn't bother about the briar scratches either that tore at their hands and legs as they kept their eyes firmly fixed on the splendour of the hall that grew nearer with each excited laugh they made.

"Where did you find the bell?" Parth's eager words whispered in Maximillian's ear and Vishnu heard.

Maximillian smiled. "I have my sources also. I might just tell you sometime," he goaded and tapped his nose with his index finger in the style of one who knows but doesn't chose to explain.

Vishnu smiled.

The steep hostile animal path melted into a field of wildflowers, and they moved through the enchantment with apprehension in every footstep as they drew near the halls foreboding presence.

Each one secretly imagined different ending scenarios to their eventual encounter with the hall; all of their perceptions had doom as a finale and their jollity began to turn to fear.

"Remember walking through the swamps of Louisiana once. A terrifying place to be – Alligators the size of a London bus - totally lost and thinking the worst but I made it out all right in the end. Lost a toe but I have nine others." Maximillian tried to console the group as they approached the flight of ominous stone steps. No one acknowledged his intervention in their fears. He shrugged his shoulders and made an expression of disinterest in their obvious apathy which didn't display his true feelings.

"Ok. A story for some other time I think," he said and turned his gaze away from them.

CHAPTER 12

Outwardly the sound of butterflies fluttering wings and the gentle billowing of flags were all that could be heard. Inwardly the loud beating of their hearts exploded in their ears and filled them all with added fear and trepidation. Glassless windows one hundred metres square were set between each flagpole on the outer walls of the hall and millions of butterflies peacefully flew in and out through them unconcerned and unhindered. As Maximillian put his left foot on the first stone step that lead to the entrance of the hall, a mammoth blood red soul butterfly rose gently from the rear of the building and hovered over the roof just above the entrance as if protecting its sanctity.

Maximillian swiftly removed his foot from the step, and they all watched the butterfly in wonder as the gentle fluttering of its massive wings created a refreshing cool breeze that tossed their hair and fanned their exhaustion.

"Is it going to attack?" Jilly pulled Cecily close to her, but Cecily struggled to get free to evaluate the situation for herself.

"It doesn't appear angry, memsahib," Vishnu replied and for the first time took off his turban and wiped his forehead with a crisp white handkerchief that he took from his lapel pocket. The others stared at him suddenly with as much astonishment as they gave the large red butterfly. He noticed their reactions and quickly put his turban back firmly in its rightful place without acknowledging the interest of the others.

"And how would you possibly recognise an angry butterfly?" Jilly added with slight sarcasm.

"Well. There's a thing. Funny you should mention that. I remember a man in Sri Lanka telling me a story once long ago about how…" Maximillian started his story and the others immediately marched, as if a starting gun had just discharged, up the flight of five hundred stone steps, leaving him alone. Maximillian gave an unconcerned cough "if you don't want to know how to tell if the butterfly is angry that is fine by me," he said, very miffed and followed along behind them, his head tossed to one side in an offended fashion.

They reached the top of the steps and from the advantageous viewpoint on the large stone balcony looked back out across the endless fields of multi-coloured wildflowers. The sight was so enchanting that each one of them regretted having to turn their gaze away.

The opening in the centre of the large stone butterfly wings minimized their stature as they passed through. Cecily wiped her hand along the smooth chiselled stone surface as she followed closely behind Jilly. The ceiling of the great hall beyond the entrance was one thousand metres high and they strained their eyes to see if they could catch a glimpse of its pinnacle, but they couldn't. The lilting sound that the butterflies made with their wings echoed through the cavernous hall and was an enchantment to their weary spirits, allowing their fears to ease a little and smiles to form on their faces. Filled with the new energy the harmonious sound gave them, they moved forward through the hall as the butterflies parted gently before them. The atmosphere radiated an aura of antiquity as the light shun in through the vast windows in long shafts of brilliant amber highlighting the wings of the butterflies. There was no furniture or any object that gave the impression that humanity played any role within the walls.

"Rawinda...Rawinda." The decibels of Parth's voice echoed to the highest points of the massively high ceiling. The echo insured his calls rang out a constant cry of Rawinda's name. A bright golden staircase wound its way around the walls of the hall and became invisible long before it reached the highest points of the ceiling. Small balconies presented themselves every thirty steps on the stairway and a door of varying bright colour slotted into highly carved cut stone arches with a butterfly motif adorned the pinnacle of each arch. The countless doors formed a multi coloured rainbow that stretched to the infinity of the ceiling and individual doors vanished to a blur in the far distance.

"She could be in any one of those rooms," Parth despaired as he looked in dismay at the immense quantity of doors.

"We will have to try them all," Vishnu said and took the first step up the golden staircase.

"This will take forever. I don't believe it will be possible to search every room," Maximillian said and shook his head in dismay.

"Come on we have to try." Jilly's earnest reaction gave them the courage they needed and they all set off running up the golden stairway. One by one they twisted the large brass knobs on varying coloured doors to vast cavernous rooms that were occupied only by different varieties of butterflies who fluttered about peacefully unconcerned with the intrusion. They called out Rawinda's name each time they entered a room and waited for a reply before closing the door and moving further on up the stairs once more.

"We will have to form a relay. We all can't stand waiting for one door to be opened at a time. Form a line of attack," Maximillian said with a sergeant major like attitude. "Right, we will all get to separate doors further up the stairs and open them on my command. We will give each room a few minutes search and then we all move forward again." Maximillian smiled in self-satisfaction at his imagined ingenious plan of action. The others stared at each other and shrugged their shoulders with no look of conviction before playing along with his idea. As any plan, no matter how ridiculous, was better than having no plan in a situation as hopeless as this. Vishnu looked at Maximillian and remembered a line he read somewhere that seemed to be apt right now. "There is no confusion like the confusion of a simple mind," he smiled but kept his deduction to himself.

When everyone was in place he shouted, "Right now open your door," in the crispest accent he could muster.

They all opened their chosen doors and looked inside and called out Rawinda's name. Some of the doors opened to rooms stacked high with gold, diamonds, and rubies but this wasn't the treasure they were looking for. On realising that Rawinda wasn't in the room they were searching they closed their respective doors on fathomless riches and moved further up the stairway reproducing the same actions over and over. Maximillian's legs began to give way and wobble as beads of sweat ran down to the point of his nose like a meandering forest stream.

"We are not getting very far up this bloody stairway," he shouted out to the others and sat down heavily on the gold step to catch his breath. All the others followed his example and sat down as well.

"This won't work. We could be here for an eternity, and we won't get half of these doors open," Vishnu said and held his head in his hands in despair.

"And who knows we could have missed her in one of those vast rooms that we already checked," Jilly said and took a deep fatigued breath that made her shoulders slump even further downwards.

"Yes, you are all right we will never find Rawinda like this." Parth almost in tears stared up at the endless stairway and the countless coloured doors that tempted the group as if knowing their efforts could never produce the result they desired.

"What are we to do?" Parth screamed out in despair. His voice returning to him many times as a cold distressed forlorn echo.

They were all silent as they fell into deep thought. Even Cecily twirled her hair faster than usual as she wished to be the one who hatched the best plan first.

The large black soul butterfly flew gently into their view, serenely flying higher and higher, peacefully moving the smaller butterflies out of its way with its wings as it ascended. It delicately landed on a balcony a few hundred metres higher up on the stairway. The graceful movement of its wings kept it's balance as it perched. The yellow door on its balcony opened slowly and Tuliana walked out, looking radiant and in perfect health. She stood for a moment as if in a trance and looked out across the hall without expression, never once noticing the Indian party or looking in their direction.

The black butterfly gently picked her up with its two forelegs and carried her off the balcony. It flew through the millions of other butterflies towards a large circular window on the opposite end of the hall and disappeared out through.

"Tuliana, Tuliana," Parth screamed over and over but she never once looked in his direction and appeared not to hear his call. He began to race down the golden stairway calling out her name as he ran. Vishnu grabbed Parth by the arm as he reached the balcony Vishnu was standing on.

"They have gone too far away now. You will not be able to find them," Vishnu said, and Parth sat down on the balcony and put his head in his hands in desperation.

"It was Tuliana. It was her. I saw her," he cried.

"Yes it was, I saw her as well." Vishnu sat down beside Parth and comfortingly put his arm around his shoulder.

Jilly, Cecily and Maximillian joined them, and they all sat huddled in a group together on Vishnu's stone balcony.

"She is alive. Isn't she?" Parth doubted what he had just seen and his eyes demanded a positive reply as he stared at Vishnu.

"She must be in the place of renewal with Rutherford. The black butterfly has brought her back there again," Maximillian said and they all nodded in agreement.

"But what was she doing here?" Cecily asked innocently.

On hearing Cecily's question all the others looked at each other in an instant.

"Rawinda," Parth screamed and jumped to his feet and ran headlong up the stairway.

The others immediately ran after him, even Maximillian attempted to run but was limping slightly and moved much slower than the rest.

"Which door was it? Am I getting near it?" Parth screamed from a distance as he ran; the desperation and expectancy in his voice made the others fear possible disappointment.

"The yellow one. Way up there," Maximillian replied, pointing and squinted as he looked towards the distant yellow door.

Parth ran even faster taking two steps at a time. He stumbled on occasions but bounced back up again immediately, feeling no pain.

"I have to sit. Maximillian sat down heavily on a step. He held his breath suddenly as he looked over the edge of the gold bannisters at the sheer drop to the distant stone floor frighteningly far below him. He suffered severely from vertigo but only his doctor knew this. He removed a tattered handkerchief from his trouser pocket and mopped some sweat from his forehead.

"I am too old for all this," he exclaimed quietly to himself and stood up again to resume his climb.

"Is this the one?" Parth shouted as he reached the yellow door on the distant balcony. His voice was faint as it reached Maximillian's ears.

"Yes, that's the one - I think," Maximillian said as loudly as his fatigued voice would allow, his words fading to a whisper on "I think."

Parth rattled the handle and pulled frantically at the yellow door his face filled with angst and the veins on the side of his neck protruding horribly as if ready to burst. But it wouldn't open. Sweat dripped onto the door handle from his brow like rain drops as he continued to push and pull at the unmoveable thick oak door. He was in the midst of having a personal war with a solid piece of immovable wood as the others joined him. They all tried their hand at opening the door in that way that people do, assuming their approach to be superior to the last effort made, but none of them had any success.

"This is the one? Are you certain?" Parth directed his question to Maximillian with undercurrents of impatience and doubt.

"Well…I think so?" Maximillian's voice quivered with uncertainty.

"Look there is a strange looking keyhole in the door," Cecily said calmly and pushed her finger into it.

They all gathered around to get a closer look at Cecily's discovery.

"Well done young Cecily. You clever little thing," Maximillian said and gave the top of her head a rub with his hand. She didn't mind this too much as her hair wasn't kept to her usual standard at that moment after all her strenuous activity.

"No normal key will fit that lock. I know a thing or two about locks," Maximillian spoke with the authority of an expert and hummed and hawed as he studied it, as most experts do.

"What will open it? Do you know?" Parth enquired as he leaned in over Maximillian's shoulder to get a better view of the problem that was taking more than its fair share of time.

Maximillian scrutinized the lock with distorted facial shapes that intimated one giving an examination with skilful authority.

"Ermm…the key should be very thin and four inches or so long." Maximillian scratched his head sounding very unlike the professional he credited himself with being.

Parth grabbed the handle of the door again and began to shake it in a further vain attempt to get it to open.

"It is no use. I am fearing it will not be opening for us." Vishnu left his hand on Parth's shoulder.

"Try the butterfly wing," Cecily said innocently and examined the keyhole for herself, daring to push her index finger into the hole for the briefest of moments. The others looked at her suddenly and gasped with amazement.

"Young Cecily could be right," Vishnu said.

Cecily acted as though this thought was not at all praiseworthy and was really a rather trivial deduction. After all she and Chet had much more complex mechanisms in Woodhouse 2. Parth produced the two butterfly wings from his pocket and very gently tried to insert one of them into the lock. They all stood around the yellow door in anticipation; all eyes wide and focused on the keyhole in frantic stares. The butterfly wing fitted perfectly and Parth, with utmost delicacy turned the butterfly wing in the lock and the door opened. They all cheered.

"Thought so," Cecily said calmly and smiled.

Parth pushed the door open and ran inside like his pants were on fire and this was the way to the fire hose. The room was completely familiar to him as it was exactly as he remembered from his previous vision. Everything was precisely as he had explained to the others and they felt they knew the room intimately as they had all privately mulled the descriptions over in their minds. Rawinda was sleeping peacefully in the large golden bed. Her complexion was restored and she looked a vision of perfect health once more with cheeks as rosy as a fresh spring blossom.

Parth leaned down and gave her a gentle kiss on the cheek. She awoke and smiled at him. Parth picked her up in his arms and, holding her tightly, swirled in happy circles, his feet barely touching the dark brown wooden floor. The sound of their laughter made the others feel overjoyed.

The sun shone in through the large stained-glass window and covered the room with a warm peaceful glow. Dust from the floorboards lifted into the air as they danced and mingled with the beams of light creating a miniature moving galaxy of tiny particles.

"Was Tuliana here?" Parth said as he let Rawinda's feet delicately touch the wooden floor for the first time.

"She is dead. How could she be here?" Rawinda froze and the jollity drained from her face.

"Who nursed you back to health? I imagined I could sense somebody in the shadows when I visited you," Parth spoke in a soothing voice and brushed a rouge strand of hair back from her eye. "Yes, there was somebody here but I could never see who it was. They were always out of sight and tended to me when I slept. I remember always suddenly falling asleep whenever they were near. It was as though they had the power to make me sleep whenever they wished. But why do you mention mother?" Rawinda searched all the staring faces looking for a response.

"We saw Tuliana leave your room. She was taken away from here by the black butterfly," Parth said and held both Rawinda's hands tightly in his own. She felt faint and sat back on the gold bed. Cecily ran to a nearby table and brought her some water that was in a pink butterfly shaped glass. Rawinda took a long drink and smiled at Cecily.

"I didn't see her at any time." Rawinda's lip quivered, and tears welled up in her eyes.

"She must have nursed you back to health," Cecily said and sat on the gold bed beside Rawinda.

"Tuliana has to be in the place of renewal. She died before her time just like my Rutherford. We have to find a way to free them." Maximillian's anxiousness grew and he paced about the floor in thought.

"Remember Atia's words. Their souls are in the ground where they died so we need to have fragments of that earth with us when we go to the place of renewal. How do you suppose we do that?" Jilly folded her arms so tightly the veins on the back of her hands began to turn blue.

Maximillian pulled up the sleeve of his safari jacket giving a clear view of a brass bracelet that surrounded his right wrist. The brass had stained the skin beneath it to a dark brown colour.

"Remember this?" He showed it to Jilly. "I had a piece of the gravel from the place where Rutherford died encased in this bracelet. I didn't tell you about it in the past; I felt it might upset you. Or you would think it strange. But I was following the rituals of an ancient custom I had heard about many years ago. In this ancient tradition a piece of earth is taken from the place where a person died tragically and it is kept sacred by the family as they thought it held that person's soul. I feel I have Rutherford with me at all times when I wear this bracelet. And now it seems my strange little indulgence has paid off." Maximillian smiled.

Parth took a small stone from his pocket and displayed it to the others on the palm of his hand. It was a plain white sand pebble that was made perfectly round by countless millenniums of crashing waves onto sandy beaches.

"I found this pebble on the exact place we discovered Tuliana's body. I never heard of the ancient custom you mentioned but having this pebble with me gave me a feeling of having Tuliana beside me always. So, I also have her soul here in my hand to give to the place of renewal. That's if we can find this place." Parth gave the pebble one final look and placed it safely back into his pocket again.

"We must go to the place of renewal now and find Rutherford and Tuliana. There is no time to waste." Jilly spoke with determination and holding Cecily's hand led the way out of the vast room and away from the compelling light that shone in through the stained glass window.

CHAPTER 13

The wasps' cave was very humid at night like somebody switched the air off and purposely set the thermostat to boil. The condensation, created by the wasps' over heated bodies, ran down the walls like rivers and gathered all over the ground in large rank pools. Oxygen levels were so thin it was almost impossible to breathe and the putrid aroma of rotting fish and miasma could only be compared to a back-alley dumpster at Billingsgate fish market in midsummer. The buzzing and flapping of wings was constant and the regular groan from the queen as she tried in vain to find a more comfortable sitting position all combined to keep Sukey and Ishmael awake throughout the long wearisome night. They lay on the stone floor in the only tiny space where the condensation didn't pool and crouched tight together to avoid the dampness. Every now and again an arm or a leg would encounter the meandering flow of condensation and they would shudder and awaken.

"Oh for my lovely comfortable bed of leaves in the jungle," Sukey would say irritably on these occasions throughout the night and kick Ishmael each time he managed to nod off.

"Bloody hell, I was just asleep there. You have no concern for anybody other than yourself. Just like that moaning old queen wasp." Ishmael gave a wearisome angry half-asleep growl at having yet another attempt at sleeping abruptly disturbed and rolled over holding his right hand under his head for a pillow.

"Ermm, let me think about that for a minute. You've got it in one. Absolutely no concern for others whatsoever and I am getting worse by the day," Sukey shouted into his openly displayed inattentive ear.

"How I hate bloody wasps," she screamed inside in her, not allowing the words to exit through her lips for fear of retribution. She imagined igniting one of her speciality bombs right in the centre of the cave beneath the queen's throne and watch a myriad of wasp parts fly in all directions. That wishful thought was getting her through this difficult moment.

"It is morning now anyway. No point in trying to sleep any more. I am so, so tired and weary," Ishmael screamed and rubbed his face manically with his hands in an attempt to revive himself. The nearby wasps rattled their stings and stared at him.

"If only I had my blunderbuss with me now loaded with lead and nails," he mumbled to himself as he returned their stares with equal anger.

"Be nice to the wasps now, Ishmael. I need that treasure. We need that treasure should I say," Sukey said in a fake over emphasised patronising tone.

"Nice to see you added the 'we'. I do exist you know. I have feelings too." Ishmael played to Sukey's sympathy and gave her a sheepish alluring smile and brushed his comb-over back to the front of his head and gave it a few pats with the palm of his hand to make it secure.

"Oh shut up you absolute idiot." Sukey stood up and stretched herself and kicked one of the ten metre high wasps hard on the bum with her purple Dr Martin boot on purpose.

"Sorry, sorry I didn't notice you there. Sorry," Sukey said in her best fake apologetic accent.

The wasp withdrew its sting and wiggled away with a slight limp into the midst of the other wasps.

"I can't take this smell anymore I swear I am going to gag. I must get air," Sukey said and walked off picking her way over the millions of wasps that covered the floor as she moved towards the large entrance. She occasionally, and purposely stood on smaller wasps killing them and then making very swift apologies afterwards to their nearby friends. The rock was firmly placed in front of the exit and there were no visible signs of any way to open it.

"And where would you be thinking of going - little womaneen? Not leaving us are you. Sleipnir appeared instantly from the mass of crawling wasps that were bunched metres high at the entrance.

He looked rested and yawned - then stretched in a satisfied fashion giving off a leisurely groan. He rubbed his two forelegs over his head and flapped his wings as if to make sure that they were still working as perfectly as always.

"I have to get out of here. This smell," Sukey said and held her hand over her nose.

"Are you saying we smell little womaneen?" Sleipnir said, and his tone began to change.

"She meant no disrespect. She didn't sleep well. She is a monster without sleep. No disrespect to monsters." Ishmaels spoke apologetically in her defence and made a poor attempt at a tap-dance on the stone flags.

"You dance?"

"Oh well." Ishmael gave a bashful grin.

"With one leg?" Sleipnir's voice changed suddenly to a deep threatening tone.

Ishmael froze like a cool box cube.

"We will have to harness this monster in her in order to fight the butterflies." Sleipnir gave a droll laugh. "We are attacking The Land of Butterflies today. We will kill those willowy excuses for life forms until every last one of their pathetic dainty wings are burned to a cinder and their bodies lie in the dust amongst their precious wildflowers. Our arsenal of weapons that we have gathered since the first war with butterflies is now supreme and far better than we could have ever hoped. Soon we will have all the nectar we need and will get out of this cave for good," Sleipnir continued and gave a few sniffs into the air and made a wincing motion with his face once he had evaluated the aroma properly.

"You may have a point on the smell womaneen. We wasps have been in this cave far too long." He marched off into the midst of the wasps again and disappeared. "No escape until I say so. No one can open that cave door except me." Sleipnir's voice trailed back to Sukey and Ishmael's ears long after he had vanished from their view.

"Are you mad? They could kill us in seconds. Leave off with the insults will you. Womaneen," Ishmael said and gave her a disapproving look, then a sarcastic grin.

"If you refer to me with that word again, I swear I will add another scar to that ugly face of yours," Sukey growled 'womaneen' below her breath and Ishmael became suddenly silent.

Sukey gave the large impregnable entrance a mournful stare just like a gambler who watched his horse fall at the first, and she sat down wearily on the wet flag floor in despair.

The queen rose from her throne in a mood that desired pampering. She had no immediate cause to be bitchy but she was anyway. She scanned for a fault; any fault would suffice, and arrogantly looked out across the moving sea of angry wasps as they crawled on top of each other buzzing furiously.

They displayed no sign of peace or harmony and occasionally attacked each other in fury for no apparent reason.

"You horrible trolls," she screamed so loud her voice cracked "I, your ever beautiful queen am about to send some of her intelligent and delicious thoughts to you filthy foul-smelling hobgoblins. The mere sight of you in the morning makes me sick to the pit of my stomach but as your magnificent queen I will fulfil my birth right and rule over you even though you don't deserve to ever witness my glorious presence or view my stunningly exquisite countenance. Listen here now you abominations, today is the day we seize The Land of Butterflies." And the queen lifted up onto her hind legs, shook her rotund body and neurotically flapped her wings. The wasps went into a frenzy of happy excitement as they listened to her speak, buzzing and flapping their wings as if in reply.

The massive wasps bumped off the ceiling of the cave and the din made Ishmael and Sukey fall to the rough stone floor and bury their heads in their hands.

"Open the armoury - Sleipnir. Open it you large foul smelling filthy wasp," the queen shouted in a sudden very deep tone that was in complete contrast to her previous pitch.

Sleipnir rose from the midst of the throng in a self-important fashion looking about him for admiring stares and flew over the cave awkwardly bumping into other large wasps by accident as he flew. His huge mass left a dark shadow on the heads of the smaller wasps below who were viewing him in admiration. He landed clumsily on a narrow ledge high up on the wall of the cave and tried with great difficulty to keep his balance. Losing his grip then gaining composure once more in a loop of manic exaggerated movements.

"Come on, come on you big fat oaf I haven't got all day to watch your pathetic performances," the queen shouted at Sleipnir.

Sleipnir jumped nervously up and down on the narrow ledge like an actor with sudden stage fright until he managed to release a lever mechanism that slowly allowed a massive entrance to open in the rock face just below where he was precariously perched. The din the wasps made grew loud and their excitement increased to psychotic proportions as the entrance fully opened to reveal a stockpile of weapons any global tyrant would be esteemed by.

"Fly or crawl you wretches, to my precious arsenal and gorge your sad carcases on my collection of butterfly killing gadgets. Go on guzzle it all up you disgusting monstrosities. Take those weapons which I, your glorious highness above all highnesses gives you and kill every last one of those worthless freak butterflies today. I don't want to hear that even one of those creatures or one of those horrid little perfect people with their pretty little faces and blissful little lives have survived beyond this sundown. My splendour will then take residence in the hall of the butterflies. I will have to tolerate its treasures and the place will be privileged to witness my everlasting nobility." The queen sat back on her throne and tossed her head arrogantly as she watched the countless millions of wasps scurry into the arsenal of weapons and choose armaments that suited them according to their stature. Even the minute, standard size wasps found small bombs made with a half drop of nitro-glycerine to match their physique. They flew with caution but on occasions collided with each other and small explosions were heard followed by wasp parts witnessed, moving at high velocity.

The larger wasps took the bazookas and machine guns, all especially adapted to suit their anatomies. Each large wasp carried a heavy black sac that held the bombs that would deliver the killer blows.

Because of their weight they found flying difficult and bumped against each other and haphazardly crashed heads every on now and again but shielded their cargo, unlike their smaller counterparts. The attack on the land of butterflies had begun.

Zona just felt the imaginary rats of his delirium tremens crawl up along his arm and sit menacingly on his left shoulder: brandishing their teeth and staring their red bloodshot eyes as they prepared for lunch. He shook off their whimsical presence one by one and brushed his shoulder repeatedly in further attempts to complete their imagined banishment.

"Lord help me I need a drink," he cried out in agony as he sat with his back resting against the rough stonework of the palace wall. He began to shake uncontrollably and wrapped his arms around himself in a vain attempt to stop the tremors. His mind's eye could see a massive angry wolf approach him from out of the jungle with its teeth bared, dripping blood and saliva, primed ready to attack.

"Ah no; no," Zona screamed and ran headlong into the palace, slipping and sliding and still holding on to himself as though he were about to shatter and fall to pieces if he let go his grip.

Chet's mind was in Hastings in 1066 and he sat on the marble floor and watched the Norman-French army of William, the Duke of Normandy, take on the English army under the Anglo-Saxon King Harold Godwinson. The battle was well under way and Chet was happy with all proceedings. He would have preferred if the marble floor was a little warmer and if he had one of Jilly's Cornish pasties but he made do. The door of the Parth's haven crashed open without grace and banged against the perfect paintwork, leaving the trace of the doorknob imprinted in the once perfect wall. Zona raced in, his eyes bloodshot and his hands trembling out of control, and he scanned the room in search of alcohol of any kind. Paint thinners was his tipple of preference in times like this but even that wasn't available to him now.

"Ishmael. Sukey. Where they be?" he demanded, with a desperation in his voice that tipped to red on the scale of wretchedness.

Chet stood up and the Battle of Hastings came to a sudden halt with neither side having taken any advantage. Chet called out for help as Zona ran to grab him but in his delirium, Zona stood on the head of The Duke of Normandy and fell over the army of the Anglo-Saxon King Harold Godwinson before landing heavily onto the unforgiving marble floor. The army of lead soldiers scattered to the four corners of the room - their battle ended for that day at least.

The myriad of colours in the wormhole sensed unease and swirled around with a boost of energy. As Chet reversed back toward it to distance himself from Zona, the colours disappeared and a white mist appeared covering the mouth of the entrance. Zona timidly reached out his bony hand to touch the mist and as he did so, millions of angry wasps raced from the entrance and filled the room like passengers on a Chinese underground train. Without options, Zona scampered into the wormhole screaming in agony as he was stung mercilessly by the enraged wasps. Chet laughed as butterflies filled the room but raced after Zona as he was enjoying Zona's frantic actions.

The exit of the wormhole opened into the putrid cave of the wasps in the Land of Dark Shadows.

Chet and Zona held their hands over their noses to block the stench as they ran out near Sukey and Ishmael who were sitting dejectedly on the cold wet floor near the sealed entrance to the cave.

Once Sukey and Ishmael saw the wormhole open they pushed Chet and Zona to one side and tried to run back inside but the wormhole suddenly vanished into a cloud of mist as they approached. As they ran around in circles frantically trying to find the entrance to the wormhole Zona stood with a simple grin on his face and looked pleadingly at Sukey.

"Zona needs whiskey." Zona smiled politely and held out both his hands. Sukey looked through him.

"So, you have returned to us again you little brat." With a leering laugh she roughly pushed Chet around in circles before her. Chet tried to fight back, swinging punches like the ones he had seen on Boxing Uk but she kept him at arm's length by holding her hand on top of his head. "You may come in useful brat. We could need a hostage again, so sit down and be quiet. Any more of your funny stuff and I will throw you out into the centre of those wasps and you know what will happen to you there." Sukey pointed out to the wasps with her long skinny index finger. Sukey gave Chet one last push and he tumbled and fell against the cave wall and stayed where he landed.

"You brought him here, so he is your responsibility. If he does anything to upset my plans you know what I will do." Sukey put her nose close to Zona's trembling mess of a face and ran her finger along his throat from ear to ear. Zona ran and sat cross legged in front of Chet and stared eyeball to eye ball with him watching his every movement.

"You have a way with people," Ishmael smiled but Sukey

ignored his remark.

"Open the main entrance Sleipnir. Your queen commands it." The queen rose up from her ruby throne and waved her two forelegs in the air and sang an anthem badly that repeated the word wasp a lot. Sukey knew it must be an anthem as some of the wasps sang along with her in a patriotic fashion. None of them were choir material.

The cold air raced in and chilled the bones and wings of every living thing in the cave once the large stone was moved by Sleipnir and the entrance open. Sukey gulped in long deep breaths of the icy fresh air greedily like a calf drinking from a bucket of fresh milk. Sleipnir landed without grace in a loud awkward thud beside Ishmael - his sting knocking Zona from his Buddha like seated position.

"You will need a ride to battle. Those skinny legs of yours are no match for the wasp's superior method of travel." Sleipnir demonstrated the power of his wings with a few sudden flapping movements. "You little one, get on my back." Sleipnir poked Chet in the forehead with his antennae.

"I haven't got the time to wonder where you and this craggy old geezer came from." Zona made a disgruntled expression. Sleipnir instructed three other massive wasps, who weren't happy with the arrangement, to carry Zona, Sukey and Ishmael out from the cave and into battle. One dropped a large tear, like a bathtub of water, in angst as the moments he had dreamt of were being impeded by a scraggy old Zona on his back. Chet put his leg gently onto Sleipnir's back - hating the feel of the wasps hot sticky fur and taking extra care to avoid his manically buzzing wings.

"The rest of you get on the backs of these brave wasps and hold on tight. This could be a very bumpy ride. Keep away from the stings. That's if you want to live." Sleipnir allowed himself a very brief chuckle.

"I can't do it. I can't. Zona need whiskey. Badly."

Ishmael picked Zona up and threw him roughly onto the back of the wasp. The wasps groaned with the sudden weight and Zona stared at the vibrating wings and screamed in terror, pretending to himself that it was all just a dream originating from his delirium tremens.

Once they were all mounted, the wasps lifted awkwardly into the air, bumping against each other by accident and dropping in altitude for moments before suddenly rising again. This made Ishmael's ears pop and he thumped the wasp hard on the back with both fists. The wasp tried to reach him with its sting in retaliation but Ishmael kept a distance from the ever eager tip.

"These idiots can't even fly in a straight line." Sukey took a quick look down from her perch on her Wasps' back to the now distant stone floor breathtakingly far beneath, as her fingers turned white from the tension of her balancing grip. Chet thought the ride was not unlike the space rocket jaunt at the fairground in Robin Hood's Bay and laughed aloud as Sleipnir bobbed up and down randomly in flight.

"Be gone you utter stinking horrors and be as brave as your cowardly looking bodies can be. Conquer for your beloved beautiful queen. Win for me The Land of Butterflies with all its nectar and all its beautiful treasure," the queen commanded as she gave a very extended regal wave; the one she had practised for the occasion, in front of her tiny hand mirror. The sky was a yellow and black canvas as wasps flew in countless millions out through the large rocky entrance of the cave and into The Land of Dark Shadows. On occasions the entrance got jammed with the bodies of over eager wasps as their fervour to advance into battle was extreme and the blood rushing to their heads intense.

Chet hung on tight as Sleipnir saw an opening in the escaping throng and dived out through the entrance to the bitter cold frosty air of the Land of Dark Shadows. The desolate landscape with its barren, bleak outlook did not impress Chet. Rock and wasteland were all his eyes could see on all sides far out to all horizons. He shuddered from the cold and crouched as low as he could between Sleipnir's vigorously buzzing wings to keep warm.

CHAPTER 14

Just like a party on the last day of school holidays when you have everything that you need to give you that jollity for life but in the back of your mind there is the thought of that dreaded awakening after the next sleep when you no longer will be in holiday mode. So, it was with the Indian party.

They delighted at having found Rawinda safe and well but now the awakening lured them and the place of renewal beckoned.

Very large soul butterflies of bright varying colours flew directly through the hall as if on important errands and didn't dally like their smaller counterparts who floated and meandered with serenity. They eased them out of their path as they flew with the draft from the wings. Cecily imagined if she jumped over the balcony their assembly would keep her afloat in mid-air as she rested peacefully on their multi-coloured graceful wings. The Indian party walked through the hall and followed the path the black butterfly made as it carried Tuliana away. After a walk that Cecily imagined must be the length of ten football pitches they came to the base of the gable wall and looked up to the enormous window the black butterfly had flown through. It was three hundred metres above them and they reclined their heads back as far as they could in efforts to get a clearer view of it.

"We will never get up there. It is much too high," Cecily said as she stared at the distant window in dismay.

"I am thinking there has to be an exit door somewhere. This is what I am thinking." Vishnu looked about him for the phantom exit he imagined.

"Look there," Cecily shouted and pointed to a red velvet curtain three hundred metres long that hung on the wall to the side of the large window "I bet you it is behind that curtain," Cecily continued and ran to the curtain and began to pull it to one side. It was so heavy she could only manage to move the bottom corner of it a few metres and coughed from the dust that lifted from its seldom disturbed surface.

"Come on give me a hand," she insisted and the others joined her just to humour her fanciful idea. They all took hold of the bottom of the curtain and pulled it to one side until it revealed the exit Cecily had predicted. It was a small standard sized door, in complete contrast to the rest of the architecture. It was painted, although a better description is daubed, in every colour on the colour wheel and signed in red at the door handle Cupid and Psyche.

"Whatever does that mean?" Jilly rubbed her finger over the signatures.

Maximillian looked at the other waiting for any of them to give their opinion first as he was growing wearisome of his best analysis being tossed to the wind. On realising their vacant stares meant they had no opinion he gave a small cough.

"Well, its Greek Mythology…" he was cut short by Parth.

"Yes of course Maximillian. The love between Cupid and Psyche. I remember. Psyche means soul butterfly in Greek am I right?"

"Yes, spot on old boy." Maximillian was none too pleased that Parth took away his forthcoming revelation.

"And what?" Jilly said unconvinced.

"We chatted about this on the plane Maximillian. Remember?" Vishnu spoke with certainty to Maximillian and then turned to Jilly to continue; "the ancient Greeks imagined the souls of their dead took the form of a butterfly that flew in the vortex of spirits around Hecate. I explained to Maximillian about the Nagas tribe from Manipur, in the Indian state of Nagaland, who believed they were descended from the butterflies and that they still ruled over humanity in a parallel universe."

Parth, eager to give of his knowledge, interrupted Vishnu who smilingly let him take centre stage

"Psyche was very beautiful and Venus was jealous of her and sent her son Cupid to tempt her to marry a very ugly man, but Cupid fell in love with her and forgot the instructions of his mother. After some tribulations and by the will of Zeus they were united in love." Parth smiled and put his arm around Rawinda.

"The wanderings of our souls with a singular desire to meet that one true love," Vishnu said in contemplation and may, for the briefest moment, have remembered the landlord's daughter Sandra behind the bar of The Red Lion.

Maximillian gave a loud cough as, yet again, his thunder was stolen and tossed out to the cold wind.

Each person ran many random scenarios through their brains to try and decipher the cryptic signatures but felt that these were thoughts for another, less important, day.

"Now I told you the door was here all the time." Cecily gave them a triumphant look of satisfaction.

"You are right again young Cecily. What would we do without you?" Maximillian gave the top of her head a gentle rub with his hand.

"Well to be perfectly honest I really don't know," Cecily replied with all sincerity. The others laughed. Cecily didn't.

They moved slowly through the exit, each one touching the signatures as they passed, and pulled the curtain closed behind them. A forest of oak trees five hundred metres tall grew at the rear of the hall. There were no other structures, just a breeze that blew generations of dead leaves in whirlwind circles beneath the base of the forest. Millions of butterflies of varying sizes drifted in and out through the trees harmoniously.

"Do you remember this forest in your vision? Is this the place of renewal?" Parth asked Maximillian.

"No, I don't remember this forest. This isn't the place, he replied as look of bewilderment covered his face.

They could see past the bare trunks of the tall trees and could look unhindered deep into the forest for many miles. The high canopy blotted out all light beneath it and the ground was covered thickly with fallen gold and amber leaves and spindles. Its unexplored presence desired to be investigated and tempted the Indian party with its sense of uncharted mystery. The occasional loud creaking of high branches, caught off guard by the breeze, made all their senses even more alert. Except for the butterflies there was no other sign of life. Jilly marched forward stubbornly holding Cecily's hand and listened as the crisp dry spindles cracked beneath her feet as she walked into the forgotten forest.

"Not a good idea memsahib. Which is the right way? We don't know. This could be a big mistake, memsahib," Vishnu pleaded but Jilly continued on ahead as if she intimately knew that the path which lay before her was the correct route to the area of renewal. Cecily was having serious doubts about the journey she was being forced to take, as she was dragged along without her permission, and she gave a concerned, pleading stare back to Vishnu.

"Are you sure this is the right way?" Maximillian's voice pleaded.

"Yes, I am sure," Jilly replied curtly and took a firmer grip on Cecily's hand that had almost wriggled its sweaty way to freedom.

The depth of the spindles on the ground grew thicker until movement forward through them was impossible. Jilly persisted and moved forward very slowly alone, as the terrain forced her to let go of Cecily's hand. On realising that the journey ahead was not an option the others stood sadly watching Jilly's futile determined perseverance. Cecily made her way back towards Maximillian.

"It is time to stop, memsahib Jilly. Come back," Vishnu pleaded and for the first time loosened his tie a couple of centimetres and opened the top button of his white shirt.

A large dark shadow slowly covered all of them, blocking out the sun's rays and leaving a cold chill in the air. Jilly stopped dead in her tracks and awkwardly balanced on top of the now very deep spindles. A breeze lifted the dead leaves and small branches from the floor of the forest into a lively dance and the Indian party, minus Jilly all bundled tightly together in anticipation. In the clearing just beyond the treeline the massive blood red butterfly they had seen earlier, hovering over the entrance to the hall, reappeared. It descended before Jilly, blocking her path forward through the forest and hovered just above her head.

"And where are you going?" It spoke in a commanding but kind voice to Jilly. She tried to shoo it off with anxious hand movements but it picked her up gently with its forelegs and then let her down beside the Indian party. The strong breeze from the butterfly's wings blew and tossed their hair and made them all huddle even tighter together.

"We want to go to the place of renewal," Jilly shouted her reply with determination.

The butterfly laughed "I see," it said and flapped its gigantic wings even more vigorously.

The resulting breeze grew to a strong wind and they all fell to the ground helplessly.

"I must find my husband. He is there," Jilly shouted as loudly she could over the sound of the gale and tried with great difficulty to get to her feet.

"And my son is there." Maximillian also tried to stand upright but both were suddenly knocked back down to the ground again by the force of wind.

"Nobody living can travel to the place of renewal," the butterfly said calmly and slowed his wings to a gentle mild flapping motion.

"But I have been there," Maximillian corrected the butterfly with a superior air, "So you are wrong" and he finally managed to scramble to his feet.

"You were there in a vision but not in real life. I can kill you if you like and ask the black butterfly to take you there but you will remain by the lake in the place of renewal for a very long time" the red butterfly replied coolly.

"I want my daddy back," Cecily said and began to cry, large salty tears streaming down her pale cheeks.

The others gathered around to console her, and the butterfly drooped its head in genuine sorrow at the sight of her emotion.

"But we have their souls. Here take a look." Parth took the small white sand pebble from his pocket and displayed it on the palm of his hand for the butterfly to see.

Maximillian pulled up his sleeve and pulled the bracelet roughly from his arm "And I have Rutherford's soul here."

The butterfly landed gracefully on the ground before them and gently took the sand pebble from Parth and the brass bracelet from Maximillian with its front foreleg.

"I will see what I can do. I don't promise anything." the butterfly flapped its wings and lifted high above the forests' canopy before vanishing like a pin head into the blue of the sky.

A feeling of pleasant possibilities filled the hearts of each of the Indian party and they sat on the comfortable dead dry leaves in thoughtful silence waiting for the butterfly's return.

"When do you suppose we will know if it can do anything for us?" Jilly said reflectively as she brushed Cecily's hair with her fingers. No one replied, fearful to build hopes too high. They all basked in thoughts that seemed too fantastic to imagine and wished beyond hope for the red butterfly to bring a positive outcome, mulling over their reactions once they were finally reunited with Rutherford and Tulianna.

These were the moments when dreams, no matter how outlandish, had every possibility of becoming a reality.

CHAPTER 15

Reflections on possibility is what makes the ticking hand of the clock appear more bearable. If all future events were to be as banal as past experiences then expectations would be the futile exercise of the deranged. The Indian party's peaceful reflection on possibility was short lived however as the first wave of wasp bombers was now in the skies over The Land of Butterflies. The previous China blue sky was now in shadow from the yellow and black bodies of wasps. They attacked in waves of massive merciless battalions that were visible clearly out to the distant Putorana Plateau on the horizon.

The larger wasps buzzed along the front line and attacked first in uneven rows that bobbed up and down, following no organised flight path. Occasionally they bumped hard into each other causing their explosives to detonate and annihilate everything within range, causing large random pieces of wasp to fall hard amongst the innocent wildflowers. The sight of their mutilated brethren didn't deter the others who hastened their speed of attack. The sound of their incessant buzzing created a ripple over the canopy of the trees and suddenly jolted the Indian party out of their daydreams. The wasps flew over the hall of the butterflies and dropped their explosives without mercy onto its high lofty roof.

"Look, millions of wasps are attacking the butterflies," Cecily screamed and the Indian party stared in horror at the invading hoards who broke the peace and viciously bombarded the tranquillity of all they despised with no semblance of remorse.

"It sounds very much like they are dropping incendiary missiles." Maximillian held his hand to his ear to make a better assessment of the sound the explosions created. Vishnu, who had seen some military action in the past, agreed with Maximillian's assessment.

"They are trying to destroy the hall. Look - the bombs

are hitting the roof," Jilly screamed as massive blue slates and burning roof joists flew high into the evening sky in a red flaming blaze.

They all ran *en masse* to of one of the largest oak trees and cowered low together in a rotten hollow that could easily house the string section of the Halle Orchestra. Maximillian held Cecily close to him and Parth did likewise covering Rawinda's head with his arm.

Some wasps overshot their target due to their clumsy flying technique and also fatigue, dropping their bombs carelessly at the back of the hall. These misfires blasted the roots of the tall oak trees knocking some of them down with a thunderous agonising roar. The dust and leaves rose high into the air and dallied there momentarily as if avoiding the chaos and carnage below. The strong pungent odour of TNT blotted out the sweet aroma of the wildflowers and honeysuckle and stung the inside of their nostrils making them feel lightheaded. Cecily thought the bombs smelled like marzipan and almonds but she was a little hungry and loved marzipan.

Chet gripped his tiny fingers tightly onto Sleipnir's furry back for dear life in the second wave of the attack. Sleipnir continuously nose-dived almost to the ground from the fatigue of the extra weight he carried but always recovered just in time as he was about to crash land. Chet screeched with laughter.

"Wahooooo," Chet screamed each time Sleipnir made his last-minute recovery. Chet was in awe as he looked out towards the magnificent fields of wildflowers and the millions of brightly coloured butterflies. His gaiety changed however once he saw the destruction the first wave of wasps had made to the landscape with their explosives. Large piles of massive oak trees were burning out of control all over the landscape and he could see the people in their, now not so white tunics, racing about frantically trying to halt the attack from the wasps. They gathered in groups, holding hands and sending powerful rays from the eyes towards the assailing wasps but their efforts were having very little effect. A whirl wind of flame raced through the wildflowers and darted high into the sky, burning everything in its path to a cinder. Chet could see fires raging furiously throughout the land leaving little intact in their wake.

"Stop. Stop. You can't do this," Chet cried and hit Slepinir hard on the back with his fists like he was beating a tom-tom drum. The impact of Chet's tiny fist made no difference to the wasp's flight as his strong thumps didn't even penetrate the wasp's fur. Sleipnir was on course to make a direct hit on the hall but because of his exhaustion and clumsiness he misjudged his flight path and flew over the smouldering roof of the hall, almost crash landing to the ground right in front of the Indian party.

"Chet," Jilly and Cecily screamed in one voice as they saw Chet perched precariously on the back of the massive wasp.

Chet saw the Indian party wave and scream in his direction. "Let me down. Let me down that's my mum," he shouted as he thumped and kicked Sleipnir with all his might. The wasp lifted high into the air above the tall forest canopy and banked itself in order to make a second attempt to attack the hall. Sleipnir steadied himself in mid-air with a look of utter determination and shuffled the explosives to a more comfortable position ready for his attack. Chet reached as far forward on Sleipnir's back as he dared go for fear of losing his grip. He stretched out his thin arm and poked his index finger straight into Sleipnir's eye. Sleipnir screamed in pain and lost the little control he had of his flight and began to nosedive. It shook all over like a dog who just come out of a stream as it plunged haywire towards the ground. Chet lost his unsteady grip and was thrown free from its back. He fell through the air, like a feather in a storm, several hundred metres to the ground.

The Indian party had been watching Sleipnir's perilous flight and they screamed as one when they saw Chet plunge to what could only be his certain death. Jilly fell on her knees holding her head in her hands and wailed a cry louder than the discord caused by the surrounding carnage. The breeze from the wings of a large white soul butterfly who had been watching the scene unfold, blew Chet into the top canopy of the forest and he grabbed on tightly to the green foliage for dear life.

"He's safe," Maximillian said with a loud sigh of relief and sank to his knees.

"Not yet, sahib," Vishnu said and ran to the trunk of the tree that Chet clung to and began to climb faster than a lace monitor lizard. The others watched as Vishnu scaled higher and higher reaching the top of the huge tree quicker than even he could have imagined. Vishnu moved out across the thin branches with the precession of a tightrope walker balancing over a mighty crevasse. He grabbed Chet who by this time was so exhausted he was just about to let go of the branch he clung to and fall to his certain death.

"Climb onto by back; there's a good little boy." Vishnu spoke in his calmest and most eloquent tone, one that would fit like a glove amongst the swish tones found on Sloane Square, and gave a smile that reassured Chet's beating heart. Chet wrapped his arms around Vishnu's neck like he would not let go even if the doomsday clock struck his name.

"You are the man from the cave. I remember your hat. You saved us before." Chet was crying and laughing at once but neither one nor the other for definite.

"Yes, but we will be talking about that later - now hold on tightly." Vishnu's tone of voice implied without words "we are not of the woods yet my lad."

Vishnu began to climb back down the tree again but not as swiftly as his ascent due to the extra weight of Chet on his back. The others watched with baited breaths, mouths open and fingernails pressed deeply into palms, fearing the vibrations from the exploding bombs could dislodge Vishnu from his position. They only felt at ease once Vishnu's feet landed safely on the heavy pile of dried out leaves at the base of the tree. Chet ran to Jilly who picked him up in her arms and cried with delight.

Cecily jumped up and down beside them in excitement wanting to give and receive a little affection. Also. Maximillian and Parth congratulated Vishnu, heaping every praise possible on his heroic action.

"It was nothing really. Nothing at all," he said in an underrated tone and shrugged off the attention as though his heroics amounted to no more than being the one who removed that extra-large spider from a bath.

Sleipnir flew around in haphazard circles, buzzing frantically and screeching like a bat caught in a fishing net as the pain in his eye grew more intense. He rubbed it continuously with his foreleg but that made the pain even more intense resulting in blurred vision that could see three halls.

Banking himself awkwardly he choose the better option of the three, and flew towards what he imagined must be the hall of the butterflies. The raging smoke and ash from the fires singed his good eye and he coughed and spluttered like an old traction engine starting up on a snowy morning. Flames from the canopy of the nearby trees were his final undoing. His impeded vision didn't notice their presence and he flew too close to the intense, raging flames. One of his wings was completely burned off in an instant as though it were candyfloss meeting a warm hungry tongue. Screaming in fear he buzzed with all his might with his only remaining wing in an attempt to fly but to no avail. He nose-dived to the earth in a swirling motion and crashed into the ground on the forest line half a mile from the Indian Party. The bomb he was carrying exploded on impact leaving no trace of Slepinir, not even his sting.

"The wasps are attacking The Land of Butterflies," Chet screamed in an overly excited voice, his cheeks a bright glowing red.

"Whatever do you mean?" Jilly said as she put him down.

Chet explained to the others all he had seen and heard in the cave of the wasps. The others listened with ashen faces and occasional nervous twitches and were silent with fear.

The second wave of the wasp attack was under way and the sound of bombs exploding filled the once serene air with anguish and abandon. The small butterflies scattered in fear but the large soul butterflies flew bravely in simmering brightly coloured legions to repel the attack. The only defence mechanism they had was the force of wind they could generate with their wings. They managed to blow some of the wasps to the ground where the bombs they were carrying exploded on impact.

Most of the wasps got through this weak line of defence however and their explosives hit their desired target causing maximum damage to the hall that was now a ball of flame right out to its extremities at opposite horizons. The people ran from their small individual settlements of yellow houses across the now ravaged fields of wildflowers towards the hall. They were silent and expressionless as they congregated at their destination. Some of their clothes and hair caught fire as they ran through the burning fields and their once neat appearance now took on a ravaged demeanour. Their faces and hands were black with ash, but they still didn't display any emotion. Atia and her people stood in front of the stone steps that lead to the entrance hall and held hands.

They looked towards the sky and focused eyes that lacked all expression, on the wasps. A force of energy charged in one single bolt from the people's blue eyes, joining together in the sky like a single laser. It zapped some of the wasps burning them to a cinder as they neared the hall but their efforts were having little effect and was only a small drop in the ocean to disrupt the never ending waves of attack.

The bombs fell on the hall like unceasing violent thunderstorm rain and the Indian party could hear parts of the magnificent ceiling crack and collapse, lifting a dust cloud that raced high into the ravaged sky. They could imagine the millions of peaceful butterflies all trapped and dead beneath the burning debris. Atia and her people decided to take up a final defensive stance at the back of the hall. They ran through the crumbling building, unaffected by the falling, burning rubble and out through the smouldering remnants of the once small multi coloured door which was previously hidden behind the long red curtain. The curtain was now burning in a large distorted heap on the stone floor and gave off a strong stifling smell like burning hair which made them cough and hold their hands over their mouths. Once at the rear of the hall, Atia's group stood firmly together holding hands once more. The energy they generated through their blue eyes began to zap the attacking wasps. They stood with steely determination their clothes and hair singed with flames but with no expressive emotion on any of their faces. Some of the people also rode on the backs of large soul butterflies and engaged the wasps head on using the force from their eyes to disorientate the eager flight of the wasps who then crash dived to the ground and exploded. The peoples' efforts were only as successful as their small group could wish for. Their endeavours were overshadowed and minimalized by the magnitude of the wasp force like a handful of peashooter enthusiasts facing down a line of cannon. Attack after attack continued without mercy - the sky yellow and black with the density of the attacking force.

Sukey and Ishmael had a very uncomfortable passage to The Land of Butterflies and found it almost an impossibility to remain securely seated on the wide backs of their respective silent and indifferent wasps. They slipped and slid from side to side in a perpetual state of pending doom. They hollered out in discomfort and banged their fists hard on the wasp's bodies. The only reaction to their pleas was the occasional sting they received on their legs from the wasps tail. They screamed in agony after each gigantic sting had left a massive red swollen lump on the offended area. The thick black smoke that rose from the endless burning fields of wildflowers made Sukey and Ishmael cough and feel ill as the wasps flew head long through.

"You fools, you have ruined all the wildflowers and the nectar. What was the point of all this madness if everything is destroyed? The land of butterflies is of no use to anybody now," Sukey screamed at her wasp but it didn't reply. It flapped its wings with increased eagerness to get to its destination and destroy the final remnants of a once peaceful and beautiful place. Zona, however, wasn't so lucky and lost his grip on his wasp's back and silently plummeted to his certain death - all the while thinking of the ramshackle pub in the jungle and the barmaid with the brown cowboy hat and peacock feather.

The queen followed cautiously, a very long distance behind the rear of the third and final wave to oversee her victory. She puffed and preened herself, rehearsing her victory speech whose sentiment grew in ever more exuberant self-praise each time she altered its content in her head. As she flew through the battle torn fields of burning wildflowers she coughed as the smoke filled her lungs and eyes to beyond the point of crying.

"I win. I win. My magnificence has won the day. Look at all these burning butterflies and their dead flowers: I reign supreme over everything. I the most beautiful and most adored of all wasps who ever lived claim this land as my kingdom and…," she coughed and cried dark sooty tears as the black smoke and ashes raced into her mouth. She flew, oblivious to the carnage her wasps had caused to the nectar she desperately needed.

The force of the bombing on the hall was so great that the tremors ran deep into the earth's core and activated a once dormant volcano that could be seen to flare up far off in the distance. Its eruption shot molten hot lava and ash miles up to the heavens and made the fire at the hall look like a tiny candle on a birthday cake by comparison. The battle stopped on both sides for moments as they all observed the eruption that now took centre stage amidst all the carnage.

Maximillian could see the volcano erupting and began to climb one of the tall oak trees to get a better observation point. Forgetting his vertigo in his excitement he reached about twenty metres high and looked out across the landscape to where the volcano was.

"Oh no this can't be. This can't be happening now," Maximillian's voice quivered with fear. The others on the ground could hear him mumbling loudly to himself and waited anxiously as Maximillian descended the tree with overanxious movements, slipping and grabbing, tearing and pulling, all the time with a look of horror covering his face like a ghoulish Halloween vizard.

"What is it, sahib? What have you seen? What has distressed you so?" Vishnu helped Maximillian down the final few metres from the tree and both fell on top of each other as Vishnu put his arms around Maximillian's wide girth to guide him safely to earth.

Maximillian held his head in his hands. The others looked very concerned and gathered around him like animals who congregate around one of their injured brethren.

"What is wrong grandad?" Chet said in a voice near tears as he had never seen Maximillian in this perplexed state in the past.

They waited in silence for his reply as the sound of the erupting volcano filled the air with menace and discord, blotting out the sounds of the wasp attack - overshadowing it as though it were a mere pop from a child's cap gun. Millions of butterflies made a forlorn squeaking sound as they expired and this intermingled with all other sounds of decimation, could have made a suitable anthem to herald in the arrival of the four horsemen of the apocalypse.

"What have you found out? Why are you so distressed sahib?" Vishnu said and stood beside Maximillian who slowly began to rise to his feet holding Chet's hand for support.

Maximillian stared at them all for a moment, his expression clearly displaying his fear for their future safety as he gently cradled Cecily protectively towards him.

"The erupting volcano you can hear is in an area which in our time is called the Siberian Traps. I know this volcano well and am very familiar with the area as I once lived at the base of it for two years on one of my expeditions. The eruption of this volcano 300 million years ago marked the annihilation of civilization at the end of the Triassic period. Almost all marine species and terrestrial vertebrate species died as a result and the basaltic lava from the volcano covered a large expanse of Siberia which, now in our time, is known as the Siberian Traps. This event we are witnessing here is known as The Permian-Triassic extinction and was one of the most significant incidents in our Earth's history. The vibrations from the wasp's attack must have caused the volcano to erupt. If I am right, and sadly I believe I am, this is the end of this world we are living in right now." Maximillian spoke solemnly and stared with a gaunt expression, observing each of their reactions to his revelation individually.

"It took nature ten million years to recover after the Permian-Triassic extinction and many of the species that were wiped out at that time never recovered and are extinct in our world today. Like many of the strange wildflowers we have seen here in the land of butterflies and many of the strange unknown butterfly species we wondered at." Maximillian spoke with regret at the pending loss of so many species.

"And those huge wasps?" Cecily asked.

"And the huge wasps indeed young Cecily." Maximillian smiled as he looked at her.

"And Atia's people," Jilly whispered afraid of the reply.

Maximillian nodded in the affirmative not wishing to relay the words from his quivering lips.

"We must all be getting out of this place soon in that case," Vishnu said with a look of urgency.

"But we must wait for the red butterfly - to see if it brings Tuliana and Rutherford back to us," Parth added with a stubborn agitated concern. They all nervously nodded in agreement.

The Indian party watched as sections of the hall burned furiously, sending fire balls thousands of metres into the evening sky. They could hear the thunderous crashing noise of the interior walls of the hall beginning to crumble and collapse. It made for a sad dismal sound. The smell of burning butterflies, vegetation and wood filled the air and they found breathing difficult. High up on the forest canopy Maximillian pointed to a raging fire that was sweeping through the upper branches of the trees, devouring all before it.

"The red butterfly will not be able to fly back through those flames," Vishnu said in alarm and stared at the high canopy that was shooting scorching flames a hundred metres into the air. The others feared he was correct and now felt the chances of seeing Tuliana and Rutherford again were very slim. The magnificent blood red butterfly flew over the burning canopy of the forest carrying Tuliana and Rutherford in his forelegs. It flew with great difficulty as smoke bellowed out from the edges of its long gracefully fluttering wings.

"It's Rutherford." Jilly held her hand to her mouth in a state of near collapse.

"Tuliana, Tuliana," Parth shouted over and over as he watched the large red butterfly descend towards them through the raging flames.

"The butterfly won't make it Daddy," Cecily screamed and began to cry.

The others stared on hopelessly wishing it the strength and luck it needed on the last metres of its descent. It reached the ground and gently released Tuliana and Rutherford. Without speaking or seeking acknowledgement for its heroic deed, it flew back to the top of the forest canopy and vanished into the smoke and embers of the raging forest fire.

Tuliana ran to Parth and Rawinda. Rutherford raced to Jilly, Cecily and Chet. They all embraced without speaking as tears of emotion filled all their eyes, leaving them unable to utter a single syllable.

"Cecily. Chet my little beauties," Rutherford said eventually as he picked them both up in his arms.

He embraced Jilly tenderly as he did so, with a kiss they both imagined their lips would never experience again. Maximillian stood by happier and prouder than he had ever been in his life. He reached to his jacket pocket for his pipe but pulled his hand away quickly on remembering its fate.

Parth and Tuliana embraced for such a long time that Rawinda had to separate them forcibly so she could give her attention to Tuliana. They all laughed and cried and laughed again as happiness surpassed all other emotions and was the order of that moment soaring far above all the mayhem that surrounded them.

"We must be getting out of this place right now," Vishnu said as he watched sections of the outer wall of the hall crumble and crash to the ground in many places along its length, sending debris and thick dust clouds flying hundreds of metres into the air. A section of the outer wall crashed down on top of the enamelled statues of the butterflies that once stood proudly in the gardens as phantom guardians over the place. The forest was fully ablaze now and beyond all control, giving off the strong vinegary aroma of burning oak. The dry spindles and leaves at the base of the forest were also fully ablaze and heading towards the Indian party like a gigantic wave of red fury. It was fanned by a scorching breeze that blew through the inferno.

"We must go now. Quickly. We have no time to dally" Jilly said in terror as she possessively looked at her family not wishing to lose anyone of them again.

Parth hastily reached into his pocket for the two butterfly wings. On only finding one he pulled his hand out quickly.

"One is missing," he said in terror, his eyes so wide the whites reflected the surrounding fire.

"We left it in the lock on the yellow door," Vishnu said and without further debate began to run fast towards the burning hall. As they all followed him, he stopped suddenly.

"No, sahib. You and Jilly stay safe out here and look after the children. We will try and get the key back. It may be difficult without you but we will try." Vishnu pampered Maximillian's ego, who looked a little miffed at the thought of being left behind but ultimately knew Vishnu was right.

Parth, Vishnu and Rutherford all ran as fast as they could into the hall. The place was ablaze and they had to tread very carefully through the flames and smoke as debris fell from the last remnants of the ceiling that could no longer block the sky from peering for the first time in countless centuries of history within.

Burning rafters crashed to the floor beside them but they kept running towards the golden stairway, undaunted by the danger that engulfed them from all sides.

"It's the yellow doorway up there," Parth educated Rutherford swiftly as they raced up the gold stairs behind Vishnu who was more than fifty steps ahead of them. Part of the stairway was missing, having been hit by falling debris from the collapsing ceiling, leaving a gaping chasm with a sheer drop of hundreds of metres to the burning floor of the hall below. Vishnu, having made it across first, pulled the others to safety. They would not have made it without his assistance. The gold banister was red hot and they all had deep burns to prove it but it didn't deter them one bit. They kept racing higher and higher as if a wild cat was gaining ground on them. Vishnu reached the balcony with the yellow door first and as he did so a full section of the golden stairs, some twenty metres long, collapsed and fell with a screaming crash hundreds of metres to the stone floor below. A large cloud of smoke and ash rose up and they held their hands over their mouths in order to breathe. This unpassable void separated Vishnu from Parth and Rutherford. Vishnu ran to the yellow door and took the butterfly wing from the keyhole. He raced back to the edge of the balcony with a gait that demonstrated life was at stake. He looked down at Parth and Rutherford.

"I am going to wrap the butterfly wing in my turban and throwing it down to you. So be catching it safely," he said and unwrapped his turban carelessly and knotted it tightly around the butterfly wing. He rolled the turban into the smallest ball possible so it was easier to throw and more importantly easier to catch.

"Are you ready?" he shouted, his voice almost blotted out by a massive part of the ceiling collapsing to the floor below, in front of their very eyes. It was so close to them that they could almost feel it graze their faces as it fell.

"I will catch. Played a lot of cricket in my time," Rutherford said to Parth without a smile and made a steady stance, firmly anchoring his feet into position in preparation for the catch. Like the cricketers photos you see in old magazines, standing always prepared for any ball.

Vishnu threw the rolled-up turban as if he were throwing his heart and Rutherford caught it securely without commotion like the good cricketer he had claimed to be. Parth took the turban from Rutherford and quickly removed the butterfly wing placing it securely into his pocket. Rutherford and Parth dreaded this moment and stood looking up at the balcony where Vishnu was standing.

Vishnu looked down sadly to where they stood. The distance between them was so great that no amount of effort could breach it. They all knew any attempt at rescue would be completely futile and certain to fail.

"Jump, we will catch you," Parth said in a pleading voice but knew that it would be impossible.

"Say goodbye to them all for me and tell them it was a

pleasure to have known each and every one of you." Vishnu smiled and gave a happy head wobble and walked calmly back into the room with the yellow door and closed it firmly behind him.

"Vishnu, Vishnu," Parth continued to shout, as massive sections of the inner walls began to collapse beside them.

"We must go. Come on now or it will be too late," Rutherford said and began to run back down the stairs.

Parth waited for a few moments, exhaling deep breaths of grief that made him feel faint, then reluctantly followed Rutherford.

Sukey and Ishmael barely hung on as their wasps flew to no set pattern, diving and ascending randomly for no apparent reason other than their nature dictated. The roof of the hall was, by now, completely incinerated and only small sections of the gold staircase remained attached to the wall like stairs you see in a bombed-out shell or in a house that has taken a lashing from the wrecking ball only in far greater proportion. The uppermost rooms of the hall were now clearly visible from the sky. Sukey could see diamonds as big as footballs and gold that shone even brighter than the fires that raged all about them.

"Look Ishmael! Look!" Sukey screamed, "Diamonds, gold and rubies. I told you there was treasure here. I told you and I was right." She bounced up and down on her wasp's back in delight.

"I am rich. I am rich. And I deserve it all as well. I worked hard for this all my life," Sukey screamed and waved her arms in the air before grabbing on tightly to the wasp's fur again, her stability in every sense coming into question.

"We are rich. Rich. I never doubted you for one moment, Sukey - not for one second," Ishmael shrieked; his smile was so wide it ironed out all his scars.

Sukey ignored his compliment; she was in range to hear his words and did, but she now had the riches she craved and Ishmael was about to become her ex-partner and a soon lost and forgotten memory but he didn't realise it yet. But to Ishmael riches meant the prospect of finally winning Sukey's affections and, maybe on some distant Christmas Eve, a time when all lovers confide, perhaps her love.

"Put us down. Put us down. This treasure is all mine. I want it now. Put us down." Sukey kicked her wasp hard on the side; she was familiar with its routine by now and moved out of the sting's way just in time.

"Put me down you great fat fly." Ishmael pulled its antennae back like a liquorice stick and bit the tip with his two front teeth.

Ishmael's wasp did not appreciate being referred to as a fly or being bitten and, hovering ten feet over the hall, both wasps unceremoniously dumped Sukey and Ishmael into an upper room where they fell with a heavy thud on top of a diamond the size of a small donkey foal. Greed overrode the pain of their injuries and they both dived into the piles of gold and rolled around screaming in ecstasy like children on the sand on their first day of the holiday.

Ishmael filled his pockets with diamonds and had to hold his trousers up with both hands because of the weight. It dawned on them after a while that they had no method of escape with their treasures as they stood on the uppermost balcony of a building which was moments away from collapse. They looked down forlornly to the piles of burning debris and the remnants of the twisted and mangled golden staircase. They both screamed once they realised they were trapped beyond rescue and that very soon they would join the mangled staircase on the floor way below. They looked out into the ashen sky, blackened by war and screamed in terror, waiting for a cracking noise or a shifting sound that would herald the final collapse of the structure. The large black soul butterfly flew calmly over the hall with both its wings on fire.

"Help! Help!," they screamed as one in high pitched sounds like mice caught but not yet expired in mouse traps.

The large black soul butterfly gently descended and

hovered over them and they ran to it and tried to jump onto its back. Sukey nudged Ishmael away roughly with her shoulder to get to the butterfly first and carried as much gold as her pockets would allow. She held more in her hands than they were designed to carry and moved gingerly to avoid dropping one piece.

"What I'd give for a bag, any old bag - or a sack – anything. Why don't I have a bag?" Sukey screamed in a child-like tantrum and stomped her foot as she tried to mount the black soul butterfly's back. The butterfly shook its head negatively, pushing them away with its forelegs as it hovered, with flames shooting from the tips of its burning wings.

"What does it want? What now? Give me a break," Sukey screamed at the butterfly as though she were in a road rage incident and she the main protagonist.

"Come on this place is going to crumble any second," Ishmael shouted at the butterfly as he heard the building give a loud moaning creak.

A voice called out with serenity and peace that belied the atmosphere around it: "You have a choice. Save yourselves and leave the treasures behind," the voice said calmly.

They looked around sharply but couldn't see the source of the voice. Sukey, with a deep regret that turned her face into a sour lemon, threw the gold she was carrying in her hands onto the smouldering floor of the room but didn't empty her pockets. Ishmael emptied half of his pockets with tears of regret draining into his wailing mouth and tightened the belt on his trousers so tight he almost fainted.

The butterfly continued to shake its head negatively in a disappointed fashion.

"This is your last chance. Make up your mind," the voice said calmly.

The black butterfly began to flap its burning wings ready for take-off. Sukey angrily emptied all her pockets, throwing diamonds and gold from her hands high into the air in a vicious temper and stomped around in an attitude not becoming of her age. Ishmael wailed bitter tears of lament as he threw the last large diamond onto the floor. They gave a bereft look back at the room filled to the brim with treasure beyond their wildest imaginings and gave a combined sigh that maybe was the deepest sigh ever heard.

"Right let's go. Get me out of this place now." Sukey mounted the black soul butterfly roughly without grace in a sulk that defined the word.

Ishmael very cautiously began to reach one leg over the black butterfly's back. Sukey grabbed him by the collar and unceremoniously dragged him the rest of the way.

"Get on you great fool." Sukey couldn't bear to look in his direction as she spoke.

He sat nervously behind her "Why did you pull me like that? I am not a rag doll you know. I need a bit of respect," Ishmael said in his best wounded voice. He gripped Sukey's waist for stability and a lecherous grin suddenly covered his face. He leaned forward allowing his chin to rest heavily on her shoulder. Sukey turned around quickly and slapped him hard on the cheek. "Get off me creep," she screamed and pushed him away from her with such force that he almost lost his balance and fell off the black butterfly's back.

"I lost my treasure. It should have been mine. I waited all my life for an opportunity like this - It is all your fault – fool," Sukey screeched in a loud manic voice and stared at the treasures that glistened at her from a distance, as if to tease and heighten her regret.

"My fault?" Ishmael screamed, "My fault?" he repeated in a howl and waved a fist at the red burning sky. He was about to thump the butterfly's back but rejigged that idea on reflection.

"You complete idiot." Sukey kicked back at him with her Dr Martin boot and caught him square on the shin. Ishmael screamed in pain and frantically rubbed the offended area as the black butterfly gracefully lifted high into the burning sky, its wings now burning out of control.

"It will never make it off the ground again. Its wings are

almost burnt out." Ishmael tried to quench the raging flames with his rolled-up jacket but his actions were having little effect as the fanning wind stoked the flames while the butterfly fluttered its enormous black wings.

The butterfly didn't fly towards the ground as they had imagined but flew higher and higher over the raging forest fire.

"Where is it going? Take us down. We want to go down," Ishmael screamed.

Sukey felt lightheaded as she looked down at the terrifying distance between herself and the burning forest below.

"Take me down. I want my feet on the ground again. Take me down." Sukey kicked out at the black butterfly as hard as she could almost losing her balance in the process.

A peaceful silence engulfed them as if trapping them inside a serene bubble and blotted out all other sounds of mayhem from their ears. Their eyes witnessed all that was happening around them in slow motion and they both felt as though they were spectators to a scene that was developing in a dimension they played no part in and did not belong to. A restful, soothing voice spoke with divine authority over their plight "Sukey, Ishmael hear my voice. Your lives as you know them are now over."

Sukey and Ishmael twisted their heads from left to right hysterically to try and uncover the source of the sound and a cold sweat covered each of their bodies making them shiver.

"Who are you? What is happening to me? My life can't be over. I won't stand for this. Take me down." Sukey screamed and for a moment looked as though she was considering jumping free from the butterfly's back.

"Show yourself. I can't see you," Ishmael shouted and waved his bony fist into the air.

"You are now going to the place of renewal. Here you will meet the many people you killed without mercy or remorse and sent to death long before their time. Each of those people know you are both coming and are now eagerly awaiting your arrival. Here you will be at their mercy. After they have finished with you they will take you to the cavern of the dead. A place of retribution for all the wrongdoing in your lives. Once there you will find out what true suffering really feels like. In the cavern of the dead you will find no peace, no reprieve and there you will both languish for a very long time," the voice said serenely.

Ishmael screamed with his mouth so wide it almost hid the features of his tormented face.

"Nooo, Nooo," Sukey cried out and completely forgot about the lost treasure she had once imagined would be her foremost thought and regret for the rest of her days.

Sukey turned to face Ishmael and threw her arms around him in a tight embrace, and they sat almost as one, screaming in unison.

The black soul butterfly with its wings now burning furiously, carried the screaming Sukey and Ishmael beyond the blazing forest to the place of renewal to meet their fate. Their screams echoed in the air for many miles.

Rutherford and Parth raced fearlessly through the falling debris and made their way back to the forest line where the others were sheltering from the intense heat in the rotten hollow of the tall oak tree.

"Well done, you have it. Great work," Maximillian said when he saw Parth displaying the second butterfly wing perched on top of a large blister in the centre of his wide-open hand.

Parth carried Vishnu's unwrapped shiny black turban in his other hand and the others stared at it with shocked expressions giving it more attention than the glistening gold of the butterfly wing.

"Where is Vishnu?" the tone of Maximillian's voice hinted he knew the answer and he looked back at what now remained of the hall.

Parth and Rutherford looked at each other solemnly and

Jilly and Maximillian knew in an instant details they didn't want the children to hear. Jilly and Maximillian looked heartbroken and fought off tears they knew they would cry at a later time.

The battle was complete and the wasps were victorious. All that remained of The Land of Butterflies was now in the wasps' control. The black smoke and ash from the fires and the volcano left the air almost unbreathable. The sad pitiful sound of dying butterflies echoed like a multitude of orchestras playing out of key and resonated from every direction, making the place that was once so serene and beautiful now a place of tragic horrors.

"We must make our escape now or it will be too late. The lava from the volcano will be here shortly," Maximillian said with an urgency in his voice.

Parth took the second butterfly wing from his pocket and held both in his hands. They all huddled together in anticipation waiting for the wormhole to reopen once more.

The queen flew over the hall and cried out in horror as she assessed the damage her army of wasps had caused; this realization hitting her now like a cannon ball for the first time. She gave continuous heavy coughs that made her gasp for air as she wiped her bloodshot eyes with her forelegs.

"My beautiful hall is ruined," she screamed amidst coughs. "Those moron wasps have destroyed my kingdom." She looked out over the burning fields of wildflowers and in the distance could see the heavy stream of molten hot lava from the volcano, fifty miles wide, coming towards her like a runaway steam train. It greedily consumed and charred everything in its path, leaving the fields where the wildflowers once grew buried beneath a hot mass of magma and ashes. The people in their once white tunics and yellow sashes all walked through the mounds of burning debris and dying butterflies towards the approaching wall of boiling lava. Atia walked at their head and as the lava neared they joined hands peacefully without fear or emotion. The lava swallowed them up instantly and continued with angry force towards the remains of hall.

The queen observed this unfold and, in her shock, flew too close to the burning canopy of the forest where her wings immediately caught fire.

"I am on fire," she cried out and buzzed her wings even faster in vain attempts to quench the flames but her efforts only assisted in fanning the blaze.

"My beauty is being destroyed. Your gorgeous queen is dying and there is no wasp to come to my aid in this, my time of trial. The world will never see beauty like mine again. I am the most perfect creature ever born or whoever will be born," she cried as she began to awkwardly lose control of her flight. Beneath her she could see the Indian party all grouped together and she dived towards them to wreak the last havoc of which she was now capable.

"Kill, kill, kill," she screamed as she dived towards the Indian party, her wings now completely burned out leaving her looking like a hideous fat sausage that has been lost beneath the barbecue for a month or so and has developed fur. "If I can't live - then nobody else will." Laughing manically, she stretched her head forward and straightened her back in an attempt to reach her target accurately.

"Look," Cecily screamed in terror as she noticed the queen's death-plummet first.

"It is diving towards us," Jilly shouted.

Parth pushed the two butterfly wings together and immediately the wormhole opened. He ushered everyone inside ahead of himself and stood watching the queen's final dive getting closer. She was now so near he could hear her give a remorseful whimpering scream just before impact.

Parth stumbled over the remains of a large smouldering wasp as he ran the last few metres to the mouth of the wormhole and as he did, dropped the butterfly wings. The queen's dive was almost at an end and she cried and screamed in penitent fear "What have I done? What have I done," she bawled as she waited for her impact with the solid merciless earth. Parth regained his composure and quickly tried to find the butterfly wings but the ground was now covered with many centimetres of heavy lava ash. He ran his hands frantically over the area where he thought the butterfly wings to be - scrambling and tearing at the earth, fanning the ash out of his way like a dog burying a bone but he couldn't find them. They were now lost in the cinders and would remain covered and forgotten for the next 300 million years until Parth would notice them once again at the bottom of the trench at the pyramid in Luxor and the cycle would repeat itself over but with changes made to the landscape of events by the lessons learned by all the protagonists involved.

The butterfly wings would be subjected to the sedimentary changes in the earth's surface - moving location as landmasses altered position throughout time, the ice age pushing them to Luxor at the base of a mountain of ice and snow.

With only mere seconds to spare before the queen's impact, Parth ran headlong into the wormhole after the others. The queen crashed without mercy near the wormhole and exploded into a ball of yellow flames and smouldering hot fur. Her whimpering screams rang to the ears of the India party who stood in confusion as they searched for the exit that should lead them back to Parth's haven but none of them could find it.

The bright multicolours swirled all around in circles leaving them in an enclosed zone with no exit or entrance. Maximillian tried to find the area where he assumed the exit should be but as he touched the bright colours they repelled his hand away with force. Undeterred he tried once again with added aplomb but this time he was tossed to the floor of the wormhole on his back as the force displayed unfathomable energy.

"Where is Dad?" Chet said and looked about him screaming "He is still outside," he continued.

"Where is Tuliana? She is not here either," Parth cried.

Rawinda fell to her knees.

"Cecily, Cecily where is Cecily?" Jilly screamed and both she and Parth tried to clamber back through the wormhole frantically attempting to get back to the land of butterflies, but their movements were now acting out in slow motion and their bodies felt so heavy they could barely lift their feet to move forward. They screamed agitatedly at their lack of mobility and tried to fight against their predicament, Jilly forcibly lifting her legs one at a time with both hands, but her actions were just like running on the spot. They weren't gaining an inch forward.

The colours closed in all around them and herded them all into a small tight circle together.

"Tuliana and Rutherford are happy and at peace now." The serene voice spoke filling the air with a soothing compassion. The Indian party held each other in the tight circle, unable to move or speak.

The voice continued: "Their work in your time is now over but their real true life is now only just beginning. They are free forever from the place of renewal. Illness and death have no power over them anymore. One day you will all be together again when your work in this life is over. Until then be happy for them and let them rest in peace. They will visit you often in your dreams, some dreams you will remember - some you won't, but you will gain a comfort and understanding from these dreams remembered or not, that will assist you throughout your lives. Speak to them on occasions as you would when they were alive, and they will hear you. But most of all be happy for them as they will be sad if they see you are unhappy. Once I open the exit of the wormhole you will all go back to your own time once more to live out the remainder of your days. Be certain to remember the kindness of the butterflies and the people and the beauty they created and cultivated. And you must also remember the anger and vanity of the wasps and the destruction and havoc that their hostility caused. You should have gained a great lesson from these groups if you are able to decipher it and I am sure you will. It is everyone's choice in life to be like either group so choose wisely and act accordingly. Cecily will be returned to you presently and all will be fine," the voice spoke kindly and softly to them and then faded out to a whisper.

The exit in the wormhole opened in a white transparent mist and they all walked calmly out into Parth's haven feeling refreshed as if they had slept the most restful night's sleep of their lives.

Once through, the wormhole vanished without a trace. They were silent as they pondered on the words the voice had spoken.

"When will we see Cecily again? When do you suppose?" Jilly stared at Maximillian who just gave her a confused smile in reply. Parth held his arm around Rawinda as though he would never let her go again and stared helplessly at the marble floor unable to give a response to Jilly's question either.

"When?" Jilly continued as tears formed in her eyes and Chet held her hand tightly.

"Soon, Jilly. The voice promised, and I for one believe it. Have faith." Maximillian put his arm around Jilly's shoulders that were now heavy and drooping with sadness.

The long white shutters on the windows of the room had been opened since their departure and a pale sunlight shone through onto the marble floor.

"It looks like winter. Couldn't be …," Parth said as he observed the dim sun light and the direction its shadows made on the floor.

"Couldn't be. We were only gone for a few hours," Maximillian said and quickly took his pocket watch from his safari jacket, fumbling open the cover to check the time and date.

He looked up suddenly, the wrinkles on his forehead deepening into furrows and scratched his head with such vigour that his comb over had to be rearranged afterwards.

"It's the 24th of December. We have been gone for five

months," Maximillian said and handed the pocket watch to Parth who gave it a second penetrating stare before moving quickly to the large rectangle latticed window that overlooked the gardens.

"Yes! You are right Maximillian. It is Christmas. My family are Christian, so the servants have decorated an outdoor Christmas tree, as they do each year, for Rawinda," Parth said as he stared out through the window to the tall tree whose fairy lights could be seen to glisten in the dusky sunlight.

"The tree is for you as well," Rawinda said with a smile.

"Well... yes... for me also," Parth agreed bashfully and smiled.

Some of the servants heard the voices in the room and came to investigate. They cheered and clapped their hands once they saw the Indian party and ran to Rawinda and kissed her.

"We hoped and prayed you would return safely to us again and you have," the old lady who had advised Parth on Tuliana's funeral said with delight.

Even though it was 22 degrees and not at all like an English Christmas eve, the group stood around the decorated tree and toasted the return of Rawinda and Chet, their amazing experience and, of course the festive season, with glasses of Thandai; a festive Indian drink the servants served on shining silver trays. Jilly was not in festive spirits and decided to try and hold her emotions together for a little longer for Chet's sake. She moved the cold glass around in her hands, nervously taking occasional sips and poked the toe of her shoe into the ground to relieve some tension. Her eyes searched the skies and the forest, waiting for the promised return of Cecily. Parth and Rawinda stood by the tree and celebrated but were aware of all the emotions that were being kept in check all around them.

"Happy Christmas," Parth said, in the best cheery tone he could muster as he held his glass aloft.

They all acknowledged his toast but with strained smiles

on their faces.

Maximillian tried to take Chet's thoughts away from Cecily's absence by handing him the small silver bell.

"My Christmas present to you. Happy Christmas Chet," Maximillian said as he placed the silver bell in Chet's small eager hand.

Chet's eyes lit up as he stared at it.

"Mine?" he affirmed and Maximillian gave him a warm smile in acknowledgement. Chet stared at the bell and then gave it the slightest shake to allow the enchanting delicate tinkling tone to escape to all the surrounding ears. The others grew silent as they listened to its ethereal toll. As the slight sound rang out their eyes were all at once drawn to the skies as the sunlight was eclipsed by a large object advancing towards them slowly from the direction of the sun's rays. The sound of its fluttering wings, growing louder as it got near, was a familiar sound to all of them.

"Look. It's the red butterfly," Chet screamed and dashed out from the group, ringing the small bell as loudly as he could as he ran. The large red soul butterfly calmly followed the sound of the bell and floated down from the sky with grace - its massive wings fluttering and shimmering delicately.

"Look… it's Cecily," Jilly screamed in delight.

The butterfly carried Cecily in its forelegs and released her gently as it landed on the ground before the Indian party. The breeze from the butterfly's wings fanned the Christmas tree, knocking some of the decorations to the ground but no one noticed. Everyone gathered around Cecily, cheering and crying with joy and affection. When everyone had expressed their emotions, Chet and Cecily finally gave each other a hug and everyone smiled.

"I will take you all home now." The red soul butterfly spoke as it continued to flutter its wings and hover just above the ground.

The Indian party looked confused. The butterfly bowed its head down low to allow them easy access to its back.

"Climb on board," the butterfly said calmly.

Cecily, who was now an old hand at being transported by butterfly, took Jilly by the hand and led her up onto the butterfly's back. Jilly made a humming noise, that followed no rhythmic pattern, in an attempt to blot out the actions she was forced to endure. She kept her eyes closed and continued to hum as she sat down meekly on the butterfly's back.

"It will be ok. Its great fun," Cecily said and smiled as she sat down beside her mother.

Chet followed next and sat in front of Jilly and Cecily watching the massive wings flutter gently on both sides of him.

"Time to go I suppose," Maximillian said and shook Parth's hand.

"We may have more adventures in future. Who knows?" Parth said with a warm smile.

"Maybe we will," Maximillian replied in a whisper "Take care of Parth for me will you. Don't know what he is going to do without me," Maximillian spoke to Rawinda who rushed to him and gave him a hug.

Maximillian climbed up onto the butterfly's back awkwardly and was helped the final few metres by Chet. They all sat holding on tightly, with white knuckles, as the motion of the butterfly's wings began to gain in momentum, fluttering along their huge length until the butterfly lifted gracefully from the ground soaring high into the blue sky. Cecily and Chet cheered down towards Rawinda and Parth waving until the white palace beneath them faded into a small dot away in the distant landscape below.

The butterfly was silent throughout the journey only speaking to point out Persepolis in Iran, Mount Olympus in Greece, the Colosseum in Rome and the Eiffel Tower in Paris as it flew over them.

Snowflakes began to blot out their view of the land beneath once they crossed the English Channel, flying high over the chalk cliffs of Dover. The butterfly descended gradually and flew at around one hundred metres above the ground as it crossed over the border into Wales. The land beneath was a carpet of crisp white snow and as dusk set in they could see the lights from the Christmas trees shining in the windows of the houses beneath them. The butterfly glided over their little village and the roof top of the rectory, covered thick with snow and gently descended to the ground near Woodhouse 2 which was just about visible beneath the white Christmas carpet.

One by one they all disembarked and watched as the butterfly's wings began to increase in momentum once more blowing the snowflakes into lofty whirlwind swirls as it rose high into the cold air.

"Goodbye. Goodbye," Chet and Cecily shouted over and over as the butterfly departed.

"And thankyou red butterfly," Maximillian shouted.

"Thank you for everything," Jilly said quietly in a whisper as the butterfly flew high into the sky, rising and fading into the thick falling snowflakes. They watched it until it dissolved into to a small red dot and then disappeared into the unknown.

Maximillian reached for his pipe but stopped as Jilly gave him a sudden stare.

"That was a filthy habit - one I should have given up years ago," he said earnestly "and come to think of it, did I ever tell you all about the man I knew in Jamestown, Virginia a long time ago, who smoked two pipes at the same time. Said he couldn't get enough smoke with one." Maximillian looked at, Chet and Cecily eagerly. "Well, it was about May I think, no it was June yes it was June and I was…"

Jilly intervened, "No we haven't heard that one before Maximillian but maybe you can tell us all about it later, after our breakfast. We are all a little bit hungry? Are we?" and she looked at the children.

"I could do with some of Atia's fish right now," Chet said with a smile.

Maximillian mumbled "Ermm... oh so you haven't heard that one before, that's good – after breakfast, so," he said. A beaming smile covered his face beneath the icicles on his frozen white beard as his eyes lit up brighter than the lights on the Christmas trees that shone brightly from the surrounding neighbours' windows.

Jilly, Chet and Cecily smiled and raised their eyes skyward out of Maximillian's view. He reached into the pocket where his pipe once resided and, mesmerised, returned his hand, filled to overflowing with large bright shining diamonds. The sound of the nearby church bell rang out eight o' clock, penetrating the falling snowflakes and softly drifted in through the peaceful candle lit windows. It was Christmas morning.

THANK YOU!

To my Reader:

Many thanks for buying *Land of Butterflies*, I hope you enjoyed reading it.

If you did enjoy it, please post a review at Amazon, Goodreads or your favourite social network site and let your friends know about this and my other novel, *The Dream Voyagers*.

Look out for more stories coming soon.

Happy Reading!
All the best
David

CONTACT DETAILS

Cover designed by: T-Rex Cover Design

Published by: Raven Crest Books
www.ravencrestbooks.co.uk

Like on Facebook:
www.facebook.com/ravencrestbooksclub

Printed in Great Britain
by Amazon